THANKS, *Carissa,* FOR *Ruining* MY LIFE

DALLAS WOODBURN

Immortal Works LLC
1505 Glenrose Drive
Salt Lake City, Utah 84104
Tel: (385) 202-0116

Cover Art by Rebecca Barney
barneydesign.com

ISBN 978-1-953491-30-5 (Paperback)
ASIN B09Q2K5573 (Kindle Edition)

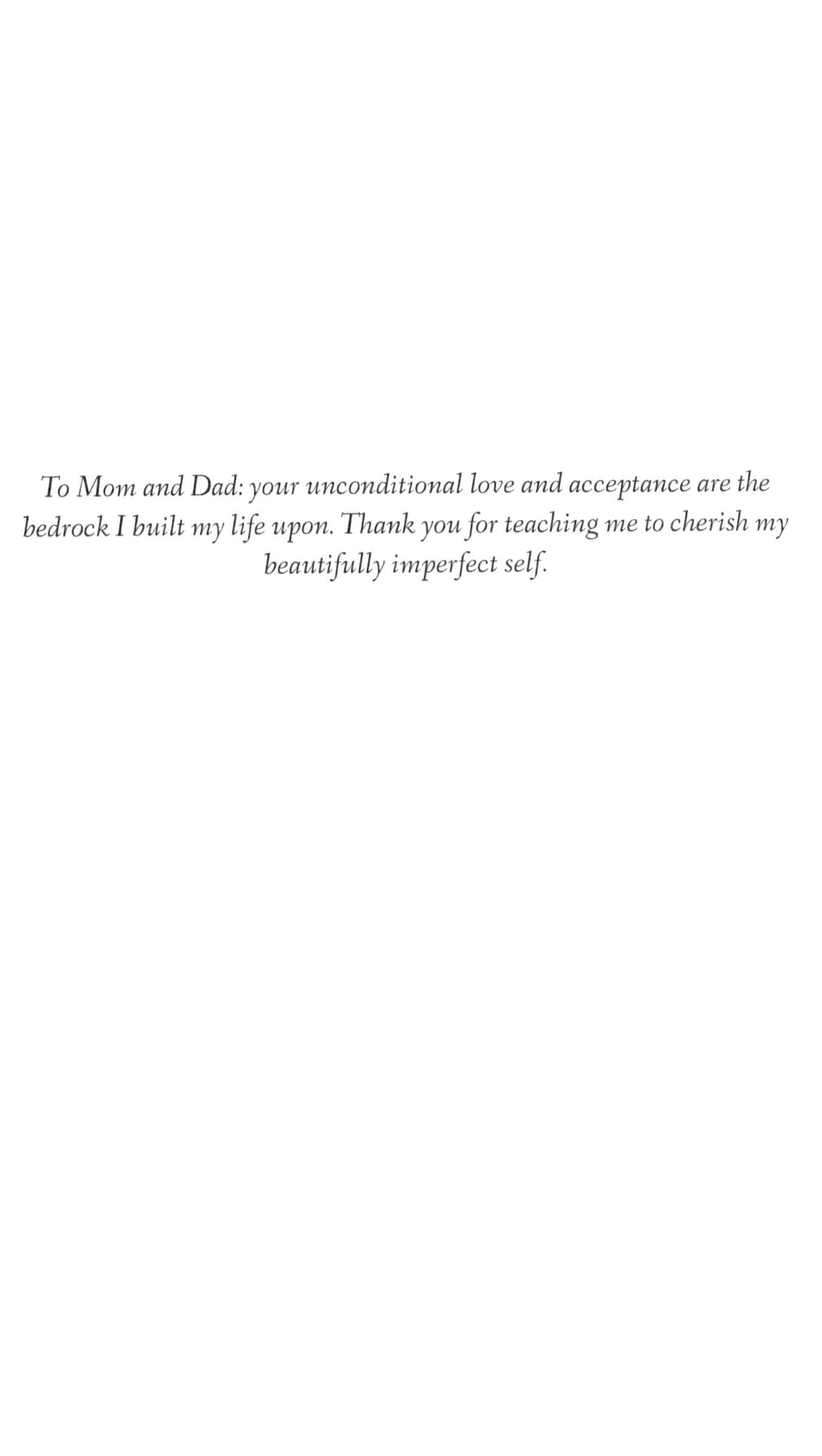

To Mom and Dad: your unconditional love and acceptance are the
bedrock I built my life upon. Thank you for teaching me to cherish my
beautifully imperfect self.

Chapter 1

Exactly one week before school started, Carissa Hayward broke up with me over chocolate-dipped soft-serve cones at the Dairy Queen three blocks from my house. We were supposed to spend our senior year together. I tried explaining this to her, but she wouldn't listen.

It's been five days since she yanked my heart out of my chest and ground it through a pepper mill. I've been calling her and calling her, but nothing I say is enough to change her mind.

I call her and try again.

"Brad, please. We've been over this a million times." She sighs. "Stop calling me, okay?" And then she hangs up.

Five days, and already she has sliced me out of her life, as cleanly as if she used a brand-new X-Acto knife. She seems surprised that I am having a harder time wrapping my head around things. I mean, we dated for eleven months. We went to Homecoming and Prom together. She was my first kiss, if you don't count Bethany Morris in third grade (which I don't, as it was during recess and Bethany was running away from me across the playground. I only caught her because the sandbox tripped her, and after I kissed her she ran away shrieking, "Eww, cooties!").

What I'm trying to say is, Carissa and I have history. You'd think all that history would take some time to unravel. You'd think I would have gotten a little warning.

But no. One minute we were sitting at our favorite table at the Dairy Queen, the one by the window next to the drinking fountain (ice cream always makes me thirsty), talking about the summer reading assignment for our dinosaur English teacher Mrs. Ostertank.

The next minute, ice cream was dripping all over my hand as I tried to comprehend the words "break up" coming from my girlfriend's perfect lips.

Carissa had finished reading *A Farewell to Arms* by mid-June, and her report was already written, edited, rewritten, printed out, stapled, and waiting in her binder.

"How about you?" she asked. "How's your report coming?"

"It's coming."

"Yeah? So, what'd you think of the ending?"

"Oh, I haven't gotten there yet." I bit into the chocolate shell. "Don't ruin it for me."

"You haven't finished the book yet?"

"Not quite."

"What page are you on?"

"Eh, like...a hundred, I think."

That was a lie. I was on page forty-six.

"Brad, I can't believe it," Carissa said, looking wounded. "I thought you were going to take school seriously this year."

"I am, I am," I insisted, still calmly unaware of what was coming next.

"You say that, but really? Page one-hundred? There's no way you're going to finish the assignment in time!"

"Don't worry, babe. I work best under pressure." And for good measure, I flashed her my signature winning grin.

She didn't smile back. Carissa was usually helpless to the charm of my signature winning grin, so when she didn't smile back I should have known something bad was coming.

"Brad," she said, looking down at the plastic tabletop. She wiped up a chocolate splotch left by a previous customer. "This isn't working for me."

Still, my internal alarm bells remained silent. I worked my tongue around the ice cream cone. "What do you mean?"

"I mean..." She sighed. "I think we should break up."

☆ ☆ ☆

HERE ARE the reasons Carissa Hayward gave for breaking up with yours truly:

1. "We're just different people."

Well, duh. Isn't everyone "different people"? This is actually a positive thing about our relationship. It means we are not clones or distant relatives. Edgar Allan Poe may have been entirely happy marrying his cousin, but he also was a creepy guy who wrote horror stories. For the rest of us, I say, *No thanks.*

2. "We have different interests."

Sure, Carissa likes taking painting classes and browsing thrift stores downtown, while I like playing video games and uploading my goofy stand-up comedy routines to YouTube. But tell me, what guy doesn't like video games and stand-up?

And okay, so I got drunk. Twice. And got a C in Chemistry because I got lazy and didn't turn in all the work. That was last year. I'll do better this year. Those things are changeable.

When you get down to it, my only real interest is Carissa. And that's what I told her that day in the Dairy Queen, but Carissa only shook her head and moved on to number three:

3. "We're going different places."

Yes, she has stellar grades and a million extracurriculars and a whole school filled with adoring teachers dying to write letters of recommendation for her. She'll get into any college she wants—and she wants a ridiculously hard-to-get-into college. In other words, a school I could never get into, not even if I somehow managed to tap into Bill Gates' bank account and steal a trillion-dollar bribe for the admissions counselor. I'll probably end up going to the community college the next town over. But that's okay. I told Carissa that we'll work it out. What matters is that we love each other.

4. "I'm sorry, Brad, but I don't love you anymore."

Okay, I admit, this one hurt. But the thing about love is, you can win it back. So that's what I'll do. I'll win back the love of Carissa Hayward.

How? I'll change my ways. I'll show her how awesome I am, and she'll remember how great we are together, and she'll fall in love with me all over again.

It's only a matter of time.

Chapter 2

In normal circumstances, I would be heading back to Buena Vista High School in exactly one week to start my senior year. Instead, I am on a bus to Fat Camp.

That's not its real name. The TV show is actually called *Help Me Lose Weight and Live Again*, but my younger brother Scotty calls it Fat Camp, and that's the name that has stuck in my mind.

Everyone else seems to *want* to be here. They're smiling and laughing and talking to each other. Not me. I'm sitting by myself at the back of the bus. This, at least, feels familiar: me, alone, on a bus, stomach roiling with anxiety. Only this is worse than ever before. This is humiliating. Sure, I feel out of place at school. And yes, I feel out of place with my athletic, yoga-loving, marathon-running family. But I feel just as out of place here, on this luxury "travel coach" with eleven other obese people. Maybe it sounds weird, but I don't see myself as one of them.

But I know the millions of people watching this show will see nothing but my weight. The cameras are everywhere. I've always hated being in front of cameras. Carissa knows this, yet still she sent in that stupid nomination to this stupid show.

"Rosieeeee! You're not going to believe this!" she had shrieked, bursting into my bedroom without even knocking, waving around that envelope as if it were a great big prize. Even from ten feet away I could read the shiny red letters, *Help Me Lose Weight and Live Again*, embossed across the front alongside our address.

"What's that?" I asked.

"The invitation to the rest of your life," Carissa declared. She has a flair for the dramatic.

"What are you talking about?" I wanted to get through the conversation as quickly as possible so I could go back to the book I was reading, *Infinite Jest*. If I had known what was coming, I would have grabbed the envelope from my sister's hands and ripped it to pieces.

"You know how much I love you, Rosie," Carissa said. "This is my gift to you." And she launched into the story: how she had seen an ad online looking for "extremely overweight contestants" for a new reality show that would help them "lose weight and gain happiness"; how she had filled out the application and sent it in with the video she had taken of me eating a giant slice of triple-fudge cake on our birthday last April; how she had known it was "a long shot" but she had figured she might as well "give it a go" because "it never hurts to try!!!"

Looking at my twin sister's radiant, slender face was like looking at a Twilight Zone version of myself. Had she ever understood me, or had we always been this different? I couldn't remember. "Wow," was all I could choke out.

"I know!" Carissa said, beaming. "I am so glad I went for it! You're welcome."

"I mean, well, that's very thoughtful of you." I put down my book and sat up straighter on the bed. "But I'm not going on that show."

"What do you mean? You're going to have an amazing time!"

"Highly doubtful. Unlike you, my ultimate dream is not to have my daily life played out on national television for millions of strangers to discuss on social media." I held up my book. "Besides, I have school."

People are always complimenting Carissa on her beautiful smile. Well, people compliment me, too—it's the one clue that we are indeed twins. But, maybe because we share the same smile, I can always tell immediately when Carissa's smile switches from genuine to fake, like a light switch abruptly flicking off. When this happens, it is not a good sign.

"I'm sorry to burst your bubble, but you don't have a choice," she said, tucking a strand of hair behind her ear. "I was hoping you'd be excited about this opportunity and see it as the gift it is, but I should have known you would react this way. Always Miss Negative."

"I'm not negative!"

"I mean, I can't blame you. You're so miserable. You can't even take the first step to becoming happy, because you don't believe you deserve happiness."

"Cut the psycho-babble, please. I'm not miserable."

"You are *obese*, Rosie."

The label stung, but I gritted my teeth and lifted my chin. "My weight is none of your business."

"Yes, it is my business, because I love you and you are killing yourself. This isn't a choice for you. This is an intervention." She explained how they were all in on it: Mom, Dad, Scotty, Grandma and Grandpa, even my best friend Holly.

"Holly too?" Betrayal squeezed a web around my heart.

"Holly is worried about you," Carissa said, her voice flat, the voice of a fourth-grade teacher dictating spelling words. "Holly cares about you. She wants you to be happy."

"I *am* happy."

"Rosie, please."

"I am."

"Can you look me in the eyes and honestly tell me that you are perfectly happy with your life exactly the way it is now?"

I ran my fingers over the cover of my book. I looked at my nubby blue carpet, my dusty bookshelves, my mirrorless bedroom walls. "Well, no—but can anyone honestly say that? I'm happy enough."

Those words sealed my fate. I might as well have thrown my arms around Carissa in gratitude. Before, she might have wavered, but now she was steadfastly certain that she was Doing The Right Thing. And once Carissa makes up her mind, she doesn't change it. Her smile flicked back to genuine, and I knew with weary resignation that I could talk in circles with my twin sister for hours but there was nothing I could do: I was going to Fat Camp.

Chapter 3
Brad

"I don't blame her for breaking up with me," I tell Leonard. He dragged me out of my house to have lunch at Tony's Taco Shack, a hole-in-the-wall place by the beach where the cooks always slip an extra taco onto both of our plates because we come here so often. I haven't been here since Carissa broke up with me. Five days —pretty much a record for the summertime. Too bad that next week school is starting up again, and I'll be back to eating soggy PB&J sandwiches for lunch instead of Tony's carnitas tacos.

"Dude, what are you talking about?" Leonard says. "You're awesome. Carissa thinks she's too good for everyone."

This is why Leonard is such a great friend: he knows when it's okay to give me a hard time, and he also knows when to just be there for me.

"Thanks, Leo." I wipe taco sauce from my mouth with the back of my hand. "But seriously, Carissa is too good for me. I'm not the guy she fell for. Not anymore."

"Listen to yourself, man. She's really messed you up."

"But it's true. She fell for me when we were doing morning announcements last year. Remember? We were so good together. Everyone said so. I made her laugh. I actually studied for my classes, because she always studied in the library after school and I started going there too. I even sold my old Playstation to get money to rent a limo for Prom."

"See?" Leo says. "You were a great boyfriend. What's she complaining about?"

"No, but here's the thing. Once we'd been dating for a while, I got complacent. I started taking her for granted. I've become nothing but a slacker wanna-be radio DJ with no money and no future, trying too hard to be funny and looking down on those people who actually care."

"Whoa, man." Leonard looks uncomfortable. "You've been spending way too much time brooding in your room. Seriously. We need to get you out tonight. Meet some new ladies. There's a party at Matt's."

"I should stay home. Finish that Ostertank report."

"Dude! It's Friday night! Our last Friday night of summer! You have all weekend to finish that report. Plus, you have a girlfriend to get over."

"I'm not getting over her, Leo. I'm winning her back."

"Even better. No one can resist the life of the party!"

I pour salsa onto my taco. "Is she gonna be there, you think?"

"Who cares?"

"I care. She won't answer my calls or texts."

"Do I need to confiscate your phone?" Leo says in a perfect impression of Mrs. Ostertank when she catches someone texting in class.

"I miss her. I know it sounds lame, but I do."

Leonard sighs. "She'll probably be there. I'm sure Matt invited her."

"Does Matt have a thing for her? Is that what you're trying to tell me?" Picturing Carissa kissing some other guy makes my whole body twitch.

"No—calm down. You know Matt. The guy probably invited our entire class. Even Carissa's sister. What's her name?"

"Rose."

"Yeah. Rosie." Leonard laughs. "Let's hope she doesn't come, eh? There'd be no food left for anyone else!"

"Don't be a jerk. Rose is the best. But she won't be there." I know this because the day before Carissa broke up with me, I went with her family to drop Rose off at the airport to catch a plane to Texas. She's going to be on some reality TV show. I gave her a hug and told her not to forget about me. I meant to say "us"—"Don't forget about the rest of us!"—but for some reason "me" came out instead. She'll be gone almost four months, all the way until December. No phone calls. No email. No texting. No social media. I remember thinking I would go crazy if I wasn't able to contact Carissa for four days, much less four months.

"So, Brad, you coming with me tonight or what?" Leonard asks.

"Yeah, okay." I drain the last of my soda. "At least for a little bit."

"That's the spirit!" He stands up and claps me on the back.

I follow him to the door, upending my tray into the trash on the way out. The trash can outside is overflowing. Sea gulls cluster around it like old ladies at a rummage sale, squawking loudly as they nose through the cardboard containers soggy with salsa.

"I have a good feeling about tonight," Leonard continues.

"Me too."

"It's gonna be epic!"

I nod along, but to be honest I don't care that it's the last Friday night of summer. I don't care if it goes down as the best party ever. To me, only one thing matters: tonight is The Night I Win Back Carissa Hayward, Just Wait And See.

Chapter 4

T he bus veers off the highway and onto a dirt road lined with oak trees. We pass under a huge sign: *WELCOME TO THE FIRST DAY OF THE REST OF YOUR LIFE!!!* Already this place has too many exclamation points for my taste.

It looks like the producers bought a summer camp, then remodeled it to make everything ritzier for TV. There's an ornately tiled pool, a campfire pit, hiking trails everywhere. More trees than I thought existed in Texas. There are two cabins, one for guys and the other for girls. At least we each get our own room and bathroom, and instead of bunk beds there are queen-sized beds. Which is good. Carissa and I had bunk beds when we were kids, and I hated it. The top bunk seemed too high—I was terrified I would somehow roll over the railing and fall off in my sleep. But the bottom bunk was no better. When I slept there, I felt claustrophobic, like a giant dark mass was pressing down on me. I would move my mattress to the floor beside the bed, relieved at the openness between the ceiling and me.

The four other women and I file into the girls' cabin. Each door is affixed with a bright pink placard with one of our names written out in bold lettering, along with "You go, girl!!!" My room is at the very end of the hallway on the left. I resist the urge to rip off my name placard and crumple it up into a ball. A cameraman tries to follow me inside, but I shut the door. I know it's useless because there are cameras in my room, but I try not to think about them.

Letting my suitcase fall onto the floor, study my surroundings. Framed black-and-white photos of fruit and vegetables adorn the cheerful yellow walls. No television or computer. They took all of our phones when we boarded the bus. I keep reaching into my pocket to check for a text from Holly, forgetting my phone isn't there.

There's a small wooden desk with an electric teakettle and two mugs. I pull out the drawers. Plain white stationery, envelopes and stamps. I guess we're allowed to write letters to people back home? Not that I especially want to do that. Well, maybe I'll write a letter to Holly.

A wide, full-length mirror faces the bed, unavoidable. The first thing I'll see when I wake up will be myself. I read somewhere that it's bad feng shui to have a mirror facing your bed.

In my normal life, I would be going shopping with Holly for school supplies right now. We both like to start a new school year with brand new supplies. There's something so hopeful about freshly sharpened pencils and crisp blank sheets of lined paper.

Holly didn't come with my family to the airport. She said it would be too hard to watch me walk off through security and then have to drive all the way home with my family. "There's no way I could drive myself, I'd be bawling too much," she said. "And that would be so embarrassing to be crying like a baby in front of your family."

The real reason is that Holly didn't want to cry in front of Carissa. Holly and Carissa have never gotten along. Carissa thinks Holly is boring and whiny, and Holly thinks Carissa is a judgmental control freak. That they actually both agreed on something—me coming here to Fat Camp—is pretty miraculous.

Holly was right that she would have bawled too much to drive. She crumpled into tears when she came to my house to say goodbye the night before I left. When I saw how genuinely distraught Holly was that I was leaving, it was hard to stay mad at her for going along with the "intervention."

"I'm really gonna miss you, Rose," she choked out. "I don't know what I'll do at school without you."

I can't imagine being at school without Holly. On the few days she's been sick and I had to get through the day alone, I was even more self-conscious than usual. During snack break I'd fiddle with my locker, pretending I'd forgotten something, open it, stare forlornly at my books, then close it again. There was no one to pass notes to in the hall; no one to laugh with about random inside jokes; no one to commiserate with about our dinosaur English teacher, Mrs. Ostertank. I ate lunch all by myself in my car.

I told Holly that I ate lunch with Carissa, so she wouldn't feel bad about me eating alone. But, as lonely as it is to eat alone in your car, eating lunch with Carissa and her group would have been even worse. To Carissa's friends, I am the definition of "loser." They smile fake smiles at me and then return to their conversations about parties and sports and gossip. The one time I did eat lunch with them, Carissa and her boyfriend Brad were having an intense argument, completely wrapped up in their own drama. The girls all gave me disgusted looks as I ate my PB & J sandwich. One guy, Leonard, offered me his Fritos, and when I said "No, thanks" they all laughed. If I had taken them, they would have laughed, too.

Carissa tries to hide it, but I can tell she's embarrassed of me. As much as she might spout nominating me for this show out of the goodness and love in her heart, I know a big part of her motivation was wanting me to become less of a family embarrassment.

The only one of Carissa's group I can actually stand is Brad. Carissa thinks he's a slacker, but he isn't, not really. He works hard at the things he is passionate about. Like comedy—he's put up all these videos on YouTube of his stand-up comedy routines. And he's really good! He has this one joke about different animals at the zoo that makes me laugh so hard I snort. I tried explaining it to Holly, but it's only funny when Brad tells it.

Brad came with my family to the airport to see me off. He gave me a hug goodbye and told me not to forget about him, which was kind of a weird thing to say, but also kind of sweet. Or maybe he was just trying to be funny. With Brad it's sometimes hard to tell.

In line for security, I turned back to wave goodbye to my family. Mom was crying. Dad gave me a thumbs-up. Scotty did a ninja kick for my benefit. Carissa was examining her manicure, but Brad was looking at me. When our eyes met, he smiled and waved.

What I like about Brad is that he treats me like I'm a normal person. Usually when people look at me, it's obvious that all they see is my weight. Like I'm a giant anonymous blob rather than a human being with thoughts and skills and emotions and ideas. But Brad isn't like that. He looks at me and sees Rose. Just Rose.

Actually, that's not completely true. Brad looks at me and sees Rose, Carissa's sister. Even if I wanted him to think of me as something more, it's hopeless. He's my flawless twin sister's boyfriend. Meanwhile, I'm thousands of miles away at Fat Camp.

There's a knock on my bedroom door. I briefly consider staying here on the bed, ignoring the knock until it goes away. But I heave myself up, stumble over to the door, and yank it open.

Another contestant stands there, smiling hugely. Her teeth are white and perfectly straight. She looks to be around my mom's age, late forties, and is wearing stretch pants and a voluminous frilly purple blouse. Her bobbed hair is pin-straight with blonde highlights. "Hello there!" she says. "I'm Doris. I'm your neighbor." She gestures at the room across the hall.

I stick out my hand. "Hi. I'm Rose."

"Rose!" she says, squeezing my hand tightly. "What a pretty name!"

"It's short for Roseanna."

"I had a terrier named Rosie once, when I was a little girl," Doris says. "But she ran away after only a couple weeks."

"How funny! I had a cat named Doris."

"Really?"

"No. I'm kidding."

Doris laughs an incredibly loud laugh. She squeezes my hand again. "Rosie, you are something else, aren't you? I like you already."

It seems pointless to explain that I wasn't trying to be likeable, I was trying to be insolent. Doris seems determined that the two of us are going to be friends. So I walk with her to the common room, where we are all supposed to meet for our first workout. Oh, goody.

Chapter 5
Brad

The first time I saw Carissa Hayward, I thought she was pretty, but not really my type. Too serious. She wore a cardigan sweater, and her long dark hair was pulled back with silver barrettes. She shook my hand as if we were high-level corporate executives entering a very serious business deal and introduced herself with both her first and last names.

I was surprised that she had been chosen to be on the school's morning announcements with me. She didn't seem like she would be very funny. I'd been tapped for the job after my stand-up routine was a hit at the school talent show. Carissa, I assumed, had been picked because of her grades, and she probably wanted the gig as another line on her resume for college applications. I figured I would have to carry the show for the both of us. Students didn't want to be lectured by an uptight goody-goody who sounded like a teacher.

But, I quickly learned, put a mic in front of Carissa and her serious demeanor melted away. I think she was as surprised as I was to discover how well we worked together on-air. She balanced out my oddball zaniness with her impeccably timed dry wit. Monday through Thursday for five minutes during first period, the two of us ruled the school. We interviewed students about school issues, gave notice about upcoming spirit days and dances, and tried to raise enthusiasm about various school club fundraisers. Carissa laughed at my jokes; I teased her about being Miss Perfect.

After a couple weeks, I began coming in earlier and earlier every morning, preparing material I thought would impress her. I actually took time to pick out my clothes and comb my hair before school. One day, as I held the door open for Carissa and we left the office together after a particularly great show, she smiled her devastatingly beautiful smile at me and said, "You know, we make a pretty good team." I knew then that I was a goner.

The rest unfolded like a cheesy Hallmark movie. I made excuses to be around Carissa any chance I got. I even asked her to tutor me in math, the one subject that actually comes easily to me, because we were both in Mr. Steward's class, just different periods. In October, in front of the entire student body during morning announcements, I asked her to be my date to Homecoming. She blushed and said yes. We kissed for the first time as we slow-danced to Usher's "U Got it Bad" under crepe paper and glitter cardboard stars in a secluded corner of the school gym. And, just like that, Carissa Hayward was my girlfriend. The two of us were Meant To Be—still are Meant To Be—or else why would everything have fallen into place so easily?

LEONARD OFFERS to pick me up, but I tell him I'll take my own car and meet him at Matt's. I want to have an easy getaway if the party is lame. And, to be completely honest, I'm hoping to leave the party with Carissa. Maybe we'll drive to our favorite spot out in the lemon orchards by her house, and we'll spend hours lying on the hood of my car, looking up at the stars, her head resting against my chest and her hair fanned out above her, shiny and darker than usual in the pale moonlight.

I'm wearing the button-down shirt Carissa gave me last Christmas, navy blue with white pinstripes, and I've combed my hair so it doesn't stick out at odd angles. Nerves clench my stomach as I park along the curb and walk down the block to Matt's house. It's only 8:30, and already a crowd is spilling out onto the porch. A couple people see me, call my name and wave. Normally I would strike up a conversation, eager for the attention, but tonight I'm not in the mood. I'm only here for one reason: to see Carissa.

Leonard intercepts me in the front hallway. He says something but I can't hear him over the loud techno music pulsing from the living room, where the coffee table and couches have been pushed to the walls to make room for a dance floor. I scan the pulsing crowd of bodies.

And then I see her.

Eyes closed, arms raised, hair bouncing long and loose on her bare shoulders. She's wearing the same pink dress she wore on Valentine's Day, when I took her out for dinner at the Macaroni Grill. Later I overheard her complaining to Stacey that the Macaroni Grill is tacky, but I thought it was nice. Sometimes Carissa and Stacey just like to complain to each other.

I thread my way through the crowd until I am right behind her. I can smell her apricot shampoo.

She turns around. Our eyes lock. For a few beats we dance like that, separated by a sliver of open space. And then I can't take it any longer. I step closer. My hands gently graze her hips. She wraps her arms around my neck. We move together—like everything is all right, the way it used to be. The way it is supposed to still be.

Suddenly, Carissa breaks away. She isn't smiling and I can't read her eyes. My life has come full-circle; she is again the serious stranger she was the day I met her.

"Carissa," I say.

She frowns and says something I can't hear, then makes her way off the dance floor.

I follow.

"Carissa, wait!" I catch up to her in the kitchen.

"Brad." She runs her hand through her hair, a clear sign she is exasperated. "Please. Don't be this way."

"What way?"

"We broke up, remember?"

"But you were just dancing with me, like normal—"

She looks down at her hands. "Dancing doesn't mean anything."

"Can we at least talk for a minute?"

"Talking isn't going to help."

"How do you know that?"

"Because." She steps back, widening the space between us. "I can't say what you want me to say."

"Carissa, where did this come from? I don't get it." My voice cracks, but I don't care. "We were so good together. Weren't we good together?"

Her eyes soften. Hope expands in my chest, thick and insistent, like bread dough rising in a hot oven.

"It's nothing against you, Brad," she says. "Really. It's me. I need time for myself right now." She turns away and heads out to the backyard, the screen door banging shut behind her.

Matt comes over and thumps me heartily on the back. "What's up, my man?" he says. "Thanks for coming out! What can I get you to drink?"

"Just a soda is fine. I drove here."

I follow Matt into his bedroom, where half-a-dozen guys from our class are playing Super Smash Bros. It's nice to let myself get carried away into the game, away from my problems. Carissa never understood that playing video games is my way of decompressing, the same way scrolling Instagram is for her.

After a few rounds, Leo comes in. "Brad, I've been looking all over for you!" he says. "Way to leave me hanging."

"Sorry, I wasn't thinking." I hold out my controller to him. "Wanna play? I was gonna refill my soda anyway."

"No," Leo says quickly. "You stay here. I'll get it for you."

Worry worms into my gut. "It's fine." I stand up. "I'll go myself."

Leo grabs my arm as I stride out of the room. "Brad, look, you don't wanna go in there—"

I hurry past him, down the hallway to the kitchen. Even before I get there, I know what I'm going to find, in the same way you launch a basketball toward the hoop and know it's going to be an air ball. The same way I flipped over the Chemistry final exam last June and knew, as soon as I read the first question, the test was not going to be a shining academic experience for me.

I whip around the corner into the kitchen. And there she is, Carissa Hayward, wearing the dress she wore last Valentine's Day, making out with Matt's older brother, Ryan. His fingers are threaded through her hair.

The next few moments blur together. All I'm thinking is that it should be *me* kissing Carissa, *me* holding her, *me* dancing with her, *me* driving her home tonight.

"Hey!" I shout, stomping over to Ryan and pulling him away. "What are you doing kissing my girlfriend?"

"Brad." Carissa narrows her eyes at me. "I'm. Not. Your. Girlfriend."

She leans into Ryan, and he wraps his arm around her waist. "I'm so sorry about this," she murmurs to him.

That kills me. "I thought you wanted some time for yourself," I say.

"Brad, I know this is hard for you—"

"Is this guy the reason you broke up with me?"

"No, don't be ridiculous. Ryan and I just met tonight."

A crowd has gathered in the kitchen, watching the scene unfold. How has my life come to this? Last week I was in love, getting ready to kick off the best senior year ever with an amazing girlfriend who—I thought—loved me back.

"Carissa," I plead, looking straight into her big hazel eyes. "I love you. I know I didn't appreciate you like I should have. I haven't been the guy you deserve. But I'm a new man now."

She raises an eyebrow. "You don't seem like a new man to me."

"But I am! I'll show you!" I mentally grope for an example to prove to her that I mean what I say. "You know that report for Ostertank? I've finished reading the book. I'm gonna have it done, no problem."

"You finished it? That entire report?"

"Well, I haven't finished it yet—"

She shakes her head. "Sounds like the same old Brad to me. Full of promises, but no follow-through."

"No, Carissa, I swear—"

"Instead of getting things done, you're out partying and playing video games."

"Wait, just listen—"

"That's fine, Brad! Really. Do whatever makes you happy. You're a free man now, I've told you." She turns on her heel, grabs Ryan's arm, and together they head out to the backyard.

"I love you, Carissa! I love you!" I shout after her.

"C'mon, buddy," Leonard says, putting an arm around my shoulder and turning me toward the front door. "Let's get you home."

Chapter 6

Rose

The common room is huge and open and high-ceilinged, filled with comfy couches heaped with pillows and throw blankets. One entire wall is nothing but windows, clean panes sparkling in the sunlight, looking out onto the oak trees. Framed inspirational quotes adorn the walls:

If I can believe it, I can achieve it.

The journey of a thousand miles begins with one step forward.

I am beautiful and strong, inside and out!

Doris and I plop down onto a gingham-striped couch with enormous cushions we sink into. Doris immediately strikes up a conversation with a pretty Black woman who looks to be in her late twenties. We exchange hellos, then Doris is off and running, trying to figure out this woman's life story. I close my eyes and sink farther down into the cushions. I could fall asleep right here.

Almost immediately, the couch sinks down to my left. I open my eyes and see a guy sitting next to me, maybe a year or two older than I am. He has shaggy brown hair, green eyes, and round red cheeks.

"Oh, did I wake you?" he says. His voice has a hint of a Southern drawl. "I'm sorry."

"It's okay, I was just resting my eyes for a moment." *Resting my eyes?* I sound like my mother.

"I'm Daniel," he says, holding out his hand. I take it. His handshake is firm and warm.

"Rose," I offer.

"Pleasure to meet you. So, where are you from?"

"California."

"I've always wanted to go to California!" he says. "Is it really sunny all the time there?"

"Well, we get some rain in the winter. Where I live, the coldest it gets is around forty-five degrees."

His eyes widen. "Forty-five degrees! You serious?"

"Yeah—I mean, I guess I'm a wimp, but that's cold to me. I've lived there all my life. Never known any different."

"Well Texas must seem like home sweet home to you, then," Daniel says. "My parents are both from Georgia—that's where my accent comes from—but I've spent basically my whole life in Montana. It gets real cold there."

"I've heard Montana is beautiful."

"It is. Especially this time of year. I'm going to miss those gorgeous autumn leaves."

"I've never seen a real autumn," I admit.

Daniel gives me a confused look.

"Palm trees don't change colors," I explain.

Daniel laughs. "Well, Rosie, you'll have to come visit me sometime!"

"Sure," I reply, though inwardly I'm retreating. I'm not used to people being so friendly. Usually I'm ignored, as if being fat makes you invisible. Or else, if people are friendly, it only means they want something. I'm not quite sure what to make of Daniel.

"Welcome, everyone!" In front of the fireplace stands a peroxide-blonde, well-dressed, impossibly petite woman. She looks like a Disney Princess come to life.

"My name is Britta Michaelson, and I am the host of *Help Me Lose Weight and Live Again*. I would like to welcome you all to the show. We are all beginning an amazing, transformative, life-changing journey together. Are you ready to get your lives back?"

A few people nod enthusiastically. Doris claps.

"I SAID"—Britta smiles at the cameras—"Are you ready to get your lives back?!"

"Yes!" people cheer. Daniel whistles. I feel like I am in a cheesy motivational video. Something tells me I should get used to this feeling.

Britta introduces our professional trainers, Mark and Leslie. They could be swimsuit models: tan, muscled, not a trace of fat on their bodies. They smile dazzlingly at us. Mark pumps his fist. Leslie distributes *Help Me Lose Weight and Live Again* T-shirts. I wiggle it on over the long-sleeved T-shirt I'm already wearing.

"Let's HIT THE GYM!!" Mark shouts.

A few people whoop and cheer. Doris claps again. Daniel leaps off the couch and reaches down to help me up. He has a nice smile.

I smile back. Maybe this won't be so bad after all.

Chapter 7

Brad

I wake up Saturday morning with an emotional hangover. Remembering Carissa and Ryan together makes me nauseous.

Instead of working on my Ostertank report, I spend the morning brainstorming. Carissa thinks I haven't changed, huh? She thinks I'm still the same old slacker loser who only cares about parties and video games? I'll show her. Pretty soon she'll be begging me to take her back.

Brad Hoffman's Self-Improvement Plan

1. *Pay attention in class. Do all homework assignments. Make Honor Roll.*
2. *Get a job.*
3. *Wake up early and go for a run every morning before school.*
4. *Learn to play the guitar.*
5. *Read a thick, impressive book.*
6. *Get a haircut. (Maybe?)*

I put down my pen and call Leo.

"Do you think I should get a haircut?"

"What? Hey, Brad, are you okay? Last night was rough, man—"

"I'm fine. Listen, I need your opinion. Would I look better with shorter hair?"

"I don't know, dude. I don't really spend my free time thinking about your hair."

When Carissa and I first met, my hair was buzzed short. I've since grown it out, not for any particular reason other than being too lazy to get it cut. Last time I got a haircut was way back in May, a couple days before I took Carissa to Prom. I remember asking her sister, Rose, if she thought I should cut my hair. I was in their kitchen, waiting for Carissa to finish getting ready for our date to the movies. Rose was sitting at the island counter reading a book.

"Do you think I should get a haircut?" I asked her.

Rose looked up from her book and studied me. I mean, *really* studied me. I felt like a sculpture in an art museum. Finally, she smiled. She has a wonderful smile.

"I like your hair both ways," she said.

"Thanks for being nice, but that's no help. Honestly, do you think I should cut it?"

"It would look good short, yeah," Rose said. "But it's also great the length it is now. You've kind of got that sexy rock star look going on."

"Sexy rock star?" I grinned.

Rose blushed. "I think Carissa likes short hair best," she said.

Right on cue, Carissa clomped downstairs in her heels.

"C'mon Brad, hurry up! We're gonna be late for the movie!" she yelled from the hallway, as if *she* were the one who had been waiting for *me* the whole time.

I ended up buzzing my hair for Prom. Carissa must have liked it, since that night was the first time she said she loved me. Of course I told her I loved her, too. I remember feeling like I could burst with happiness. But I was anxious, too—like it was the sort of happiness that could vanish in an instant. Did I sense, even then, how things would end between us?

I push my thoughts away from Carissa and back to Rose. Had she even gone to Prom? I don't remember seeing her there. Why hadn't she come with our group? Rose is way better than the rest of Carissa's friends. You can actually have an intelligent conversation with Rose. She's one of those people who, when she looks at you, truly *sees* you. When I showed Carissa's family some of my stand-up routines on YouTube, I could tell Rose was genuinely laughing. Carissa giggled, but she kept glancing across the room at her mom and dad, trying to read their faces. Sometimes I got the feeling she was embarrassed of me.

I guess I should have been prepared for what happened. I should have realized our relationship was on autopilot. I should have stepped up my game sooner.

But better late than never, right?

"Next time you see me," I tell Leo, "I'm gonna be a changed man." I hang up the phone. Then I drive to The Beachfront Cut & Curl.

"Buzz it all off!" I tell the hairdresser, a leather-faced woman with perfect corkscrew curls, as she adjusts a smock around my neck and shoulders. "It's time for me to look presentable."

✩ ☆ ✩

"You look like a freshman," Leo says when we meet up at Tony's Taco Shack that afternoon. "And not a college freshman. A *high school* freshman."

"Shut up."

"Or like you just joined the Marines. Is that your plan, dude? To make Carissa think you've joined the Marines?"

"Laugh all you want, Leo. Carissa likes short hair."

Though I admit, the hairdresser did buzz it pretty short. Even she said as much. "You've got a good-shaped melon," she pronounced, surveying my freshly shorn head as she whipped the smock off me. "You're lucky. Not everyone would be able to pull off a haircut like this."

Now, Leo points at me, lettuce falling from his mouth. "Dude, I've got an idea. Why don't you shave your initials and Carissa's initials into the back of your head?" He cracks up.

I flick a chunk of salsa at him, but soon I'm laughing too. I'm glad Leo is back to teasing me. It must mean I'm starting to pull myself together.

Last night, after I saw Carissa with Ryan, I was a complete mess.

No one was teasing me then. Leo insisted on driving me home, taking my car keys and sliding behind the wheel. "It's fine," he said. "I'll get my car from Matt's tomorrow." The drive to my house was silent. I turned away toward the window, tears sliding down my face. I didn't want him to know I was crying, but I think he heard my pathetic sniffles. When we pulled up in front of my house, Leo hesitantly patted me on the arm, got out, and walked the two blocks to his house.

Like I said before, Leo is a great friend. And it was really nice of him to take care of me like that. Still, it was awkward. I'm glad he's back to teasing me today.

I stuff the rest of my taco in my mouth, crumple up my used napkin, and chuck it across the table at him. "Later. I've got an Ostertank report to finish."

"Good luck!" he calls after me. "You're gonna need it!"

Chapter 8

The gym is the biggest building at camp, newly built and painted a brilliant white. Inside, a maze of shiny metal machines look like torture devices.

Which, I soon find out, they are.

We've only been in the gym for fifteen minutes when I come to the realization that I am going to die. Here in this shiny new gym with all these cameras rolling.

Unlike Carissa, I do not tend toward melodrama or exaggeration. I honestly feel like I am going to topple over and collapse. My arm muscles ache. My legs are as wobbly as the flan at Tony's Taco Shack, my favorite restaurant back home. My heart is pounding wildly, and I can feel my pulse thrumming in my neck. Pulses are not supposed to thrum so loudly you can hear them in your ears.

Still, Mark reaches over and pushes the "up" arrow on my treadmill, increasing the speed further.

"No!" I gasp. "I can't!"

"*Can't* is not a word in our vocabulary!" Mark barks, loud enough for everyone to hear.

Normally I would be embarrassed to have attention called to me, but right now I am too exhausted and hot and sweaty and frustrated to care. Besides, I don't think the other contestants notice—they are too busy struggling through their own personal hells. I glance at Daniel on the treadmill to my right. His face is bright red, and he is breathing heavily, but his jaw is set in determination as he keeps plodding along. I wish I had his strength.

All I can picture is Carissa's haughty face when she said, "You're so miserable. You can't even take the first step to becoming happy, because you don't believe you deserve happiness." *Well, sis, I'm more miserable now than I've ever been in my entire life.* She acts like she knows everything. Like she has all the answers. But she doesn't. Carissa has no clue what it's like to be me.

Despair tightens my chest. How can I ever expect to find someone who understands me and accepts me for who I am, if even my twin sister doesn't?

I grab onto the treadmill bars with both hands. "I can't do this!"

"Yes you can!" Mark bellows, his mouth inches from my ear.

"No I can't!" And with that, I let go and stumble backward off the treadmill, falling square on my butt. Tears spring to my eyes, and then I'm up and limping toward the exit, sobbing freely now, a quitter and a baby for all of national television to see.

Outside, the sky is a brilliant blue. The saying is true: everything *does* seem bigger in Texas. The sky stretches high overhead, and the horizon wavers blurrily in the distance. I walk slowly past the common room, past our cabins, down the long dirt road that leads out of camp. No one comes after me. No cameras follow me, unless they are hidden somewhere in the silent trees lining the path. I squint up at the leaves, but I don't see anything.

August in Texas is hot. Very hot. Outside of the air-conditioned gym, the air is heavy and oppressive. My double layer of T-shirts, already soaked through from sweating on the Treadmill of Hell, stick to my back and shoulders. My hair is knotty and damp. I want to cut it all off. I want to collapse into a giant pool of ice-cold water. I want to drive to the ocean and jump in the waves with all my clothes on. Back home, we live only ten minutes from the beach, but I can't remember the last time I went there.

Actually, I do remember. In eighth grade, my school held Beach Day for the entire graduating class. I didn't want to go. All the awkwardness that is an unavoidable part of middle school was magnified and compounded by my weight, which felt like an inescapable part of my identity. Maybe not to my inner self, but to how other people saw me.

I didn't want to go to Beach Day, but I knew I had to. Because if I didn't go, Holly would be alone. I tried convincing her to skip with me, but Holly is the type of person who gets anxious riding the school bus because there are no seatbelts. For her, skipping a mandatory school event was out of the question. So we went to Beach Day. I kept my T-shirt and shorts on the whole time.

Holly and I actually had fun, at first. We built an enormous sand castle and splashed in the waves while the rest of the girls in our class sunbathed and played volleyball in their tiny bikinis. Carissa wore a purple-and-white polka-dot bikini that had cost her two months of babysitting money. Even in middle school, I was saving all my money for college. My dream is to study Broadcast Journalism at UCLA, work super hard and land a bunch of internships at different stations in Los Angeles, and then graduate with honors and get a job I love. I want to host my own radio show—interviewing people, offering advice, talking about issues of the day. When you're on the radio, it doesn't matter what you look like.

Brad is the only one who knows about my radio career ambitions. It slipped out one day after he showed me and Carissa a video of his latest stand-up comedy routine. He films them and posts them on YouTube. In the middle of it, Carissa's cell phone buzzed with a call from one of her friends, and she fled to the kitchen to talk. Through the wall, we could occasionally hear her exclamations of "No way!" and high shrieks of laughter.

Brad told me that after he graduates from high school, he's planning to take his clips to a local radio show producer and maybe get his own show lined up, even for one of the late-late-late or early-early-early time slots.

"I don't care when it is," he said. "I just want to be on the air! It would be so cool."

"Tell me about it!" I said. "If you have a radio show, it means you have a voice. You say things and people actually *listen*."

"Exactly! That's why I want to get into the business. To connect with people. To change the world." He sighed. "Carissa thinks I'm naïve."

"Well, Carissa thinks I'm nothing but a boring fat girl." As soon as the words left my mouth, a warm blush flamed across my cheeks. Why had I said that to Brad, of all people? I didn't even talk to Holly about my relationship with Carissa. The only place I felt comfortable being so painfully honest was in the pages of my journal, late at night. I didn't dare look at Brad.

He cleared his throat. "Well," he said, "Carissa doesn't always know what she's talking about, does she?"

And then, to dissipate the awkwardness, he showed me a YouTube video of his impression of Mrs. Ostertank, the terrible junior and senior English teacher who perpetually sucks on cough drops and hands out detention slips like they're raffle tickets. Brad is awesome at impressions. Before long, I was laughing so hard my eyes watered.

Later, right before he left, Brad came into the kitchen where I was doing homework. "Hey, Rose?" he said.

I looked up from my math homework, surprised to see him there in the doorway. "Yeah?"

"I think you'd make a great radio host," he said.

"Thanks, Brad. You too."

"Hey, maybe someday we'll have a show together. Brad and Rose Take Over the Airwaves."

"The Brosie Showsie."

"Ha! Yeah."

I smiled. "That'd be great."

He smiled back, said goodbye, and left. I had trouble concentrating on my math homework the rest of the night.

If only Brad knew how badly I had wanted to be on morning announcements with him. Again and again, I had checked the notice boards for audition information, but I never glimpsed a single announcement or sign-up sheet. Turns out the music teacher, who was in charge of lining up the morning announcement hosts each school year, was out on maternity leave and auditions fell through the cracks. Three weeks before school let out for the summer, the Vice Principal tapped Brad because his Talent Show stand-up act had been such a hit, and Carissa because—well, because everyone loves Carissa.

Carissa told us the news over dinner. Our parents were very proud, of course. Scotty asked if he could come on the morning announcements and tell one of his knock-knock jokes (he was big on knock-knock jokes last spring; now he's into riddles). I choked on my spaghetti, said I wasn't feeling well, and escaped to my room for the rest of the night. The next day, though, I pulled myself together and made Carissa a "Congrats" cake, complete with a microphone drawn on with chocolate icing.

She hugged me and said I was the best sister ever, but she couldn't eat any of it because she was on a diet. "I've gotta fit into my Prom dress!" she said. "It's a beautiful cake though, Rosie. Thank you." She kissed my cheek. Her lips were sticky with lip gloss.

I wasn't going to Prom, so I didn't have to worry about fitting into a dress. I ate the entire cake myself. It tasted delicious, but afterward I felt awful.

Not as awful as I feel now, though. I stop to rest, leaning against a tree beside the path. Its leaves rustle slightly in the breeze. I close my eyes. I don't feel as awful physically as I did when I first left the gym —my breathing is coming easier, my heartbeat has slowed to almost normal, and the sweat is cooling on my back in an almost-pleasant way. But I feel awful inside. What will my parents say when they watch me quit the workout and storm out of the gym? What will Scotty think? And Carissa? For all I resent her for signing me up for this show, she is my sister, and she does care about me. Just when I start to forget, she finds ways to remind me.

Like on eighth-grade Beach Day. Holly and I were tossing a

beach ball back and forth, the waves washing over our feet, lapping gently against our shins. She threw the ball and a gust of wind blew it over my head. I jumped up and caught it, but I came down on a rock, slipped, and twisted my ankle. When I tried to stand, I couldn't. My ankle throbbed like painful, bass-booming speakers were implanted in the bone.

Holly sprinted up the beach to get a teacher. Carissa was the first person to reach me. I was crying, out of embarrassment as much as pain. Carissa wiped my cheeks like our mom would have if she had been there, with a quick synchronized swipe of her thumbs.

"It's okay, Rosie." She reached for my hand. "Here. Let me help you up."

"No, I'm too heavy. You can't."

"Yes I can. Come on." And my twin sister grabbed my arm and pulled me up, slipping my arm around her thin shoulders.

"Lean on me," she said. So I did.

Together, we slowly made our way out of the water and up the beach. Carissa didn't complain once about my weight. She acted like I was light as a feather. I think she knew I would have been mortified to lean on any other student, even a strong football player, much less a teacher. She was trying to protect me.

Maybe I don't give her enough credit. Maybe she really did sign me up for this show because she wants me to be happy, and this is the only way she knows how to help me do that.

I open my eyes and wipe my face with my T-shirt sleeve. Then I take a deep breath, turn around, and make my way slowly back up the dirt road to the gym.

Chapter 9

Brad

Monday morning comes way too soon. My alarm blares at 5:45, and I stumble out of bed, nearly tripping over my clothes and shoes discarded around the room. I was up past midnight finishing that dreaded Ostertank report—but I *did* finish it.

Now, as I read through it a final time and click PRINT, a wave of pride washes over me.

I actually did it.

I *am* changing.

It's only a matter of time until Carissa sees it, too.

I lace up my running shoes and step out the front door into the cool, misty morning. I can't remember the last time I was awake this early, much less out in the world. The sun hasn't risen yet, and there's a dark stillness in the air. As I jog past the quiet houses on my street, I think of all the people sleeping soundly in their beds. Being up this early, it's like I'm privy to a secret world most everyone else sleeps through.

I turn out of my neighborhood and cross the street to the park. The freshly mown grass is springy under my feet. I pick up the pace. I'm wide awake now. My legs are strong. My lungs pump clean, cool air through my chest. I feel like I could run forever.

After two loops around the park, I'm breathing heavy and dragging my feet. I guess it takes a while to get in shape. Still, I'm proud of myself. This is the start of something.

I reach my neighborhood and walk down the street to my house. Daybreak. The sky blazes with pinks and purples. Down the street, a neighbor stumbles out of his house, pulled along by his eager golden retriever. I wave. He smiles and waves back. A sense of hope, of goodness, burgeons in my chest.

I shower, shave, and put on my favorite T-shirt, a faded "WAVE 104.3 Radio" shirt I won in a call-in years ago, before I met Carissa. This shirt has been with me through it all.

The closer the clock gets to 8:00, the more my confidence fades to a knot of nerves clenching my stomach. Just a week ago, I was actually looking forward to school starting. As much as I love summer, there's something about a new school year that seems so promising. A blank canvas stretching out in front of you. With Carissa by my side, I knew I would have at least one good thing in my life, no matter what else the year threw at me.

Now, everything is uncertain. I force a smile as I study my reflection in the bathroom mirror. I have no clue what to expect from today. As far as I know, Carissa and I will both still be doing morning announcements this year, though the job doesn't start until next week. I am anxious to see her again, especially after Friday night. Remembering her and Ryan together makes my head ache.

I try to convince myself it was a one-time thing. When I see Carissa, she will be blown away by my new haircut and new sense of responsibility. She will throw her arms around me and beg me to take her back. She misses me so much and can't believe she ever let me go.

I imagine myself pulling away from her, making her sweat. "What about Ryan?" I'll ask.

"Oh, he's nothing compared to you, Brad!" she'll say.

So I'll wrap my arms around her and kiss her, and we'll walk the hallways holding hands, and everything will be back to normal, the way life *should* be.

I force my smile wider, but it doesn't reach my eyes. I turn away, grab my backpack off the floor, and head downstairs and out the front door. 7:43. Usually I'm late to everything, but that was Old Brad. New Brad is early, even to school.

✩ ☆ ✩

Carissa got a haircut, too. And it's all anyone can talk about.

"Your hair!" Stacey shrieks. "I love it!"

"Wow, you're so brave, Carissa!" Lindsay says. "It looks fabulous, but I don't think I'd ever have the nerve to chop my hair off like that."

"It was time for a change, you know?" Carissa says. "Something new."

Her long brown hair now falls just below her ears, framing her face and making her eyes somehow appear even huger than before.

"Plus, I was able to donate it," Carissa continues. "I've always wanted to do that."

"Aww, that's so sweet of you," Stacey says. "Always thinking of others."

It's lunchtime, a beautiful sunny day, and our group has claimed one of the senior tables outside, in prime location by the snack bar and the girls' bathroom. Leo waves me over to sit by him, but I head toward Carissa. I can't help it. She is captivating. She looks like a model. Or an actress.

"You look like Natalie Portman!" Mel says.

"Oh, please," Carissa says.

"No, really, you do," I say, sitting down next to her. Carissa half-smiles at me but doesn't say anything. An awkward hush falls over the table.

"Brad got a haircut, too!" Leo puts in, too loudly.

"Oh yeah, I guess you did, huh?" says Lindsay.

"What did your hair look like before?" Mel says. "I can't remember."

"It was longer," I say. "It's, uh, shorter now."

Things are kind of weird with our friendship group now that Carissa and I aren't together. Last year, when we started dating, it seemed natural for her friends and my friends to sit together at lunch. And everyone really hit it off. Now Danny and Mel are a couple, and Leo's been flirting with Stacey forever—they're practically a couple, for all intents and purposes—and Lindsay and Tim bonded over their mutual love of surfing and snowboarding. Now the problem is that everyone hit it off *too* well. We're hopelessly enmeshed. No longer is it "my friends" and "Carissa's friends"—separate entities. Now it's "our friends." But since Carissa and I broke up, everything seems different.

It's like I'm living in a strange alternate universe, waiting for everything to snap back into place, back to the way my life *should* be. Everywhere I look, I'm reminded of her. Of us. The bench where we used to sit, my arm around her, during snack break between second and third period. The tree we stood under that drizzly morning before class, when I kissed her for the first time and she wrapped her arms around my neck and kissed me back. I remember how it seemed unbearable to go a couple periods without feeling her hand in mine. As soon as the bell rang, I'd shoot out of my seat, meet her in the hallway, and envelop her in a hug. She'd laugh and kiss my cheek or playfully bite my ear, and we'd amble our way to the lunch tables, together, my arm around her waist and her hand in my back pocket.

Does she miss it too? Does she miss us? At all?

I've been on edge all morning. Every period, I hurry in and scan the room, hoping Carissa might be in my class. First period I thought for sure she'd be in Ostertank's class with me, but I guess this year there are so many seniors in A.P. English that it's spilled over into two classes, and of course Carissa is in the other period. Our entire schedules seem to be off that way. By the time lunch rolls around, I'm desperate to see her, to talk to her, to show her I've changed, that I'm Brand New Brad.

I'm sitting beside her so close my knee brushes against hers. She's turned away from me, talking to Lindsay on her other side. Without glancing my way, she scoots a few inches away.

Frustration burns in my chest. Why is she acting like I don't exist? Like I've done something wrong? *She's* the one who broke up with *me. She's* the one who broke *my* heart. But from the way she's acting, you'd think it was the other way around.

I poke her arm. "Hey, friend."

She ignores me. Across the table, Leo shoots me a look.

I poke her again. "Hey, friend!"

She turns, squinting in the sunlight. "What is it, Brad?"

"Just wanted to say hi. See how your day's going. You know—as a *friend*."

She sighs. "Brad..."

"You said, if I remember correctly, that you still want us to be *friends*. So that's what I'm trying to do." I pull my peanut-butter sandwich out of my lunch bag and take a big bite, even though my stomach's churning and I'm anything but hungry. Mouth full, I smile close-lipped at Carissa, as if today is any other lunch period, as if this is any other school year, as if I'm not heartbroken in the slightest.

Carissa eyes me warily. "I'm fine," she says. "First day of school is always boring, going over the class rules and everything."

"I finished my report for Ostertank," I put in proudly. "Turned it in this morning, first period."

"That's great, Brad," she says, and actually smiles at me. "I'm proud of you."

"And I went on a run this morning. Before school. I'm getting in shape." I hadn't meant to tell her this yet, hadn't planned on throwing all my cards on the table at once, but I can't seem to stop talking. I so desperately want to coax another smile out of her. Another beautiful Carissa smile directed right at me.

And it works. "Wow, Brad. How far did you run?"

"Two miles. I mean, it was only the first day. I'm gonna increase the mileage. Work my way up to a 10K."

"10K? How far is that?" Danny asks.

"Just over six miles."

"Woo!" Stacey whistles. "Go Brad!"

"Maybe you could talk about it on morning announcements," Carissa says.

"Yeah," I agree. I spot my chance and lunge for it. "Hey, speaking of that, we should get together this week sometime. You know, to plan the show—what we're gonna talk about and everything."

"Oh, I don't know," Carissa says, looking down at the table instead of at me. "I don't think we really need to do that anymore. We're old pros. How about you prepare your part and I prepare mine, and we'll put them together when we get on the air?"

"What do you mean, 'parts'? We always used to prepare the show together."

"It's too time-consuming. This is senior year. It's gonna be super busy. We'll both find some things to talk about and bring them in and we'll be fine. Plus Mr. Marshall always gives us a list of school announcements, so that takes up a lot of time."

"But—"

"I mean, really, Brad." Now Carissa does meet my eyes. "It's not that big of a deal. It's just morning announcements."

"What do you mean, *just* morning announcements?" She knows how important the morning announcements gig is to me. And it's important to her, too. At least, it was—to the old Carissa. To the cool, sweet, fun girl who used to love me.

"I guess you're too good for everything now, is that it?" I ask.

"Brad, don't be like this. I'm sorry I hurt your feelings—"

"No," I interject. "You know what, it's no big deal. If doing morning announcements is such a drag for you, I'm sure Mr. Marshall can find someone else to take over. Or I can do it all by myself."

"Don't be offended." Carissa sighs, which only infuriates me more. "I like doing morning announcements. All I'm saying is, this year is gonna be busy."

I crumple my lunch bag and stand up, untangling my legs from the bench. I don't know where I'm going, but I know I need to get out of here, fast, before the humiliating tears building behind my eyes leak out.

"Sorry to take up your precious time," I spit out. "I guess I'll be going."

Carissa doesn't say anything, just lets me walk away.

Leo calls out, "Brad, hey!" but I don't turn around. No way I'm letting Leo see me cry twice in one week.

Sitting in my car in the student parking lot, waiting for the bell to ring that signals the end of lunch, I think of Carissa's sister, Rose, who I once saw eating her lunch out here by herself in the car she and Carissa share. I wonder how Rose is doing. It's strange, but she's about the only person I could stand to see right now.

Chapter 10

"**I**s anyone sitting here?" Daniel asks.

I shake my head and he sits down next to me.

Dinner is baked chicken breast (with the skin removed), steamed broccoli, and mixed green salad. We're not allowed to serve ourselves; instead, the chef brings our plates to us.

"How you feeling?" Daniel says.

I focus my attention on cutting my chicken into super-small bites to make it last longer. "I'm okay. You?"

"Already sore. Tomorrow's gonna be brutal."

"Yeah." I can tell Daniel's trying to be nice, but I don't feel like talking. About anything, and especially not about workouts. When I re-entered the gym this afternoon, it seemed like everyone paused to turn and look at me. A cameraman scurried over, red light blinking, no doubt expecting drama. Trainer Mark glanced over but stayed where he was, spotting Doris on a weight machine.

I stood there, feeling awkward and out of place. I thought of Carissa. What would she do? She never lets anything ruffle her. Channeling my sister, I lifted my chin and strode quickly over to the treadmills. I climbed back up on my treadmill beside Daniel, who flashed me a smile, and then I pushed the green "Start" button. The belt beneath me gathered speed.

A few minutes later, Mark sauntered over. I steeled myself for him to yell at me like he had before, to push the "Up" arrow and make the belt go faster and faster. *This time,* I vowed, *do not break. Do not let him get to you.*

But Mark smiled at me—a smile taut with condescension—and simply said, "Glad you're back."

"Thanks," I huffed.

Mark nodded and walked away.

But I have a niggling feeling he has more to say.

After dinner, everyone migrates to the common room to sit around the fireplace and talk. I don't feel like joining in, but I also don't want to set myself apart as the outsider any more than I already have. So I sit beside Doris on a different overstuffed gingham couch and half-listen as she and Marcella, a sixty-year-old grandmother from the Bronx, swap hair-styling tips.

"My hair's naturally wavy," Doris confides in a low voice. "But I straighten it."

"You straighten it? Why? I would kill for wavy hair!"

"If I don't straighten it, my hair gets so frizzy." Doris smooths her hands over her hair as if worried the mere mention of frizz will cause her strands to pouf up uncontrollably.

"See, here's what you do," Marcella reaches out and rolls a strand of Doris's hair between her fingers. "At the end of your shower, before you step out of the tub, turn the water to cold and count to thirty."

"Thirty seconds?" Doris shrieks. "That's an eternity! I'll freeze!"

"Trust me. My daughter has wavy hair and she swears by this. The cold water seals the hair follicles against frizz."

I am making a mental note to try this myself when there is a tap on my arm. I turn, half-expecting to see Daniel's warm smile, but instead I look up into Mark's tan, chiseled face. There is, predictably, a cameraman right behind him.

"Hey Rosie," he says. "Do you have a minute? Wanna go for a walk?"

What else can I say but "Okay"?

✧ ☆ ✧

"So what happened today?" Mark asks.

The last rays of sunlight slant through the trees. I try to give Mark the benefit of the doubt. Maybe he really *does* want to make sure I'm okay. But, for some reason, I don't feel comfortable talking to him. I don't trust him. There's something about his smile that reminds me of Carissa's friends watching me eat my PB&J that day at lunch, snickering behind their teeth. Not to mention the camera guys clomping along beside us, microphones extended so they don't miss a word. They don't exactly ease my nerves.

I cross my arms over my chest and shove my hands under my armpits. "I don't know," I say. "I just... I didn't feel like I could do it."

"So you quit," Mark says.

I nod and look down. Tears burn my eyes. I would give anything to be away from this place, back at home in my room, getting ready to begin senior year with everyone else.

"But then...you came back," Mark says. He raises his voice, addressing the cameras more than me. "You. Came. Back."

I'm not sure if I'm supposed to respond or stay silent. A breeze rustles the leaves of the trees. The clouds are edged in fuchsia.

"Why did you come back?" Mark asks.

"Because." I swallow, forcing the tears down. "Because I didn't want to be a quitter."

"You're not a quitter, Rosie."

"Thank you."

"You proved that today. You proved to us—and to yourself—that you want to be here. Right, Rosie?"

"Yeah."

"What's that?"

"Yeah. Yes, I do."

"You do what?"

"Want to be here."

"Did you send in your application to come onto this show?" he asks.

I shake my head. "Hey, should we go back inside?" I say. "It'll be dark soon."

Mark waves my words off. "Who sent in your application?"

"My sister."

"Your older sister?"

"We're twins, actually. Carissa is a minute younger than me."

"Are you two close?"

I shrug. I'm not sure what to say. We were close as kids. Lately, not so much. But all I want is to end this conversation and retreat to the solitude of my room, so I keep it simple and say, "Yeah."

"Does Carissa struggle with her weight, too?"

"No. She's perfect."

"Ahh," Mark says. His eyes gleam in the waning sunlight. "Nobody's perfect, Rosie."

"Well, you haven't met my sister. Everyone loves Carissa. She's got perfect grades, perfect clothes, the perfect boyfriend—"

I bite my tongue, aware once again of the cameras. Texas might seem far away from Carissa and home and my real life, but it's not. All of this—any moment caught by the red blinking light of the cameras—is fair game. Who knows what the producers and editors will choose to include in each episode when the show is televised in January.

"Have you ever had a boyfriend, Rosie?" Mark asks, lips curled into a smirk.

The sky looks bruised. I am flushed and teary and exhausted. I can't deal with this anymore.

"Listen, Mark," I say, breaking away from the path and turning back toward the gym, the common room, the cabins. "I'm really tired all of a sudden. I'm gonna head to bed."

"Rosie, I hope I didn't upset you," Mark says.

"No, no," I lie. "I'm just really tired."

"Good night," he says.

I flee up the path, thinking of my warm bed, eager for the privacy of my room.

"Rosie!" Mark calls after me.

Inwardly cursing, I stop and turn.

"I'm glad you're here!" he yells.

I force a smile, wave, and continue on my way. *Of course you're glad I'm here. The timid twin with the dazzling sister. The fat girl who's never been kissed.* I've always skirted the spotlight, but here I'm already becoming a one-woman drama mill, my insecurities nailed down and splayed wide open for everyone to see. When Mark looks at me, he sees a boost in ratings waiting to be tapped into. *The ugly duckling hoping to become a swan.*

Chapter 11

Brad

When I wake up, it's already light outside. Panic doesn't immediately set in because I figure it must be the weekend. Then, like dominoes, a series of realizations crash over me:

1. It's not the weekend, it's Monday morning.
2. And not just any Monday morning. The first day of morning announcements.
3. It is 7:57 A.M.
4. Morning announcements begin at 8:00.
5. *Craaaaap I'm going to be late.*

I leap out of bed, throw on a sweatshirt and jeans, grab my backpack, and bolt to my car. Stupid unreliable alarm. What happened? I *know* I set it last night.

Miraculously, I am blessed with a record number of green lights and pull into the school parking lot with my dashboard clock reading 8:08. Adrenaline on overdrive, I sprint to the office and yank open the door to the broadcast studio, which is basically a closet with a P.A. system.

Carissa flashes me an unsurprised smile and says into the mic, "Well, guess who just walked in—it's my always-dependable co-host, Brad Hoffman! Good morning, sunshine."

I plop down beside her, breathing heavily. "Sorry I'm late. My alarm didn't go off for some reason."

"I thought maybe you weren't coming," she says.

"Why would you think that? This gig is my life!" I mean it as humor, but it sounds pathetic. Carissa makes it even worse by letting a couple beats of awkward silence elapse before she speaks.

"So..." Carissa says, her tone bright. "I have an announcement from Mrs. Erickson about senior portraits. I know it's only the second week of school, but appointments fill up fast. All seniors should go to the office to sign up before September fourteenth if they want their pictures included in the yearbook."

"I need to figure out the pose I'm gonna do for my senior portrait." I flex my muscles at Carissa, trying to remind her of the funny guy she fell for.

She doesn't laugh. Doesn't even crack a smile. "What pose?" she says. "You sit there and they take your picture."

"I thought you get to do a cool pose. Like...Superman or something."

"Superman?"

"Without the cape."

Carissa smirks. "Brad, you are, like, the furthest thing from Superman."

"Ouch."

"I mean—if you were Superman, you wouldn't have been late this morning. You could have flown here."

"I wouldn't have needed an alarm clock. I would have just woken up."

"Exactly."

"Usually I've been waking up early, you know," I put in. I want to remind her that I'm changing. I'm an early riser. A go-getter. Responsible. Being late this morning, that was a stroke of bad luck. "I've been running every morning before school."

"You told me," she says. "You're training for a 5K, right?"

"A 10K. Six miles. They hold a race downtown every Christmas to collect canned goods for people in need."

"That's really nice of you."

"What can I say? I'm a nice guy."

"You're the nicest guy I know." But she isn't looking at me. She's smiling into the microphone. Putting on a show.

"I guess it's true what they say, then."

"What do you mean?" Carissa asks, eying me warily.

"Everyone says nice guys finish last. I guess it's true." I know I sound bitter, but I can't help myself. I hate this—it feels all wrong. Fake. Me and Carissa, carrying on in front of the entire school as if everything is the same. All my good memories of us are being tainted. Was she pretending then, too? Was she pretending the whole time we were together?

"Brad, please," Carissa sighs. "Now isn't the time."

"Then when *is* the time, Carissa? I never get one moment alone with you to talk about things."

"Brad—"

"All of a sudden—wham. You're done. Now you act like I'm invisible."

Carissa covers her mic with her hand. "Stop it," she hisses. "You're embarrassing me."

That's when I lose it. "Oh, my bad, Carissa. Sorry I'm so *embarrassing* to you." I'm speaking loudly now, practically shouting. "Sorry that our relationship actually *meant* something to me. Sorry I can't just turn off my freaking feelings—"

Carissa cuts in. "I apologize to everyone for this unprofessional turn of conversation."

The studio door slams open to reveal a purple-faced Principal Marshall.

"That's all for today's morning announcements," Carissa quavers into the mic.

"Brad Hoffman," Mr. Marshall bellows. "My office. Now."

✧ ☆ ✧

I STUMBLE through the rest of the day in a haze. I avoid my friends—even Leo. I can't face his worried eyes. I want to be alone. At lunch, I sit by myself in my car and slowly chew my food without tasting it. I try to take notes in class, but I keep zoning out. When the final bell rings, I make a beeline to the school parking lot and head straight home.

I can't remember the last time I felt so relieved to be in my own messy room. I collapse into bed, kick off my shoes, and close my eyes. I want to drift away and forget everything.

I wake up with a jolt. My phone alarm blares. Weak light streams through the blinds. The clock reads 5:45. For a moment, I am overjoyed. *The whole day was a terrible anxiety dream, and now I get to live it again, the right way.*

"Brad, is that your noise?" my mom calls from downstairs. "Turn it off! It's almost time for dinner!"

It's not morning.

It's evening.

Five-forty-five P.M.

Only the second week of senior year, and already I feel like I'm running on a treadmill that keeps going faster and faster. Carissa Hayward is no longer my girlfriend. I eat lunch in my car because I feel awkward around my friends. And today I was kicked off morning announcements for "being inappropriate" and "making a scene." Not for a week, or even a month. For the entire rest of the school year.

"You're lucky not to be suspended, young man," Mr. Marshall had said. "Harassing Carissa like that on air. What were you thinking?"

"I don't know," I replied. "I'm sorry. I don't know what came over me."

Now, I turn off my alarm and flop back down into bed. So much for a Whole New Brad. So much for Winning Carissa Back. Ever since she dumped me, I've been slipping further and further back on the treadmill...and today, the inevitable happened. I fell off.

Chapter 12

Rose

Daniel was right. When my alarm blares, I have trouble getting out of bed. I'm so stiff and sore that moving is painful. My limbs feel heavy, like my muscles are sandbags, and there's an uncomfortable tightness in my chest and shoulders when I stretch.

I throw on my sweatpants and T-shirt and barely make it downstairs in time for a breakfast of apples, bananas, and protein bars.

"Morning, sunshine!" Doris says. Her blonde hair is a pouf of curls pulled up into a high ponytail.

"Hey, I like your hair," I tell her. "You have such pretty curls."

"Thank you, sweetheart," she says, beaming.

I unwrap a protein bar. I must make a face when I take a bite, because Daniel laughs.

"A bit chalky, huh?" he says, holding up his own half-eaten bar. "Try washing it down with orange juice, then it's not so bad."

"Thanks," I say. "How do you know this stuff?"

"I used to be a runner," Daniel replies. "In middle school. I know you can't tell now, but I was a pretty fast little guy."

"Wow. How far did you run?"

"Well, my races were the one-mile and the two-mile, but to train I'd run a lot farther—five or six or even seven miles sometimes."

"Wow." The farthest I've ever run was a mile for the Fitness Standards Test in P.E., and I had to walk some.

"So why'd you stop running?" I ask.

Before Daniel can answer we're interrupted by Leslie, who shouts in her Barbie voice, "C'mon, everyone! It's time to HIT THE GYM!"

I throw the rest of my protein bar in the trash.

"Hey, Rosie?" Daniel asks as we walk over to the gym. "Do you wanna be work-out partners? Team up?"

"Oh, I don't know..." I think of Daniel's sympathetic smile when I came back to the gym yesterday. He's so nice, but I don't want his pity. And I don't want to be a burden on his workouts. I can take care of myself.

"The thing is, I have trouble staying motivated," Daniel says. "It's only our second day here, and already my energy is slipping. I thought, you know, if you and I worked out together and helped each other... "

Daniel stops walking, so I stop too. He looks me right in the eyes. His eyes are a deep green, like sea grass.

"I know you would keep me motivated, Rosie." His face is so serious. He swallows while waiting for my response.

Is he nervous? No, he can't be. No one ever gets nervous around me.

"Okay," I say. "Yeah, that sounds great."

"Really?" Daniel smiles like sunshine breaking out from behind a bank of clouds.

I smile too. "Workout partners."

"Workout partners it is." We shake hands and continue on our way to the gym.

A few minutes later, when Daniel holds the gym door open for me and says, "After you, teammate," I'm still thinking about how warm his hand was, and how nice it felt when his fingers enclosed my own.

☆ ☆ ☆

THE WEEK WHIZZES by in a blur of sweat, heat, aching muscles, sandbag limbs, chalky protein bars, and healthy meals that never seem quite filling enough. I yearn for a dish of rich vanilla ice cream, mashed potatoes and macaroni and cheese, dark chocolate and buttery popcorn, and more chocolate.

But, as sore and tired as my muscles are, I *do* seem to have more, not less, energy as the week goes on.

Or perhaps that energy comes from working out with Daniel. When I feel exhausted beyond belief, Daniel smiles at me and says, "Good job, Rosie! One more! Do one more!" And somehow, I find a hidden well of strength that allows me to do one more sit-up, one more weight rep, one more minute on the treadmill.

Sunday morning is our last workout before the first weigh-in session. Daniel and I jog side-by-side on elliptical machines.

"Are you excited for the weigh-in?" he asks.

"More nervous than excited."

"I'm sure you'll do great," Daniel says. "Before you know it, you'll be running a 10K!"

"A 10K? What's that?"

"It's a race. Ten kilometers."

"How far is ten kilometers?"

"A little over six miles."

"Six *miles*?" I laugh and shake my head. "There's no way I could run six miles."

"Don't put limits on yourself," Daniel says. "Just you wait. At the end of all this, you and I will do a 10K together, easy."

"Okay," I huff. "It's a deal."

According to my elliptical machine, I've gone 0.7 miles. I'm already gasping for breath on jelly legs. As hard as I've worked this week, I still have *soooo* far to go.

✧ ✦ ✧

I'M NOT sure what to expect at the weigh-in. I'm so uncomfortable that I'm not really thinking about the scale. I'm focused on crossing my arms over my bare stomach to try to cover as much of myself as possible. The guys are all shirtless; we girls are only allowed to wear shorts and bright pink sports bras, a color Holly and I both swore we'd never wear.

I wasn't the only one who balked during dinner this evening when Britta went over the last-minute "Weigh-In Pointers" and got to the part about the dress code. We're all here because of how uncomfortable we feel in our own skin—and that's with clothes *on*. It seems sadistic to magnify every ounce of insecurity we possess about our bodies by forcing us to step onto a scale half-naked on national television.

"I don't see what the big deal is, you guys," Britta said, waving her pencil-thin arms. "The goal of the weigh-in is to get an honest calculation of your weight, which means you should be wearing as little extra weight as possible. This also puts everyone on an equal playing field. Everyone is being weighed with the same exact parameters."

We've only been here a week, but still I'm surprised by how easily all the other contestants go along with whatever Mark and Leslie and Britta say. It's like they are All-Knowing Fitness Gods. Or maybe I'm the only one who didn't sign myself up for this—who isn't filled with pure, all-encompassing joy to be here.

I feel numb as I watch the other contestants walk up one-by-one onto the stage to be weighed. Marcella loses eight pounds. An ecstatic curly-haired Doris drops nine. A few of the biggest guys lose major weight—fourteen pounds, sixteen pounds. It's only been one week! This is unbelievable. My stomach turns anxiously. Is it even healthy to lose so much weight so quickly? What is this doing to our bodies?

Even though I'm more skeptical of Mark and Leslie and their methods than the other contestants seem to be, I'm not immune to the peer pressure they've created. My thoughts spin. What if I go up there and I've lost a pitiful two pounds? What if I haven't lost any weight at all, even after all the grueling workouts I've put in this week? What if none of it was enough? What if the fat clings to my body like sea barnacles cling to a mossy ocean rock? Or what if—my cheeks grow warm at the thought—what if I've *gained* weight? That would be humiliating.

Now that I've thought of this possibility, I'm convinced it's going to happen.

"Rosie!" Britta announces, flashing her bright white smile to the cameras. "You're up!"

Daniel must glimpse my terrified expression, because he pats my arm gently. "Be confident," he says. "You've worked so hard this week."

I swallow and try to nod. My legs shake as I make my way up the steps of the platform.

I turn around slowly, looking out at the other contestants. Doris gives me a thumbs-up. Marcella waves. But it's Daniel's face I latch onto, Daniel's smile I fixate on as I take a deep breath and step onto the scale.

Right foot, left foot. I try to exhale all my breath.

The scale beeps as the numbers whir past. I can't look.

Suddenly, the beeping stops. Daniel's smile broadens. The room erupts into cheers. Heart thumping wildly, I slowly turn to read the giant numbers lit up on the screen beside me.

"Congratulations, Rosie!" Britta says. "You've lost ten pounds!"

Ten? Ten pounds? I stare in disbelief at the numbers.

"How do you feel?" Britta asks.

It takes me a moment to find my voice. "I—I—great!" I finally say. "I feel great!"

Everyone laughs and claps some more. Doris yells, "You go girl!"

I pump my fist in the air, then walk down the steps and take my place beside Daniel in the row of contestants.

Daniel wraps me in a big hug. "You rock!" he says in my ear.

"Thanks," I reply. "I'm so happy!"

And I mean it. For the first time since I arrived here, I don't wish I were back home instead.

Chapter 13

Wednesday. I'm sitting in my car in the school parking lot, waiting for the clock to creep to 8:15. I don't think I can handle hearing Carissa on the morning announcements with her new co-host, a sophomore named Sam who undoubtedly is harboring a huge crush on her. Last year, Sam played one of the lead roles in the school musical. The guy can sing, and I've heard he's funny, too. Probably has Carissa in stitches. I don't want to hear it.

So I'm waiting until morning announcements are over before I venture onto campus. Yesterday I told my first-period teacher, Mrs. Sussman, that I had car trouble. She must have been feeling generous, because she didn't give me a tardy. Something tells me she won't be so understanding when I walk in late again today. I don't have an excuse ready. All I can hope is she'll see the anguish on my face and won't press it.

8:08. I glance around for something to occupy the next few minutes, to keep myself from obsessing about Carissa and Sam. On the passenger's side of the dashboard hulks *Infinite Jest,* the 1,100-page tome I bought last weekend for its thick impressiveness. I thought I would be lucky if I could slog through the thing by the end of the school year, but it's a surprisingly entertaining read. I devoured the first thirty pages sitting right there in the Barnes & Noble coffee shop. Then I forgot it in my car and haven't touched it since.

I reach over and grab it. I like how heavy, how weighty it feels in my hands. I open the book to where I left off, but pause when I see what I used as a bookmark.

Brad Hoffman's Self-Improvement Plan

1. Pay attention in class. Do all homework assignments. Make Honor Roll.

> *2. Get a job.*
> *3. Wake up early and go for a run every morning before school.*
> *4. Learn to play the guitar.*
> *5. Read a thick, impressive book.*
> *6. Get a haircut. (Maybe?)*

Seeing the list makes me even more miserable. I was working toward everything on that list. Well, except learning to play the guitar —I'm saving up my money to buy one. To do that, I need to get a job, and I haven't heard back from any of the fast-food places where I applied. But everything else, I've been actively working on. And it didn't help one iota. In fact, things have only gotten worse.

I slam the list facedown onto the dashboard.

At least I have this book. Something to escape into. Carissa's sister, Rose, always had her nose buried in a book. I never really understood the appeal, but now I do.

Rose. I wonder how she's doing. I wish there was some way I could contact her. To talk. Not even about Carissa. Just about...life. It would be nice to have someone to talk to outside of all of this mess. Rose is a great listener. I always found myself telling her things I didn't tell anyone else. She's one of those people who makes you feel comfortable. Like she really cares about what you're saying.

I remember one time, I was over at the Hayward house and Carissa was off in another room doing something. Probably getting ready to go out somewhere, or on the phone with one of her friends. It was just me and Rose, and we started talking about radio. Turns out Rose wants to go into radio, too. She'd be great at it. She could have one of those talk shows where people call in and you give them advice. She'd be wonderful.

Anyway, I told Rose about how when I graduate, I'm not even sure I want to go to college. I want to get a job working at a radio station. I know I'd have to start out low on the totem pole—getting coffee, doing research, managing the phones—but I wouldn't mind. Working at a station, being in that atmosphere, would be *so* cool. And I'd work my butt off. With any luck, eventually I'd move up, get a show myself. That would be awesome. A dream come true.

"Why wait till you graduate?" Rose said. "You could do that now, at one of the local stations."

"Oh, I don't know..."

"I'm serious." Enthusiasm lit up Rose's face. "You have lots of experience doing morning announcements. And it's obvious you have passion. That's what people like to see more than anything."

"But I'm in school all day."

"So go in on weekends. Even a couple hours a week would add up into great experience."

"Okay, I admit it." I leaned forward and our legs brushed under the kitchen table. "That's an awesome idea."

"Why thank you."

"You should do it."

"What?" She blinked at me.

"Why don't *you* go for an internship like that?" I asked. "You'd be amazing."

Rose looked down at the table, her expression unreadable. "Oh, I...I couldn't. I'm super busy with school. Besides, I don't have experience like you do. They'd just laugh at me."

"I doubt that."

Abruptly, Rose pushed back her chair and stood up. "You want some tea?"

"Um, sure. Thanks." She clearly didn't want to talk about it, so I didn't press the issue.

Maybe she felt the same way I did: I loved dreaming about having a radio show, partly because the dream was still far off, in the future. Thinking about actually trying to make it happen—walking into the local radio studio with some of my clips, trying to convince a stranger to hire me—that was terrifying. Imagining it made my heart rev up uncomfortably.

I turned the conversation to the broader subject of radio as a vehicle for change. "That's why I want to get into the business," I said. "To connect with people. Change the world. Carissa thinks I'm naïve."

"Well," Rose said, reaching up to grab two mugs from the cupboard. "Carissa thinks I'm nothing but a boring fat girl."

Hearing her say that made me so angry at Carissa. She has a sweet exterior, but she can be really cruel. Thoughtless. She doesn't realize how the words she tosses out can cut people deeply.

"Carissa doesn't know what she's talking about," I said. I could tell Rose was embarrassed, so I didn't say anything more. Instead, I went onto YouTube and clicked on one of my dumb stand-up comedy routines in an effort to make Rose laugh. Which she did, because she's nice like that. She always laughed at my comedy routines, no matter how dumb they were.

Now, I try to turn my attention to *Infinite Jest*, but I can't get Rose's face out of my mind. Her earnest expression, the excitement in her voice. *Why wait till you graduate? You could do that now, at one of the local stations around here.* Like she actually believed I could.

As if on cue, my "Self-Improvement Plan" flutters down from the dashboard and onto my lap. My own handwriting stares up at me. Hopeful.

The tardy bell rings. 8:15. Morning announcements are over. I'm safe.

I set *Infinite Jest* down on the passenger seat but slip my "Self-Improvement Plan" into my jeans pocket. Then I grab my backpack and power-walk toward Mrs. Sussman's classroom.

✦ ✰ ✦

WHEN LUNCH ROLLS AROUND, Leo bombards me at my locker.

"Brad, man, where have you been? Listen, we don't have to sit with the gang today if you don't want to see Carissa. We can find somewhere else to go. You don't have to sit off by yourself somewhere. I'm here for you, okay?"

I slam my locker shut. "I was thinking of eating lunch off campus today. Wanna come?"

"Sure," Leo says.

Ten minutes later, over carnitas tacos at Tony's Taco Shack, I practice my pitch on Leo.

He claps when I'm done. "That was great, man! How could they say no?"

"Thanks," I say, wiping my palms on my jeans. "I'm nervous. It's a total long shot."

"I'll drive over with you. Moral support."

"Really?"

"What are best friends for, right?"

"Thanks, Leo. That means a lot." I check my watch. "The bell's gonna ring in eight minutes."

We wrap up the rest of our lunch to go and make it to fifth period —Econ, the only class I have with Carissa—as the bell rings.

I try to pay attention in class, but the butterflies in my stomach migrate to my brain and make it hard to focus. I keep replaying over and over what I plan to say until I have it memorized.

"Brad, can you enlighten us?" Mr. Gallo says from the front of the room.

"Uh—what?"

"Will you enlighten us as to what Adam Smith meant by 'The Invisible Hand'?"

"Umm... " *Crap.* I read the assigned chapter last night, but my mind was focused on Carissa, replaying my morning announcements meltdown, so I hadn't really absorbed much of what I read. I meant to review the chapter at lunch, but with everything else going on, I forgot. Now I sound like a complete idiot.

"Didn't you do the reading last night?" Mr. Gallo asks, frowning.

"Yeah, I just...um, I must have missed that part."

"It was the focal point of the entire chapter! It's the foundation of capitalism!"

"Sorry," I say lamely. "I'll have to review it."

"Yes, I think that would be a wise course of action," says Mr. Gallo. Across the room, Carissa shakes her head at me.

My cheeks burn in embarrassment, but I try to calm myself. I need to be confident if I want my pitch this afternoon to come off well. I picture Rose's face, her smile, and it makes me feel better.

After school, I meet Leo in the school parking lot.

"You ready to do this?" he says.

"As ready as I'll ever be."

Climbing into my car, I am filled with a sense of purpose. I'm terrified, yes, but it's a good kind of terror, the kind that comes from moving forward with nothing else to lose.

Chapter 14

I wake up to a tapping at my window. At first I think it's the wind rustling the leaves against the glass. I almost roll over and sink back down into sleep. But then I hear it again.

Tap, tap, tap. Tap, tap, tap.

I sit up and peer into the darkness.

Someone is out there. A chill runs through me.

I'm wide awake now.

Slowly, my eyes adjust to the dim light of the room. Heart thrumming, I get out of bed and slink over to the window. Up close, I see a face.

Daniel.

I release a lungful of breath I didn't even realize I was holding in. Daniel grins and motions for me to open the window.

I undo the lock and push it open. "You scared me!" I say, laughing.

"I did? I'm sorry," he says. "I didn't know you'd be asleep yet."

I glance at the clock on my nightstand. "It's past midnight! We need to be at the gym in seven hours!"

"I guess I was too excited to sleep. C'mon." He holds out his hand for me to take.

"What?"

"We had an incredible week, Rosie. I lost fifteen pounds!"

"I know you did. I'm proud of you."

"Thank you," Daniel says. His eyes shine in the moonlight. "And that's not all. You lost ten pounds!"

"Yep."

"*Ten pounds*, Rosie! In one week! That's amazing!"

I laugh. "It feels amazing."

"So?"

"So...what?"

Daniel reaches for my hand. "We need to celebrate!"

"Now?"

"When else do we have any time to ourselves? You're awake now, aren't you?"

"I guess."

"C'mon then!"

My instinct is to close the window and scurry back to my safe, comfortable bed. I've never been much of a risk-taker.

"What if someone sees us?" I whisper. "Won't we get in trouble?"

"As far as I know, there's no law against going for a midnight walk. It's not like we're prisoners, Rosie."

The breeze is cool against my face. Daniel's broad smile sends a tiny shiver up my spine. Maybe Old Me would have been scared and fled back to bed. But New Me squeezes Daniel's hand.

"Okay," I say. "Give me two seconds."

I slip my bare feet into flip-flops, throw on a sweatshirt over my PJs, and pull my sleep-mussed hair into a ponytail.

"Should I bring anything?" I ask.

"Just yourself," Daniel says.

So I grab his hand and hoist myself out of the window into the fresh midnight air. Climbing out of a ground-floor window may seem like an ordinary feat, but to me it is exhilarating. I can't remember the last time I climbed anything.

I stumble a bit on my landing and grab Daniel's arm for support. "I've got you," he says. He feels sturdy. Dependable. I imagine both his arms around me, holding me close, and a warm blush creeps up my neck.

"So what does this celebration entail?" I say when I've regained my balance and let go of Daniel's arm.

"I was out walking by myself the other day," he says. "And I found this really cool place. It's not far. I want to show it to you."

THERE'S a peaceful hush over the camp in the moonlight, with everyone asleep in their beds. During the day everyone is in motion, a constant flurry of activity, with the cameras everywhere and Mark and Leslie shouting and the heat and the sweat and the pain of aching muscles. But now, at midnight, all of that noise and busyness is wiped away.

"This is like a different place," I say.

"Nice, isn't it?" Daniel agrees.

We walk down the dirt path leading out of camp, not saying anything, both of us soaking up the quiet. The oak trees stretch above us in a protective way, their leaves rustling gently in the breeze. We've only walked a couple hundred yards when Daniel abruptly turns off the path, cutting through the trees. He disappears into the shadows.

I try to follow him but quickly lose my bearings. The thick tree branches block out the moonlight. I can't see where I'm going. My heartbeat quickens. What if I get lost?

"Hey!" I call. My voice sounds small. "Daniel? Where are you going?"

No answer.

Alone, the night takes on a spooky quality. The trees seem menacing. This was a stupid idea. I wish I were back in my bed. Sleeping, safe, like everyone else.

"Daniel!" I shout.

Still nothing.

I turn back and stumble in what I think is the right direction. But it's hard to tell. It's so dark. All the trees look the same.

Suddenly, I feel something on my arm. I jump.

"Rosie?" I turn and look up into Daniel's face. "Where did you go?"

"Where did *I* go?" I'm on the verge of tears. "Where did *you* go? You left me."

"I thought you were right behind me."

"I wasn't. You took off all of a sudden."

"I'm sorry," he says.

"It's really hard to see. I have no clue where I am."

"I'm sorry," he says again. He grabs my hand. "I've got you. It's not far, just through these trees. Can you see, there's a little path here on the ground?"

"I can't see much of anything."

"It's okay. Follow me. It's worth it, I promise."

I hold onto Daniel's hand and concentrate on not tripping. After a couple minutes, the trees open up into a little clearing.

My breath catches.

Rosebushes. Rosebushes everywhere. Pink roses, yellow roses, white roses, red roses, all tangled together, growing wild. Like a garden was planted years ago and then left to its own devices.

"Wow," I whisper. "It's beautiful."

"Isn't it?" Daniel says. "My second day here, I went for a walk and discovered this place. I've been coming back most nights. It was pretty in the daylight, but it's even better at night. It feels... I don't know..."

"Magical," I say.

"Yeah. That's exactly how it feels." He takes a few more steps into the clearing, still holding my hand. Here in this clearing, the moonlight is bright enough that I can see fine. But I don't say anything. It feels nice holding his hand.

"There's a bench over here somewhere," Daniel says. "Aha! There it is." He leads me to a stone bench nestled among the roses.

"My sister would love this place," I say, sitting down. "Roses are her favorite flower."

"What's your favorite flower?" Daniel asks, sitting down beside me.

"Used to be roses, too. I mean, when your name is Rose, your favorite flower is pretty much set at birth." With my free hand, I tilt a rose close to my nose and breathe in. "But, that's Carissa for you. She couldn't even let me have this one thing for myself."

"I imagine it's hard being a twin," Daniel says. "Especially an identical twin. You said you're identical, right?"

"Technically, yes. But...well, I'll put it this way: it is very easy to tell us apart."

"So you two never had a case of mistaken identity?"

"Carissa's thin. She's popular. She's everything I'm not."

"I don't know," Daniel says after a moment. "Maybe you're not as different as you think."

"Yeah, we are. You haven't met Carissa. All the good genes went to her, and she knows it. She's so confident about everything. So certain she's right."

"That's not always a good thing."

"Good luck telling Carissa that." My hand, still entwined with Daniel's, is sweaty. I pull it free and smooth my palms on my pajama pants. "Anyway, she's the reason I'm here. She's the one who signed me up for this show."

"I'll have to remember to thank her, then," Daniel says, flashing me a smile. I love his smile because it lights up his whole face. He smiles like a child does: nothing to hide, nothing to hold back.

"How about you?" I ask. "Why are you here?"

"I knew I had to make a change. My life was in shambles. I felt helpless, Rosie. The last few years, I've been a wreck."

"You don't seem like a wreck."

"Well, thank you. I'm happy here. I'm moving in the right direction. Regaining a sense of who I am, you know? Who I used to be."

Daniel gazes off into the dark smudge of trees. For all his openness, for all his optimism and enthusiasm and sweetness, there's something weathered about him. Sad. No, *sad* isn't the right word. It's more than sad. He seems...haunted.

I search my mind for something to say, but nothing seems right. We've known each other only a short time. I don't want to pry.

All of a sudden, he breaks his gaze and looks over at me. "Sorry," he says. "Zoned out for a second there."

"It's okay." I stretch. "Are you tired?"

"Yeah. That means this did the trick."

"What trick?"

"Most of the time, I have trouble sleeping. That's why I go walking at night. It tires me out so I can fall asleep."

I stifle a yawn. "I never have that problem!"

"You're lucky."

"My problem is waking up."

"We should probably get you to bed then. Ready to head back?"

"Okay." I stand up. "Thanks for bringing me here, Daniel."

"Of course. As soon as I stumbled across it, I knew I had to come here with you."

We make our way through the trees. Daniel grabs my hand as if it's the most natural thing in the world. It seems natural to me, too. But when we reach the dirt path leading back to the cabins, he lets go. Maybe he doesn't mean anything by it. I'm always reading way too much into things.

Daniel walks me back to the girls' cabin. My window looks higher than it did when I climbed out an hour ago.

"You can do it," Daniel says. He kneels down and laces his fingers together to make a step. "Here," he says. "I'll give you a boost."

I hesitate.

"What's wrong?"

"I'm too heavy," I whisper.

"What?"

"I'm too heavy."

"No, that doesn't work with me, Rosie. C'mere. I've got you."

I slip off my sandals and toss them through the window. Then I tentatively place my bare foot into Daniel's hands.

"I'm a strong guy. Don't worry. Put your weight on me," he insists.

So I do. I grip the windowsill with both hands, Daniel gives me a boost, and I tumble sideways through the window. Not the most graceful of landings, but at least I'm back safe in my room.

Daniel pokes his head in. "You okay?"

"Yeah." I stand up and attempt a nonchalant smile. "Thanks."

"Goodnight, Rosie Hayward."

"Goodnight. See you in…" I squint at the clock on my nightstand. "Five and a half hours."

"Yikes."

"Yikes is right. Do me a favor and come bang on my door if I'm not at breakfast, will you?"

Daniel laughs. "Will do." He waves and ducks away into the night.

I step away from the window and shrug off my sweatshirt.

"Hey, Rosie?"

I turn. Daniel is back.

"I forgot something," he says.

"What?"

"I wanted to tell you that I'm really glad we're friends."

I smile. "Me, too," I say. And I mean it.

But a minute later, as I snuggle back under the covers, I remember the warmth of Daniel's hand in mine and feel more confused than ever. Is *friends* really all we are?

It's weird, but of all people, I wish I could talk to Carissa right now. She would know. She would tell me what to do.

Chapter 15

Brad

I open the plate-glass door to WAVE 104.3, my stomach in knots. I've never been inside a radio station before. As I step into the room, I half-expect the DJs to be right there, headphones on, mics at the ready.

Instead there's a wrap-around desk, potted plants, and some chairs and magazines. It reminds me of a doctor's waiting room. Except in a doctor's waiting room there'd be someone sitting behind the desk, waiting to help you, but this room is completely deserted.

I walk up to the desk, scanning around for a bell to ring. No dice. I glimpse a laptop and haphazard stacks of paper, but no half-eaten yogurt cups or sweaters or soda cans that suggest someone momentarily leaving the room but coming back soon.

Well, what else can I do but wait? I sit down in one of the stiff-backed chairs and rub my sweaty palms against my jeans. There's a doorway over to the right—probably leads to the studio—but no way am I walking through unannounced. I have a feeling even Rose, whose brave idea this was, would shake her head at that.

There's a clock hanging on the wall opposite me. I watch the second-hand tick, tick, tick. Two minutes, three minutes, six minutes pass. *One more minute and I'm leaving,* I tell myself. *I'll come back some other time.* Even though I know, deep inside, that I won't. I can already feel most of my courageous resolve leaking away.

Suddenly, the door to my right opens and a skinny balding man with a ponytail strides into the room. I stand up, but he doesn't appear to notice me. He crosses behind the desk and shuffles through papers.

I cough nervously.

"Can I help you with something?" he says, not looking up from his manic shuffling.

"Is this...uh, am I in the right place? Is this WAVE 104.3?"

"Yep." His T-shirt says *Still in Band Camp.*

"Ah, um... I'm looking for a job?" I hate the way I sound. When I'm nervous, I tend to talk in questions. Carissa used to get on my case about it, like when I met her family for the first time and I got caught up in a political argument with her father. Rose, not Carissa, was actually the one who came to my defense. I remember talking to Carissa about it the next day, asking why she had left me hanging out to dry like that. "You've got to learn to be more assertive, Brad," she had said. "It's the nature of a debate. You can't talk in questions."

But the man with the ponytail doesn't really seem to care about the inflection in my voice. "Do you have any experience in radio?" he asks.

"Yes, sir. Over at Buena Vista High."

"Didn't know the high school had a radio program."

"Well—it's not officially a radio show—it's more like a morning announcement type of thing—"

But he's already taking big strides toward the door that leads into the studio. I watch him walk away, unsure what to do. *Was that my job interview? Did I already blow my big chance?*

The ponytailed man turns and looks at me. "You coming or not?"

I hurry after him, filled with nervous excitement.

Other than morning announcements—which are broadcast from a small room in the school office—I've never been in a radio studio before. It looks every bit as cool as I've dreamed about. Big microphones, over-ear headphones, a soundboard with more buttons and dials and switches than I can count, framed band posters on the wall. There's a real live DJ working right now, adjusting the microphone, probably getting ready to go back on the air after a commercial break. He has dreadlocks and hipster glasses and looks to be in his mid-twenties. He waves to the pony-tailed guy, who waves back and continues walking down the hall. I do a half-wave/cool-guy-nod combo. Totally lame, but I don't even care.

I follow Ponytail Guy behind the radio studio into a small room. The counters are littered with empty soda cans, crumpled receipts, stacks of papers, and leaning towers of CDs.

Mr. Ponytail raises his arms in an exasperated way. "It's been kinda hectic around here lately, as you can see. We have this great intern, Meghan, but her school schedule's tight this semester so she won't be able to come in as often. We need another intern to help research topics, book guests, answer phones, get coffee, that sorta thing. We aren't able to pay much, but you'll get lots of experience for your resume. Whaddaya say?"

"Ah, um, yes?" I'm still talking in questions, but I'm too excited to feel embarrassed.

"Great. Let's say after school on Mondays, Wednesdays, and Fridays. If you prove you're reliable, maybe we'll even give you the early shift on weekends to help run the morning show. Think you can handle that?"

"Um, yeah, I mean, when should I start?"

Mr. Ponytail looks at his watch. "How about tomorrow? Four P.M.?"

"Okay. Sounds great." I reach out my hand. "Thank you so much, sir, I promise I won't disappoint you."

He shakes my hand and flashes a quick smile. "You can call me Jerry. What's your name, kid?"

"Brad."

"Look forward to working with you, Brad. See you tomorrow. Don't be late."

I'm smiling so wide my face might crack open. I turn and float out of the break room, past the radio studio where I give a thumbs-up to the DJ—my new coworker!—and out the front door into the bright September sunshine.

I can't believe it! I have a job at a real radio station! The world seems brand-new, filled with opportunity.

I open the car door and plop down into the passenger seat.

"Well?" Leo says, his tone a mixture of hope and fear. "How was it?"

I'm so pumped I can't even build up the suspense by pretending that it went terribly. All I can do is smile goofily and give him a thumbs-up, too.

"YEAH!" Leo shouts, giving me a fist-bump. "Way to go, my man! That's how it's done!"

We drive with the windows down to Tony's Taco Shack for some celebratory horchata. For the first time since Carissa broke up with me, I feel excited about the future.

Chapter 16

For the first time in a while, I have trouble sleeping. I'm actually grateful when my alarm blares because I'm frustrated with trying to fall asleep. My brain simply refuses to shut down and rest. I know workout is going to be awful today, but at least it will make me so tired I shouldn't have any more trouble sleeping.

I leave my room for breakfast at the same time Doris leaves her room across the hall.

"Hi there, Rosie," she says, a teasing lilt to her voice. "Late night?"

Wariness makes me close my door harder than usual; it slams. I try to make my voice normal. "Not especially. Why do you ask?"

"Around midnight or so I walked over to the kitchen to get a glass of water. And I swear I saw *someone* sneaking into your room. Through the *window*."

Crap. Busted. "Oh, uh, that was me," I stammer. "I, uh, went out for a walk."

"Seems late for a walk."

"I had trouble sleeping."

"Did it work?" Doris asks.

"Yeah, I was pretty tired by the time I got back."

"Good thing you had Daniel to give you a boost back into your room."

"Yeah, it was." As soon as the words leave my mouth, I realize my mistake.

Doris smiles. "I've been noticing you two getting cozy lately," she says, winking.

My cheeks flush. "Oh, it's not like that."

"Sure looks that way to me."

"It isn't." I don't feel comfortable talking to Doris about this. Something tells me that whatever I confide in her will find its way around to all the other contestants. Probably to the cameras, too.

I cast around for some explanation to appease her. "The truth is, Doris—will you promise not to tell anyone about this? I don't want people to think I'm weird."

Doris steps in closer, her eyes intent on mine. "I won't tell anyone, I swear."

"Well, I..."

"You can talk to me, honey."

"I've been feeling really homesick lately. I miss my family. Daniel's accent reminds me of my dad's."

Doris puts her arm around me. "Oh, Rosie, that's not weird. We all feel homesick. You're not the only one."

She keeps her arm around me the entire walk from the girls' cabin to the dining commons. When we walk through the double doors, I manage to break free.

"Thanks, Doris," I tell her. "I'm gonna grab a protein bar."

"Okay, honey. I'll see you later."

She doesn't say anything about Daniel, but later I see the two of them talking in the gym. And that afternoon, when Daniel and I are running side by side on treadmills, Doris walks by and shoots me a very obvious wink.

✧ ☆ ✧

THE DAYS FLOW into each other, merge together. I lumber through workout after workout. My muscles ache, and I wake up each morning with stiff limbs, but I can tell I'm growing stronger. I can run two miles on the treadmill without stopping. I can do more weight repetitions than I thought possible. I've done more sit-ups in the past week than I'd done my entire life before I came here.

I go to bed each night hoping to wake up to Daniel's tapping on my window. Instead, each morning I wake up to my blaring alarm clock and sunlight poking through cracks in the curtains. One morning, at breakfast, I almost ask him about it.

"Hey Daniel?" I ask, mixing granola into my fat-free yogurt. "Are you—"

But then Doris interrupts, leaning across the table and thrusting a banana in our direction.

"Good morning, *you two*!" she says, winking at me. "Do either of you want this? I'm not gonna eat it."

"I'm okay," I say, but Daniel thanks her and takes it.

"What were you saying?" he asks.

Doris is still smiling at us. I look down into my yogurt and concentrate on stirring, trying to calm the blush I can feel spreading across my cheeks. "Nothing," I tell Daniel. "Never mind."

I don't know what I would say to him, anyway. I don't want him to think I'm some pitiful loser, waiting up all night hoping he'll come to my window. I guess now that he's shown me the rose garden, there's no reason for him to come over again.

As the week wears on, he is friendly as ever during meals and workouts. I honestly don't know what I would do without Daniel's warm smile and encouraging words every day. But he makes no move to hang out with me alone.

I definitely read too much into things. We are only friends. No doubt about it.

Which is fine, I tell myself. *At least you have him as your friend.*

And I try to convince myself that I'm okay with that. I try to quit daydreaming about holding his hand. I try to stop imagining what it would be like to kiss him.

Then comes Sunday night. Our second weigh-in.

"The second week is often when we see some disappointment," Britta shares. "After losing so much weight the first week, contestants expect a lot. Remember, *any* weight you lose means you are on the road to a healthier you!"

She's right—after everyone lost so much weight last week, the numbers on the scale today are smaller than I expected. This time, Daniel is called up before I am. His eyes find mine. I give him a thumbs-up. The scale blinks a whir of numbers and finally settles.

"Congrats, Daniel!" Britta shouts. "You lost ELEVEN POUNDS! That's the most out of everyone so far today!"

Everyone cheers and claps. Daniel beams.

"How do you feel?" Britta asks.

"Fantastic!" Daniel says. He points at me. "And a big thanks to my work-out partner, Rosie. Couldn't do it without you, girl."

More cheers and claps. Doris whistles. I blush.

"That's the perfect segue," Britta says. "Rosie, come on up here! Your turn to be weighed in!"

I pass Daniel as I walk up the steps to the scale and he walks back down to join the group. He gives me a huge hug and kisses my cheek, in front of everyone. In front of the cameras.

My heart pounds, and my brain races on overdrive. I watch the scale numbers whir up and down, but for the first time since I've been here, I'm not really thinking about my weight. I'm only thinking of Daniel. Why is he so confusing? One moment I'm convinced we're only destined to be friends, and I'm okay with that. But then he does something that gets me all mixed-up. Makes me restless. Makes me yearn for more than friendship.

Daniel is the first guy who has actually paid me interest. I mean, the rose garden? C'mon. How could I not fall for him? I thought it was safe, because I thought he liked me too.

Embarrassment rushes through me. I'm probably so obvious about my feelings. A little girl with moony puppy-dog eyes. I mean, Doris already knows. Who else knows? Probably everyone.

I suddenly feel like crying. *I am a total fool. This is exactly like—*

But no. I refuse to think about Brad. I look down at my sneakers to avoid looking at Daniel. Because I know my traitorous eyes would find him in the crowd.

That's the thing about unrequited crushes. Once they start, they take on a life of their own. They never go away. No matter how many miles you run, they linger.

My first week of work at the radio station is a blur: answering phones, emptying trash, filing papers and old receipts in Jerry's massive file cabinet. On Friday, I spend the entire afternoon online, researching the candidates for the upcoming school board election and writing down notes about the main issues. It's the kind of assignment I would have totally failed last year in history class, but doing it now for the radio station is completely different. I'm not scouring websites for random information so I can get a few red checkmarks in the margins of my paper and a passing grade at the top; I'm taking notes for an *actual radio broadcast.* I'm helping spread information to the people about important issues. I'm actually doing work that matters.

Something whacks the back of my head, interrupting my thoughts. "Ow!" I jerk my head up and whirl around.

A girl stands in the doorway between the break room (my makeshift office) and the radio studio. She looks around my age. She's wearing a Rilo Kiley T-shirt and has streaks of purple in her long blonde hair. "I'm so sorry!" she yelps, hurrying toward me, hand over her mouth. "I didn't notice you there. My aim is terrible."

"Actually, I think your aim is pretty good," I say with a smile. "You nailed me right on the head."

"I was aiming for the trash can!" She points at the small wastebasket, three feet to my left. A half-eaten apple rolls across the linoleum floor toward my feet.

We both reach down to pick it up at the same time. Our hands touch; then she grabs the apple and thunks it into the wastebasket. Her fingers are long and thin, her nails painted black.

"I am so sorry," she says again. "That is not how I wanted our introduction to go."

"I'm Brad." I reach out to shake her hand.

"Meghan." Her thin fingers close over mine, and my gut is filled with a light, pleasant ache.

"Oh, so *you're* the famous Meghan," I say, leaning back in my chair. "I've been hearing about you from everyone." It's true. All week, it's been Meghan this, Meghan that. *Last year, Meghan stayed late for two straight weeks to catalogue the entire album collection. Meghan used to have a fresh pot of coffee waiting for the afternoon DJs when they came in. Meghan once booked Chantrelle for an in-studio concert, live over the airwaves.*

Meghan laughs when I mention the Chantrelle concert. "That was before Chantrelle was famous," she says dismissively, waving her hand like it's no big deal. "She was in town to do a concert at the mall. *The mall,* Brad! The only reason anyone cared about her was that she was opening for the Arctic Monkeys."

"The Arctic Monkeys! What were you, ten?"

"Eight," Meghan clarifies. "I was a cute little kid. Chantrelle couldn't say no to me."

"You mean you've worked here since you were eight?" I say. What I'm thinking: *Is that even legal?*

"Not technically working. You know Jerry? Well, he's good friends with my dad, and he would let me hang out here when my dad had to work late. I sort of grew up in the studio."

"Wow, that's awesome. I'm jealous."

"You should be."

Is she flirting? My heart speeds up. I haven't flirted with anyone but Carissa in a long time. I want to respond with something witty, but my brain has stage fright—it's suddenly blank. I smile at her in what I hope is a smooth, nonchalant way.

"Here, come with me," she says, reaching down to grab my hand and pull me up. "I'm supposed to teach you how to use the studio equipment."

"Really? Jerry asked you to do that?"

She shrugs. "He didn't ask me *not* to. Friday afternoons are pretty dead around here, if you haven't noticed."

She's right—I've been here three hours, and I haven't seen anyone else in the studio. There isn't a live show on the air, just a loop of Top 40 hits playing.

There's nothing I want more than to explore the studio and fiddle around with the equipment, but I hesitate. I know I'll sound utterly uncool, but I can't help myself. "Are you sure Jerry's okay with this?" I blurt out.

Meghan rolls her eyes. "It's fine, I promise. You have to learn sometime, right?"

That is true, Jerry said he wanted me to help out in the studio eventually. And honestly, I am dying to learn how to work the soundboard. Why not now?

Plus, okay, I admit it: I want to spend more time with Meghan. I follow her into the studio, absentmindedly rubbing the back of my head. Carissa used to tease me about that. I guess I always do it when I'm nervous.

"Are you sure you're okay?" Meghan asks. "Do you need an ice pack for your head?"

I whip my hand down to my side. "Oh yeah, I'm fine. It didn't hurt so much as surprise me."

She nods, looking sincerely concerned. But as she opens the door and ushers me inside the studio, I glimpse a twinkle of mischief in her eyes that makes me wonder if maybe her aim isn't so bad after all.

✧ ☆ ✧

WHEN I PULL up to my house, darkness is settling like a blanket over the trees and roofs of the neighborhood. It's past seven and I'm already formulating excuses and apologies in my head. My mom always makes a big deal out of having a "nice family dinner" on Friday nights, served at 6:30 sharp. I grab my phone from the cup-holder: no missed calls or triple-exclamation-point texts, which is surprising. I shove the phone into my pocket and slam the car door, hurrying up the front walk.

The porch light is on, but the front door is locked. *Oh, no—Mom must really be angry, locking me out.* I ring the doorbell twice, but no one answers. Finally, I rummage around in the hanging flower planter and find the spare key.

"I'm sorry!" I yell as I open the door and step inside, dropping my backpack on the hall floor. The house is dim and quiet. "Mom? Dad? Sorry I'm late!"

Uneasiness crawls up my spine. I hurry past the living room and into the kitchen. Darkness, emptiness. Where are my parents? What's going on?

Heart thumping, mind filling with every horror movie I've ever watched (mostly with Leo, since Carissa thinks horror movies are "juvenile and lame"), I flick on the lights. Then I pull out my cell phone and speed-dial my mom. It clicks immediately to voice-mail. When I dial my dad's number, it rings and rings and rings.

I try to calm down. If it wasn't a Friday night, this wouldn't be strange at all—it's only because my mom is so obsessed with having these weekly family dinners that I was sure they would both be home, waiting for me with disappointed expressions. Dad's been working a lot lately, I remind myself. Something about a new client he's trying to impress. And Mom could easily be out with Aunt Jayne or one of her book club friends. They probably made other plans and forgot to tell me. Or maybe they did tell me, and I wasn't listening. Very possible.

My phone rings, and I jump. Literally jump into the air. The hairs on my arms are standing at attention. I take a deep breath and answer the phone, half expecting to hear the raspy, creepy voice of a maniacal killer.

But it's my mom. "Hi, honey, you're home? Did you just call me? Your dad and I are on our way home right now."

My heartbeat slowly returns to normal. "Where are you guys?"

"We had that meeting today, remember I told you?" She sounds distracted. "About, um, refinancing our home loan?"

I glaze over the grown-up talk, already bored. "Oh, yeah. When will you be home?"

"Five minutes. We picked up Chinese for dinner. Will you set the table? Thanks, honey."

Inwardly, I sigh with relief. *Everything is okay. Everything is normal.* I grab forks from the silverware drawer, daydreaming about Meghan—her purple-streaked hair, feather earrings, sardonic smile. The butterfly tattoo I glimpsed, peeking out above her hip, when she reached up to flick a switch on the soundboard and her T-shirt rode up a little. I imagine the jealous expression on Carissa's face if she saw us together. I imagine kissing Meghan at a school dance, in front of everyone. Carissa would narrow her eyes and toss her hair, the way she does when she's upset but pretending not to be. I smile to myself. Jealous Carissa—that would be awesome.

"Hello, hello!" Mom calls, entering the kitchen with a plastic take-out bag that smells amazing. My stomach growls. "How are you, sweetheart?" Her voice is bright, but her eyes look tired and far away. Has she been crying?

"I'm fine," I say, wanting to ask her the same question but afraid to hear the answer. Instead, I reach over and help her unpack the food.

Dad comes in and claps me on the back—his version of a man-hug. He's a strong guy, six feet tall, solidly built, mountain-man beard. I stagger slightly under the weight of his energetic back-clap, glad that none of my friends came over for dinner tonight. It's embarrassing when your dad is ridiculously stronger than you are. Welcome to my life. Was it Rose who would always say that? *Welcome to my life,* with the teeniest hint of a smile lifting up the corners of her mouth.

"Hey, kiddo, thanks for helping your mom," Dad says, grabbing a beer from the fridge.

My mom doesn't even glance up at him. She's extremely focused on scooping white rice and chow mein into bowls, as if serving dinner is the most important task in the world.

I can sense a heavy sadness in the room, as if it slipped in through the front door behind them like a gust of wind.

And that's when the realization hits me. *Crap.* A pit in my stomach opens up just like it did that day at the Dairy Queen when Carissa announced our break-up. *How am I always so oblivious to the truth?*

My mom's tight smile and downcast eyes. My dad's angry grip as he wrenches open the bottle of beer. Foreboding fills my whole body. *Are my parents getting a divorce?*

Chapter 18

Rose

Instead of tossing and turning, waiting fruitlessly for a *tap-tap-tap* on my window, I throw on a sweatshirt and decide to go for a walk myself.

Being outside in the cool night air makes me feel better. An empty bedroom can seem so lonely. Outside, all I have to do is look up and I have the stars for company. It's an especially clear night—I can see the Big Dipper, the Little Dipper, Polaris, Cassiopeia.

When I was little, my family went camping for a week in the summer. One night, as we sat around the campfire, my dad pointed out all the constellations to Carissa and me. I was amazed at how many he knew. Carissa wasn't very interested. After a few minutes, she complained about being cold and ducked inside the tent to go to bed.

"Am I boring you, too?" Dad asked me.

"No," I insisted. "This is fun!"

More than anything, I was excited to have some time alone with my dad. Not me-and-Carissa. Just me.

Every night the rest of that week, Dad and I stayed up late, necks craned back, gazing at the stars. I made up funny stories about all the different constellations and my dad laughed in all the right places. I felt so proud. Back then, one of my favorite things in the world was making my parents laugh. In fact, it still is.

Tonight, the moon is bright as a spotlight. Without really thinking, I veer off the main dirt road and onto the small path through the trees that I last traipsed with Daniel. Was that really only a week ago?

This time, I'm not scared. I have a sense of where I'm going, and the moon is fuller tonight, filtering comfortingly through the treetops. In no time at all I'm stepping out into the clearing. Roses tilt their blooms up toward the stars, even more beautiful than I remembered.

I let out a deep breath. It isn't until now, when I've found the rose garden empty, that I realize I was hoping Daniel would be here.

Stupid, stupid brain. If only I could turn you off.

I sit down sideways on the bench and draw up my knees, hugging them to my chest. Disappointment seeps through me. For all the changes I am seeing in myself, there is still so much I want to change.

I don't feel like looking at the stars anymore. Instead, I rest my forehead on my knees and close my eyes. I must doze for a little bit. Suddenly, I feel a *tap, tap, tap* on my shoulder. I jerk awake and lift my head.

Daniel.

"Sorry if I scared you," he says. "I didn't realize you were sleeping."

I sit up, trying to rein in my smile. "I was resting my eyes for a minute."

"Okay if I join you?" Daniel asks.

"Of course." I scoot over to make room for him on the bench.

He sits down. We are both silent, looking up at the stars. I feel shy.

"Didn't expect to find you here," Daniel says. "It was a nice surprise."

"I was hoping you'd come," I say without thinking. "I mean—we need to celebrate. How does it feel to have lost the most out of everyone this week?"

"It feels great. And what about you? Eight pounds! That's terrific, Rosie!"

"Thanks." When Britta announced it earlier, I thought I heard her wrong. I still can't quite believe it.

"I'm real proud of you," Daniel says.

"I'm proud of you, too. I couldn't have done it without you."

"Same."

I meet his eyes. "That was nice what you said in there. About me."

"Meant every word." Daniel stretches his arm out on the bench behind me. But he does it in a casual way. Friendly. "I miss my family," he says abruptly.

"You do?"

"Yeah."

"Me too," I say. And it's true. I do miss them.

"You and your dad are close, huh?" Daniel asks.

I can't remember mentioning my dad to him. "Yeah, I guess. I mean, I'm probably closer to my dad than my mom. But... I dunno. It's hard to talk to either of them."

"I know what you mean," Daniel says. "Sometimes my mom would try to start a conversation about my weight, but I never wanted to go there. What is there to say? Then she would start crying, and I would end up promising to do better, to make a change. But I never would. I wasn't ready."

"Yeah," I say, thinking about the way my mom would look at me sometimes, bewildered, as if I was an alien life-form she had no idea what to do with.

"It's nice to be able to talk to you like this," Daniel says, gently squeezing my shoulder.

"I know. I've missed it."

"Me too."

I turn to him. "Why didn't you come to my window anymore, after that first night? I was hoping you'd come, but you never did."

Daniel blinks. The whites of his eyes look very big in the darkness. "I didn't want to bother you," he says.

"Bother me? Why would you think that?"

"I don't know."

"We're friends, Daniel." I force a smile, inwardly wincing at the word. *I want to be more than friends.* "You don't bother me."

"Thanks," Daniel says. "I'm glad we're friends. I've never really had a close female friend before."

"Me neither. Male friend, I mean. Other than Carissa's boyfriends."

"You're friends with Carissa's boyfriends? I'm surprised."

"You're right—I'm not usually friends with them. She tends to go for jerks. But her latest boyfriend is actually a great guy. Brad." I worry I've revealed too much, like my feelings for Brad are evident in my expression, my tone of voice. I hastily try to downplay things: "And, you know, he and Carissa have been together *forever*, so he's around all the time—it'd be kind of impossible for us not to be friends at this point."

"I always wished I had a sister," Daniel admits. "Maybe then I'd feel more comfortable around girls in general."

"You seemed comfortable around me right away. You were so friendly that first day in the common room."

"I was nervous!" Daniel laughs. "I had to force myself to talk to you."

"Really?"

"Really."

"Well, I'm glad you did."

"Me too."

"You're my best friend here. I don't know what I'd do without you."

"You're my best friend, too," Daniel says. And, in that moment, with the cicadas humming around us and the stars winking above, I resolve to forget about kissing him and be content with the way things are. Friends. It's probably better this way. Easier. Neither of us will get hurt.

"Doris told me," Daniel says softly.

My heart jolts. "What? What did Doris tell you?"

"About the real reason you hang out with me. And it's okay."

"Daniel," I say, steeling myself to deny any accusations that my feelings for him are more than platonic.

"I mean," he continues, "we all get homesick sometimes."

This is not what I expected to hear. "Wait...what?"

"You like to hang out with me because my accent reminds you of your dad. It's cool. I guess I don't really care why you like to hang out with me, just as long as you do."

"No—Daniel!" I burst out laughing. "My dad was born and raised in *Southern California*. He doesn't have an accent like yours."

"He doesn't?"

"No! I told Doris that because, well—you know how she is. Always asking nosy questions. I was hoping if I made up some story, she'd leave us alone."

Daniel grins and shakes his head. "I can't believe it."

Realization dawns on me. "Wait—is *that* why you stopped coming by my room? Because of what Doris told you?"

Daniel shrugs. "Like I said, I didn't want to bother you."

"Oh, Daniel!" I give him a playful shove. "You're not a bother. Okay? You're never a bother."

"Okay."

I can't help myself; I want to extend the moment. Push the boundaries of what we are. "I like you, all right?" I say, trying to make my tone flippant.

Daniel meets my eyes. "I like you, too," he says softly. His tone is not flippant at all. Nerves suddenly squeeze my chest.

I stand up and stretch, faking a yawn that turns into a real one. "Ready to head back?"

"If you are."

He walks me to my room and boosts me through the window. I tell myself that I don't care if Doris sees us. I don't care about her winks or raised eyebrows. She can think whatever she wants.

"Same time tomorrow night?" Daniel asks.

"It's a date," I say. Unsure, even to myself, what exactly I mean by that.

Chapter 19
Brad

My Saturday routine used to go something like this: sleep in till noon, play video games for a couple hours, hang out with Leo and Carissa, maybe go to a party or movie at night. Basically, Saturday was my chance to *relax*, to wind down from the school week and enjoy my freedom.

Now, Saturdays are stressful. At least, Saturday mornings are. My alarm blares at 5:45 and I groggily roll out of bed, throw on clothes, grab a granola bar, and drive to the studio just in time to get things ready for the early morning show.

Usually both the morning hosts, Manny and Cindy, are already here when I arrive, but today the studio door is locked. I find the spare key where Jerry showed me under the planter box. Unlock the door. Hurry inside, flicking on lights. The studio clock reads 6:21.

Turn on the soundboard. Cue up the intro music. Nerves clench my stomach. 6:23. Where is everyone?

At 6:25 the phone rings. I grab it.

"Oh, Brad, I'm so glad you're there. It's Cindy. Listen, there's a big traffic jam on the freeway. Lanes blocked in both directions. We're at a standstill. I'm not gonna be there in time."

"You're not? What am I supposed to do?"

"You mean Manny's not there either?"

"No."

"I guess he's caught in this mess, too. I knew I should have taken surface streets. Well, hon, hold down the fort for us, okay? I'll be there as soon as I can."

Numbly, I set the phone back in its cradle. *Maybe Manny will get here. Maybe he's pulling up in the parking lot right now.*

The clock stares down at me, the second hand ticking. 6:28.

The only thing to do is sit down in Cindy's chair and put the headphones on. I adjust the microphone toward me. My heart is pounding so loudly in my ears, I swear the audience will be able to hear it over the airwaves. It's 6:29 in the morning, and I've never felt more awake.

At 6:30, I play the intro music. My pulse leaps at the familiar auto-tuned chords. *Good morning,* croons a synthesized voice backed by a dance beat. *Good moooorning.* I keep glancing toward the door, hoping Manny will rush in.

But he doesn't.

It's only me.

A year of doing morning announcements didn't prepare me for this. That was only a few minutes, plus I had a person sitting next to me, someone I could talk to on the air, someone who could take the lead if I became tongue-tied.

Right now, I have no one but myself.

The music fades out. I press the button to turn on my microphone.

"Hi, everyone," I say, trying to keep my voice from ascending to a high-pitched nervous shriek. I clear my throat. "Welcome to the morning show at your favorite station, WAVE 104.3. I'm Brad Hoffman, in this morning for Manny and Cindy, who are stuck in a traffic jam on the 101 freeway. I guess that means it's a good time to go into our traffic report: the 101 is at a standstill, all lanes, both directions. I'll keep you posted as I get more information. In the meantime, here's some Beatles to get your morning started off right."

I turn on the playlist I've been listening to for weeks, the one I created to yank me out of my melancholy after Carissa dumped me, when it seemed like my whole world was falling apart. Track one: "Here Comes the Sun."

I cue up the next track, a catchy pop song that's topping the charts. Next I pick out some classic Michael Jackson, then the latest Maroon 5 hit. I've always liked Maroon 5. I remember one time last year, I was over at Carissa's house and we were headed upstairs to her room to watch a movie. When we walked past Rose's room the door was open a crack and we could hear Rose singing along to "Sugar." Carissa smirked at me and gently pushed the door open, peering in at her sister. I glanced in, too. Rose was folding laundry, her back to us, singing loudly and swaying a little to the beat. She has a lovely voice.

I wish Rose could see herself from the outside. You know how some people think *waaaay* too highly of themselves? Rose is the opposite. She has no idea how smart and funny and cool she is. She and Leo are pretty much the easiest, most genuine people to be around.

Anyway, the moment was ruined when Carissa ran into the room and grabbed a shirt off the pile of laundry on Rose's bed. She waved the shirt around like a flag and danced up against Rose, screeching loudly and off-key to the lyrics. It was clear Carissa thought she was being hilarious. But she was being mean.

And Rose—Rose *shrank*. She abruptly stopped singing, snatched the shirt back from Carissa, and resumed folding her pile of laundry, like Carissa was a bee she was hoping would fly away if ignored long enough. Carissa tried to grab another piece of clothing from the pile, but Rose stopped her. "Please, Caris—don't."

"Rosie, lighten up, will you? We're just having fun!" Carissa said.

The *we're* got me. I wanted no part of Carissa's actions. I wished we'd never peeked in that cracked-open door. I wished Rose was still in her room by herself, singing along to Maroon 5 in her lovely uninhibited voice.

But Rose heard the *we're* too. She turned to the doorway, where I was standing like an idiot. And, like an idiot, I waved hello. "Hey, Rose." I didn't know what else to do. I'm sure I was grinning like an idiot, too.

The look on Rose's face. Disappointment, betrayal, embarrassment. Her cheeks were bright red. She held the shirt she was folding against her chest, like a shield. "Hey, Brad," she said, though she might as well have said, "You, too?" I could tell she thought I was complicit in Carissa's teasing. And, hey, I guess I was. I didn't stick up for Rose. I didn't step in to stop Carissa. Rose was the one who had to eventually say, "Can you guys give me some time to myself, please?"

I grabbed Carissa's hand and tried to usher her out the door. "You have a great voice," I said to Rose, grasping at goodwill. Trying to show her that I hadn't meant any harm.

But Carissa had to ruin that, too.

"He's right, Rosie," Carissa interjected. "If you lost some weight, I bet you could go on America's Got Talent!"

I pulled her across the hall into her room, shutting the door behind me. "What's the matter with you?" I hissed, surprised at how angry I felt.

"What do you mean?" Carissa said. She was still in a silly mood, a dopey smile on her face. She lifted up my shirt and traced her finger against my bare skin, fiddling with the waistband of my jeans.

"Why do you put Rose down like that?"

"I'm joking around! We've always teased each other. You don't understand what it's like between sisters."

"She looked upset."

"She wasn't upset, she was just embarrassed that you heard her singing. You know, I think she has a little crush on Leo. Poor Rosie... like Leo would *ever* date her."

I was surprised that Rose would be into Leo, but the more I thought about it, the more it made sense. Leo's a great guy—a hard worker, a supportive friend, funny and smart. Not a slacker coward like me.

I let Carissa pull me over toward her bed. When she kissed me, I kissed her back. Her lips were soft and her skin smelled like wildflowers. *She's your girlfriend,* I told myself. *Out of everyone in the entire school, she chose you.* And it felt good to be chosen. Still, I couldn't quite rid myself of a heavy disappointment, like a waterlogged coat weighing down my shoulders. I couldn't quite push away thoughts of Rose—that awful, embarrassed look on her face when she turned and saw me in the doorway. After a couple minutes, I told Carissa I was feeling sick and left.

Even remembering it now, months later, there's a sad, heavy feeling in my gut when I think about how I disappointed Rose that day. I wish I had knocked on her door on my way out and apologized. The truth is, Rose deserves someone like Leo. And Leo deserves someone sweet and funny like Rose, especially after Stacey ditched him for that protein-powder-crazed football player, Andy, at the Homecoming dance. *When Rose gets back from her TV show, I'll try to set them up,* I decide.

Why does the idea make me a little rattled inside?

I push away thoughts of Rose and Leo and Carissa and try to immerse myself in the music I'm cueing up. I keep glancing toward the studio door, both hoping and not hoping someone will come in and take over. On the one hand, if Cindy or Manny get here, this nervous pit in my stomach will go away and my palms will stop sweating like crazy. On the other hand, this is what I've always wanted: me, Brad Hoffman, on the air. A real live radio show. Playing music, sharing the news, giving traffic reports to help people get to where they need to be.

After the first commercial break, I settle in a little. And I start to hope that maybe I've found my stride.

At 10:30, I'm heading out of the studio when Jerry comes strolling down the hall toward me. I nod and smile, expecting him to hurry past with barely more than a glance like he usually does, but this time he stops right in front of me.

"Good work this morning, Hoffman," he says.

"Th-thank you," I stammer, caught off guard. I shift my weight to my other foot. "But, I mean, it wasn't that big of a deal. Cindy was here in like twenty minutes."

Jerry shakes his head, shushing me. "Stop," he says. He jabs his finger at me as he talks. "You were here when we needed you. Kept the show moving. Good instincts. And you know what?"

"What?" I say, my heart pounding.

"You actually sounded decent on air. Didn't try too hard to be the funny guy. Just sounded natural."

My heart fills with pride. "Thank you, sir."

"What's your schedule like Sunday nights?" he continues.

"Sunday nights? Um, not too much going on."

"Well, we've got a free slot open. Eleven P.M. to midnight, Sundays. What do you say?"

"You want me to come work the soundboard?" I remember the promise I made to myself: *Whatever they ask me to do, I'll say yes with a smile.* So, even though working late Sunday nights will make Monday mornings awful, I smile. "Okay," I tell him. "I can do that."

"No, no, not the soundboard," he says. "Well, you'll have to work the soundboard, too, I guess. But the point is, you'll be on the air." He scowls, glaring at me. "I'm trying to offer you your own show here, Hoffman."

"My own show?" The world has gone quiet. This moment hangs delicately in the air, a raindrop about to fall. "Really?"

"Say yes before I change my mind."

"Yes! Yes, of course. Are you kidding? My own show!"

Jerry's mouth twitches, as if he wants to smile. "You can start this Sunday. Eleven P.M. Don't be late."

"Thank you, Jerry! Thank you!"

As soon as I escape into my car, I pump my fist in the air, my body surging with adrenaline. What would Carissa think of me now? I'd love to see the look on her face when she learns that I, Brad Hoffman, the guy she called a "slacker loser," now has his own hour-long radio show on WAVE 104.3 every week.

Actually, I can picture Carissa's face: the little sneer of her lip, the unimpressed look in her eyes. She would either feign overly dramatic excitement, as if I were a child needing constant praise, or she would stare at me blankly, stifling a yawn of boredom, offering a flat-voiced, "That's great."

Maybe there's a reason I always felt Carissa was out of my league. Maybe that's how she *wanted* me to feel. Maybe the reason I always thought she was too good for me was that she was actively working to make me feel that way.

It's like a blindfold has been torn away from my eyes. I straighten my spine, throw back my shoulders. I breathe more deeply than I have in months.

If Carissa Hayward asked me to take her back, I wouldn't want her.

Chapter 20

Rose

I started out on Monday more motivated than ever. I'm on a great trajectory. I want to keep working my butt off so I can climb up on that scale again on Sunday and feel proud of myself.

But by Wednesday, I'm lagging. My muscles ache. My feet are covered in blisters. My sweat-drenched clothing chafes my skin. No matter how much water I drink, I am constantly hot and parched.

"Rosie!" Trainer Leslie bellows, her face inches from mine. "Pick! It! Up!"

For some reason, Leslie has pulled me aside today for one-on-one work. Sprints on the treadmill. One minute as fast as I can, then one minute walking, then repeat, and repeat, and repeat, until Leslie tells me I can stop. It's amazing how slowly the seconds creep by when I'm running fast...and how quickly they fly by when I'm walking, trying to regain my breath before another minute-long sprint.

My legs are lead. I focus on lifting my knees, pumping my arms. My breath is ragged.

"Thirty seconds left!" Leslie yells, jabbing the "up" arrow on the treadmill's speed barometer.

I grit my teeth, but I can feel myself slipping further back on the treadmill belt, close to the edge.

"Don't fall off, Rosie! This is a sprint! C'mon, Rosie! Sprint!"

As much as I distrust Trainer Mark, I prefer him to Leslie. This woman is scary. She is the human equivalent of a pot simmering on a stovetop, constantly on the verge of boiling over.

A camera hovers in the background. Leslie steps forward and leans even closer to me, her eyeliner-rimmed eyes level with mine. I am trapped. There is nowhere else for me to look. Sweat pours down my face. The pounding of my legs makes my whole body jiggle.

"You've got to *want* it, Rosie," she whispers intently. "You've got to *work* to change. How does it feel to be the fat sister? The ugly twin? To never have a date to school dances?"

I'm breathing too hard to respond. I don't know what I would say if I could. When Leslie sees me, all she sees is a caricature. She thinks she knows what it's like to be me. She thinks she is an expert on my life, my problems. But she has no idea.

All of a sudden Leslie shouts, "How does it feel to watch your beautiful twin sister lead the life you want? Huh? How does it feel, Rosie?"

It seems everyone in the gym turns to look at us. I stare straight ahead, mentally counting my steps. *One, two, three, four.*

Frowning, Leslie jabs the "down" arrow on the treadmill speed barometer until I'm at a walking pace. I put my hands on my head and concentrate all my energy on not toppling over.

"How does it feel?" she says again.

"I think I'm going to be sick," I wheeze, and stumble on jelly legs to the bathroom, where I collapse into a stall and let myself cry.

I hate Leslie. I hate treadmills. I hate cameras. Why won't they leave me alone and let me work out in peace?

That's why I like being with Daniel. He doesn't badger me with questions or prod about my family or try to "get to the bottom" of my weight issues. He just encourages me. Builds me up. Cheers me on with that smile of his. He doesn't care what brought me here. All that matters is that we're both here, helping each other, getting healthier and stronger week by week.

I'M ONLY in the bathroom for ten minutes, but when I emerge the gym is empty. Except for Daniel. He's leaning against the far wall, guzzling water.

He waves and heads toward me. "You okay?" he calls.

"Yeah," I say, hoping my eyes aren't too puffy. I don't want him to know I was crying. "Where is everyone?"

"Almost time for dinner. We've got about half an hour till they want us in the dining room."

"Good, I'm starving."

"Listen," he says, putting his arm around me. "That was rough. Leslie was totally out of line."

"It's okay." More than anything, I want to move on and forget about it.

"No," Daniel insists, "it's not okay. I think in her mind she was trying to motivate you, but it was completely inappropriate."

"Pretty warped sense of motivation."

"I mean, I get what she's trying to do. We all have issues, and we only overcome them by working through them, not denying they exist."

I stop walking and shrug out from under Daniel's arm. "Are you implying what I think you're implying?"

"Now Rosie, hold on—I'm saying, I think Leslie was going about it completely the wrong way, but her heart's in the right place. She wants to help you work through stuff."

"What stuff? I'm overweight, yeah. But that's only because I like food a little bit too much."

Daniel's eyes say, *I don't buy it.*

"What? Don't look at me that way."

"I'm not looking at you in any way," Daniel says calmly, which only aggravates me more.

I throw my empty water bottle at the recycling bin; it ricochets off the edge and lands on the floor, rolling a couple feet away. "Why does everyone keep pressing me for all this irrelevant personal information?"

"What do you mean by 'irrelevant'?"

"Well, Carissa for example. Everyone keeps asking about her.

Why does it matter that I have a twin sister? What does that have to do with my weight?"

Daniel picks up my empty water bottle and drops it into the recycling bin. "I don't think it's irrelevant," he says. "There are emotional factors that contributed to where you are now. I'm sure it was hard growing up with a twin sister. You've said yourself that you and Carissa are different."

"We are."

"So wasn't it hard? Her having no issues with her weight, while you struggled?"

"Really? You too?" I can't believe he is comparing me to Carissa like everyone else. He hasn't even met her! None of these people have! "You have no right to make judgments about me. Don't pry into my home life. That's personal, okay? You have no idea what it's like to be me."

"I'm only trying to help—"

"That's your idea of helping? How about you, then? Let's delve into all your weight issues."

"Okay. What would you like to know?"

"I mean, you used to be a distance runner. What 'emotional factors' contributed to your coming here?"

"My best friend died," Daniel says, sitting down slowly on a weight-lifting bench.

I put my hand to my mouth as if I've been slapped. "What? When?"

Daniel looks down at his hands in his lap. "Three years ago," he says. "Summer before my freshman year of high school. We met in second grade and went all through school together."

A lump rises in my throat. "I'm...so sorry."

"So I bet you're wondering, what does this have to do with my weight?"

"You don't have to tell me, Daniel. I'm sorry."

"No, no. I want to tell you. David and I were training for the high school cross-country team. Try-outs were in September, and we wanted to be ready. Not that David had to worry about not making the team. Man, could that guy run! I was pretty fast, but he could run circles around me. That day, we ran loops around the park by his house and then headed home. Usually we'd jog together slowly on the way back, as a cool-down, but that day he was feeling really great so he decided to stretch it out, keep going hard for as long as he could. Before I knew it, he was out of my sight.

"To get back to David's house, we ran through a residential area and then spent half a mile on this narrow two-lane road before turning onto his street. David was on the two-lane road when an SUV lost control and barreled right into him. It was eleven in the morning. A gorgeous day. The driver wasn't drunk or fiddling with his cell phone or anything. He just lost control. David died instantly. I was so far behind him, I didn't get there for at least five minutes. Had no idea anything was wrong. I saw the SUV and thought the driver had pulled over with car trouble.

"After that, I stopped running. I couldn't do it anymore. Without David, everything lost its meaning. I sunk into depression, replaying that day over and over. I should have been there. I should have been with him. Maybe things would have been different, you know?"

My throat is dry. It's difficult to swallow. "No—you can't blame yourself," I manage to say. "If you were with him, both of you might have been killed."

Daniel kicks his shoe against the rubber-matted gym floor. "I used to wish that's what had happened," he says softly.

"Oh, Daniel." My voice sounds loud in the empty gym. I don't know what to say. I reach out to touch his arm, but I hesitate and draw back. What if it's the wrong thing? What if he breaks down in tears right here in front of me? I don't think I could handle something like that. Not right now. Not after everything that has already happened today.

Daniel wipes his eyes and clears his throat. "So," he says. "That's my story. That's why I'm here." With some effort, he stands up. "You know what I think?"

"What?"

"We should head over to the dining room or we'll be late."

"You go ahead. I'll meet you there in a minute."

I can't look at him. Tears are building behind my eyes, steady as flood waters rising behind a dam, and I don't want Daniel to see me cry. Not after everything he's told me. Compared to Daniel, my problems seem silly. My self-pity is pathetic. I do not deserve to ever cry again. Yet the tears are building, and I know I won't be able to stop them from bursting forth in a matter of seconds.

"You sure?" Daniel asks, his brow furrowed.

"Yeah, I'll catch up with you." I force my lips into a watery smile and wave him off.

"Okay. I'll save you a seat."

Then he is gone, and the dam breaks, and for the second time in less than an hour I am sobbing into my hands. Thinking about Carissa. For all of her self-centeredness and blind ambition and shallowness, for all of my insecurities and frustrations and issues, I can't imagine what it would be like to lose her. If she died, I would be bereft. It would be like losing a part of myself.

I would give anything in the world to see Carissa right now. I can't remember the last time I hugged her. *Really* hugged her.

✩ ✩ ✩

WHEN I ARRIVE at the dining commons, the meal is almost over. Daniel, as promised, has saved a seat for me beside him. I pretend not to see and slip into a chair on the other side of the room. I look down at my plate and pick quietly at my chicken marsala.

"Hi everyone!" Britta Michaelson screeches from the center of the room. Since the first day, she hasn't been around except on Sundays for our weigh-in sessions. Everyone trades glances, wondering what's going on.

"Are you all ready for the weigh-in?" Britta exclaims.

"Um, today's only Wednesday," says Tony, an older man who

used to coach football but had to stop two years ago when he had a heart attack in the middle of a game.

Britta flashes her smile, so bright it could be an ad for teeth whitener. "Are you implying you're not ready for the weigh-in?"

Everyone looks around, unsure what to say.

"Okay," Britta announces after a couple moments of uncomfortable silence. "I guess we won't have a weigh-in this week! You don't have to worry about getting up on that scale!"

"Really?" Doris says. "Are you being serious?"

"Of course I am," Britta says.

Marcella claps. Tony cheers. I take a big bite of my chicken marsala.

"And the reason," Britta continues, "is that you won't be here."

"Who won't?" says Daniel.

"None of you."

My pulse quickens. What does she mean? I am surprised by how much I dread the thought of leaving this place.

"Pack your bags!" Britta shouts. "Next week, you're all going home!"

Chapter 21

Brad

The station is quiet, as usual, on Saturday afternoon. Yesterday, I spent an hour deliberating over guitars at Gary's Guitarland, and ended up buying a used Gibson with a small crack in the body. Gary said I could easily repair the crack myself if I want, but I think I'll leave it. A scar. A battle wound. I like the reminder: even with the crack, the guitar can still make great music.

But even used and cracked guitars are expensive. I ended up forking over nearly all the money I've made the past month at the radio station. I keep telling myself that it's worth it. I'm now a guy with his own guitar! I spent half an hour strumming it before I went to bed last night. Playing guitar is harder than it looks. My fingers already hurt. Still, I can't wait to get off work and play around on it some more.

About halfway through my shift, Meghan comes into the back room. I'm sleepily sorting through ancient stacks of promotional materials for concerts and giveaways that happened years ago. At the sight of her, my pulse speeds up.

She beams. "Hey, stranger!"

Is she this happy to see me? Or is she happy because it's the weekend?

She plops down on the arm of my chair. I can smell her perfume, something faintly spicy. She's wearing seashell earrings today. She leans into me, our arms brushing.

"So," she says, "how much do you *looove* me?"

My chest tightens. Is it *that* obvious I'm crushing on her? Could Jerry tell? Did he say something to her? What if now he wants to fire me? Meghan mentioned he's like an uncle to her. Which would make her his pseudo-niece. Uncles can be very protective of their nieces.

I'm on the verge of hyperventilating. I sputter out a series of "Ums" and "Uhs" until Meghan rescues me by whipping out two tickets from her purse. She holds them in front of my face, but I can't focus enough to read the tiny print.

"Because," she says, "I scored us two tickets to see Turquoise 7 tonight! They're playing downtown!"

My heartbeat slows a little. "Turquoise 7? Who's that?"

"Bradley. Howard. Hoffman," she says, hitting my arm. Her face is serious. "Don't tell me you haven't heard of Turquoise 7."

"Sorry. Never heard of them."

Meghan laughs, her serious façade dissolving instantly. "Me neither! I mean, before this afternoon. I guess they're a cover band of Maroon 5?"

"Ahh. The name makes more sense now."

"Yeah, kinda funny, right? Anyway, the lead singer came by and dropped off these free tickets. Jerry said I could have them. So...do you have plans tonight?"

"Nope, no plans." Which is the truth. Some Saturday nights Leo and I get together for tacos and then an epic video game/horror movie marathon, but tonight he's hanging out with the Mark/Mel/Stacey crowd, and I don't feel like seeing those people.

"So you'll come?" Meghan says. Her purple-rimmed eyes look right into mine.

I need to move forward. It's time. And I do like Meghan. Leo would be smacking me on the head right about now. Here is this beautiful, awesome girl who loves live music and understands my obsession with the radio station. Why would I not be thrilled to go to a concert with her?

I'm standing at the door of an open airplane, parachute strapped to my back, preparing to leap out.

And then I do.

"Sure," I say with a smile. "Sounds like fun."

"Great!" She hands me a ticket. "Want to get dinner before?"

"Okay."

"Should we carpool together from the station? That's your car out front, right?"

I nod. I'm excited, but also a little overwhelmed. Part of me wants nothing more than to kiss Meghan at the end of the night. The other part of me is thinking, *I'm not sure I'm ready for this.*

✧ ☆ ✧

So HERE I AM, a few hours later, on my first sorta-kinda-maybe date since Carissa dumped me. I park in the downtown parking garage, and Meghan and I stroll along Main Street, surveying the variety of restaurant options.

"How about Indian food?" I suggest, pausing outside the Taj Mahal restaurant.

She scrunches up her face. "I don't handle spicy food very well."

It's not all spicy, I think, but I don't say anything. We pass a Thai place, a barbeque saloon, two bars. Meghan grabs my hand and yanks me across the street.

"Have you ever been here? They have the *best* food," she says.

We've stopped in front of Nature's Café, an organic foodie bistro. I don't have a problem with the place—their food is pretty good, actually—but it's one of Carissa's favorites. She used to drag me here all the time, professing to be "starving out of her mind." Then she'd order a tiny salad. It used to drive me crazy. I'd tell her she could order a tiny salad anywhere. We used to fake-argue about it—you know, the kind of arguing where you're teasing each other but there's real annoyance underneath. I haven't been back here since our break-up.

Now, standing in front of Nature's Café with the potted palm trees and familiar menu board advertising the daily specials, I hate to admit it. But the memory of our bickering makes me miss Carissa a little.

Meghan must see something on my face, because she says, "Is something wrong? We don't have to eat here."

I put on a smile, forcing Carissa's ghost away from my thoughts. "No, I'm fine," I tell Meghan. "I've been here before. Their food is great."

"Are you sure?"

"Yeah, let's do it."

We nab a booth in the corner and, looking across the table at Meghan's expressive eyes and wide smile, I'm happy I'm here. We talk about school—she goes to the other high school across town—and the radio station. She tells a hilarious story about Jerry blanking on Ringo Starr's name during a 24-hour Beatles show he used to do every year.

"I love The Beatles!" I exclaim, and begin telling her about my dream to travel to London one day and see the Abbey Road Studios where they recorded their albums. But I cut my monologue short when I notice Meghan's eyes wandering around the room. She doesn't look very interested.

"Oh, I just think The Beatles are kind of overrated," she says. "No offense."

I'm speechless. The Beatles? Overrated? Who says that? I ask about her favorite music, and she describes a lot of indie-pop bands from Los Angeles that I've never heard of. At least we agree on some classic stuff: Rolling Stones, Bob Dylan, The Who. She turns her nose up a little at James Taylor, calling him "too vanilla." I'm about to protest, but then our food comes.

I get my usual enchilada platter, and she's ordered a messy turkey burger that falls apart in her hands. She licks her fingers. It's so the opposite of Carissa's dainty salad nibbles that I want to laugh. The ache in my chest relaxes.

We move on to a discussion of favorite movies and TV shows, and our tastes have a lot more overlap. Meghan laughs at my impression of Job from *Arrested Development*. She describes once seeing Tom Hanks at a frozen yogurt shop in Los Angeles. I feel good, like Carissa is far away, like I'm wiping away painful memories and claiming this restaurant as my own.

When the bill comes, I reach across the table. "I've got it."

"Are you sure?" she asks, her wallet in hand.

"My pleasure," I tell her, and she smiles and thanks me and puts her wallet back in her purse.

A smile spreads across my face as I tuck my debit card into the slot. *She let me pay. That must mean this is a date.*

I imagine later tonight, driving up to Lookout Point, the radio playing softly, sitting beside her as we gaze out at the ocean. I imagine leaning over, brushing Meghan's hair from her face, feeling her lips on mine. I'm filled with a giddy sense of possibility. Who cares if she doesn't like The Beatles.

✧ ✩ ✧

I CAN'T QUITE BELIEVE it, but a few hours later I'm walking hand-in-hand with Meghan down the quiet, dark boardwalk alongside the beach. The waves crash against the shore in a steady rhythm. My ears are still ringing from the concert. The band was much better than I expected. They actually did sound a lot like Maroon 5, and the dance floor was packed with people shouting along to the lyrics. Meghan and I stood close together, bodies jostling around us. That was when she first laced her fingers through mine, so we wouldn't get separated in the crowd.

Now, she squeezes my hand and leads me up the stairs onto the pier. The wooden planks creak under our feet and the white lights strung overhead glow faintly through the fog. We walk all the way down to the end. The ocean stretches below us and in front of us, out and out, like it goes on forever. Meghan sits down on a bench, wrapping her sweater tighter around herself as a cold breeze sweeps in. I sit down beside her.

"So," she says.

"So." My heart is beating wildly. I want so badly to kiss her, but I'm also terrified to make a move.

"Thanks for coming with me tonight," she says. "I had a lot of fun."

"Me too. Thanks for inviting me."

The air is charged between us. We sit for a few moments in silence, both of us looking out at the ocean. She shivers. I put my arm around her and she leans her body into mine. Can she feel my heart beating through my sweatshirt? She tilts her face up and looks at me with a small, coy smile. And then we're kissing, her hands warm against the back of my neck, my arms wrapped around her waist.

Toward midnight, after dropping Meghan off at her apartment complex, I slip into my own darkened house. My curfew is technically eleven but my parents have been so caught up in their own drama lately, I didn't think they'd notice if I was a little late.

I was right. Other than one table lamp left on in the front hallway, the house is dark and quiet. No one is waiting up to lecture me. I'm relieved, but a small part of me is strangely upset. Only a couple months ago, my mom was curfew-obsessed. Now she doesn't even care. I turn the lamp off and sneak past the living room.

And then I hear something. A...snore?

I peek into the room and can barely make out a blanket-covered lump stretched out on the recliner. Another snore confirms it: my dad is sleeping in there.

It's even worse than I thought.

I sneak upstairs and collapse into bed, refusing to think about my parents' relationship problems. Tonight was amazing. I want to hold on to that feeling. I close my eyes and think about Meghan: the feel of her fingers laced through mine, the soft brush of her hair against my face, the smell of her perfume.

I slip into a dream where I'm back at the pier, kissing a girl, only it's during the daytime. I hear the calls of seagulls and smell the salty ocean air. My bare arms are warm from the sun. I feel so lucky to be here with this girl. I can't believe she wants to kiss me—*me*, of all people!

Then she pulls away, and surprisingly, it's not Meghan staring back at me. And it's not Carissa, either.

It's Rose.

Rose. Of course.

My heart is full to bursting. Her eyes are so beautiful, brown irises flecked with gold. She looks insanely happy. I am filled with the desire to make her this happy always. I lean forward and kiss her again. Her lips are soft and warm, and I pull her closer.

Chapter 22

I'm in the middle of packing when there's a knock at my bedroom door. I sigh, expecting it to be Doris. Ever since I confided to her about my "homesickness," she's been coming over to say goodnight. But when I open the door, Daniel stands there. His green T-shirt makes his eyes seem even brighter than usual.

"Hey," he says.

"Hi."

We didn't really speak last night or this morning, ever since he told me about David. I haven't known what to say. I still don't.

Shame festers inside me. I can't even look at him.

"Um," I address the flowered carpet. "Do you want to come in?"

"Thanks." He follows me inside.

I push my suitcase off the bed and sit down. He sits down beside me.

"I know you're busy packing," he says. "I don't want to bother you. This won't take long."

"N-no, it's fine," I stammer. "It's good to see you."

"I couldn't leave for home without talking to you," he says, eyebrows furrowed. "I know I'd go crazy this week if I didn't at least *try* to figure out what I did wrong."

"You didn't do anything wrong." I pick at a thread that's come loose from my bedspread. "It's me. I just—I'm sorry, Daniel. I'm not good at this stuff."

"What stuff? What are you talking about?"

"I clam up. I don't know what to say."

"Is this because I told you about David?"

"I'm such a jerk." I keep picking at the bedspread. I still can't look at Daniel. "I blew up when you asked about my family. I totally shut you out. And then you—you've actually *gone through* something. I can't even imagine what you went through. And you're so generous and open about it. You shared everything with me the minute I asked."

"You're easy to talk to. I feel safe with you."

"I feel safe with you, too." Finally, I meet his eyes. His face softens. I want so badly to bury my face in his neck, to feel his arms around me. Because I do feel safe with him. But the thing is, it scares me to feel so safe. So vulnerable. Especially with someone I've only known for two months.

I sigh. "I wanted to apologize," I continue, "but I get so awkward. I couldn't think of anything to say."

"It's okay, Rosie."

"It's not. It's really not. I'm an idiot."

"Don't say that. I sprung it on you all at once." He gently touches my shoulder. "Believe me. You're not the first one to get tongue-tied when David comes up."

"Well, I want to tell you something, if it's not too late."

"I want to tell you something, too."

"Oh—do you want to go first?"

"No, no. You first," he says.

"Okay." I force myself to quit fiddling with the bedspread. I fold my hands in my lap and look straight into Daniel's kind green eyes. "I wanted to tell you that I think you are an incredibly brave person, and I'm really proud of you."

"Thanks. I'm proud of you, too."

"I also wanted to say that you inspire me to be a better person. My weight issues are all tied up with my feelings about my twin sister. It's complicated. Stuff I've buried for a long time, and I'm not really comfortable talking about it yet. But I'm starting to work through everything. And I'd like to talk to you about it later. When I'm ready."

"I understand," he says. "And I'm here, whenever you want to talk."

"Thank you."

Daniel smiles at me, and the last residue of awkwardness between us melts away. It is such a relief to have my friend back.

I flop backward onto the bed. Daniel follows suit.

"Now you," I say, turning my head to look at him.

"What?"

"Now it's your turn. You said you had something you wanted to tell me."

"Oh, I did say that, didn't I?"

"Are you changing your mind?"

"Well..."

Now, more than anything, I want to hear whatever it is he has to say. But I channel Carissa and feign nonchalance. "If you don't want to tell me, that's fine. You don't have to."

It works. "No, no," he says. "It's the reason I came over here tonight. To tell you this."

My chest seizes with panic. Does he have more to tell me about David? I try to remain calm. I place my hand on his arm and wait.

Daniel's eyes search mine. I stare back at him. It's as if he's weighing something in his mind, going back and forth between options.

"Rosie," he says quietly. His breath is warm and smells of toothpaste.

"It's okay," I whisper. "I'm not going anywhere."

Something shifts in Daniel's expression, like he's made a decision, and I'm worried that maybe I've said the wrong thing when all of a sudden he leans forward. His lips brush mine.

I close my eyes and kiss him back. It's my first-ever kiss. And in that instant, out of nowhere, Carissa's boyfriend Brad pops into my mind.

Horrified with myself, I try to push away all thoughts of Brad. Daniel threads his fingers through my hair and pulls me closer. His lips are soft and he smells nice and I like the way our breathing is synchronized. I touch his cheek. I'm not really sure what I'm doing. Can Daniel tell that this is my first-ever kiss? Am I bad at it? Sometimes I wish I could turn my brain on mute and just let myself experience things without constantly over-analyzing. I try to relax and pretend that I am a kissing pro. Like Carissa.

Which would mean that Daniel is Brad.

Stop it, brain. Stop it stop it stop it.

Daniel pulls away and smiles at me. "I've been wanting to do that for a while," he says.

"Really?"

"Yep. Since the day I met you. But I was worried I would screw things up. Scare you off. I didn't want to ruin our friendship."

"What made you do it now?" I ask.

"I guess because things felt so weird between us. You weren't talking to me. It was like there was this wide gulf separating us, and I didn't know where our friendship had gone. But it made me realize— I couldn't keep living in fear. I had tried so hard not to ruin our friendship, but it seemed I had managed to ruin it anyway."

"Sorry about that."

"No, it was a good thing. Because I thought I might as well be honest with you about my feelings. I might as well give it a shot."

I lean back against the pillow. "I can't believe it. All this time I thought you only saw me as a friend."

"Rosie, come on. It was pretty obvious."

"No it wasn't!"

"I snuck over to your room at night. I held your hand. I took you to the rose garden."

"I don't know. I thought you were being friendly."

"I fell for you the moment I met you," Daniel says, brushing a strand of hair behind my ear. "The moment I saw your beautiful smile."

My whole body is jittery, like I've binged on caffeine. For weeks I've been imagining what it would be like to kiss Daniel, and now that it's actually happened, it feels wonderful and surreal and a little bit scary. Because I never imagined what it would be like *after* Daniel and I kissed. What's going to happen now that we've crossed this line? I have no clue what to expect.

"I'm gonna miss you," Daniel murmurs into my ear. "What am I gonna do for all these days without my workout partner?"

"I'll miss you, too," I say. Secretly, though, I'm relieved to be going home. It'll give me time to digest everything. See my family. See Holly. I cannot wait to talk to Holly. I can practically hear her voice, squealing to *slow down, start at the beginning, don't leave out any details, oh this is so exciting!*

And Carissa. I'll finally have a guy to tell Carissa about.

And Brad. Of course I'll see Brad. The thought sends a shiver of excitement through my belly, but I push it away and pull Daniel closer.

Chapter 23

Brad

After school on Wednesday, I spend an hour working the soundboard at the station. Then, after my shift ends, I help schlep equipment over to the local food pantry. The station is broadcasting from there all evening to spread the word about the pantry's canned food drive.

As soon as I climb out of my car, I spot Meghan outside the front entrance of the building, setting up a folding table and chairs. Other than a couple five-minute conversations in the station hallways, we haven't spent any time together since our date. I call out her name. She smiles and waves.

"Hey, stranger," she says as I set a speaker down on the table. "I've been thinking about you."

"Me, too. I mean, not me—you. I've been thinking about you."

We stand there grinning at each other. I want to lean down and kiss her, right here, even with all these people around. Does the station have rules against employees dating? I heard a rumor that the two morning hosts, Manny and Cindy, used to be a couple.

Screw it, I think, placing my hand on her back to gently draw her close. But at that moment Jerry barges around the corner, bellowing out assignments. I drop my hand down to my side.

"I'll get Pete to carry the rest of the sound equipment over," Jerry says. "Why don't you kids set up this tent, okay? Erika's insisting on shade while she broadcasts."

Erika is our diva-y weeknight host. The "tent" appears to be nothing more than a bunch of metal rods and a blue tarp shoved into a cardboard box.

"Are there any instructions?" I ask.

Jerry waves my question away. "You'll figure it out. After you're done, I told Marlene that the two of you would help out in the food pantry."

"Who's Marlene?" Meghan asks.

"The lady in charge around here. Please, Meg, don't complain. Not today."

"I'm not complaining."

Jerry's cell phone trills. He points his finger at Meghan, then at me. "Please help out, okay guys? It'll be good PR for the station." Then he disappears back around the corner, phone pressed to his ear.

"I wasn't complaining," Meghan says to me, dumping out the contents of the tent box. "I just hate how Jerry will volunteer us for stuff without even checking first. It's not like we're getting paid overtime for this."

I murmur agreement, concentrating on fitting two metal rods together and fastening them securely.

"I mean," Meghan continues, "maybe we have something better to do on a random weeknight than hang out with smelly homeless people."

I glance over. *Did I hear her right? Smelly homeless people?* She's busy fastening the blue tarp to a metal rod with hooks.

"Um...Meghan... I don't think...um, that was pretty uncalled for..."

"Brad, I was joking." She laughs, poking me in the ribs with her black-painted fingernail. "I thought you, of all people, could take a joke."

I turn back to my task of assembling the tent, but the energy between us has shifted. Now, uneasiness squirms inside me. I try to push it away. I try to remember what it felt like to kiss Meghan, that night on the pier, the salty ocean breeze stirring her hair. Her soft lips. The calls of seagulls. My bare arms warm from the sun...

I realize I'm doing it again. *Crap.* It's been happening all week— whenever I start daydreaming about kissing Meghan, my thoughts turn back to the dream I had of kissing Rose. My brain keeps going there, even though I know I closed that door a long time ago when I started dating Carissa. I mean, it's not like Rose would have wanted to date me in the first place...but she would *never* date me now that I've dated her sister.

I never even realized they were sisters until I went to pick up Carissa for Homecoming and saw Rose reading a book in the living room. I already knew her, because she sat behind me in World History. I had a crush on her in the same way you crush on a celebrity —like, you know that nothing would ever happen between you, so the crush kind of becomes irrelevant. Rose is so smart and genuine and easy to talk to. Not to mention incredibly beautiful. I know she would shake her head and look down at her feet if I told her that, but it's true. She is beautiful. Her smile, her eyes, her hair—it's like this light shines from her.

Anyway, when I woke up the morning after my dream, I told myself it was only because the concert had been a cover band of Maroon 5. Obviously Rose was on my mind; my subconscious was remembering that time I glimpsed her singing "Sugar." But now I can't stop daydreaming about her. And every night when I collapse into bed, there's a small insistent voice in my head hoping I'll slip back into the dream again.

Stop being ridiculous. I know Rose would never think of me as more than a friend. She's sort of...*above* the rest of us. Not stuck-up; not like she thinks of herself as better than anyone else. More like she's got more important stuff going on. She knows that the social scene in high school is cliquey and pretentious and she doesn't want to bother with any of it. I once heard my mom say that Rose has an "old soul"—I think that's the best way of describing it.

And an old soul would never want to be with a clumsy, clueless soul like me.

"Brad? Earth to Brad?" Meghan says. "What are you thinking about?"

"Oh, uh, nothing. Just trying to get this tent put together."

She grazes my arm with her fingers. "C'mon, admit it. I know you were thinking about me. You had this adorable dopey smile on your face."

I don't say anything, which makes her laugh again.

Ten minutes later, we've finished putting up the tent. Meghan half-jokes about hopping in my car and bailing, but when I head inside the food pantry, she follows.

The food pantry is crowded with rows of shelves, barely far enough apart to make narrow aisles that a person can walk through. The shelves are lined with cans and boxes of food.

A short gray-haired woman rushes past us, carrying a large box.

"Can I help you with that?" I ask.

She pauses and turns. "Thanks, sweetheart," she says, allowing me to shift the box's weight into my arms. "You can put it right over there."

I set the box down where she directs me, and then Meghan and I introduce ourselves.

"I'm Marlene," the woman says. "Thank you so much for helping us out today. We've also got some girls volunteering from the high school. National Honor Society, I think? Here, honey," she says, ushering Meghan to the other side of the room, "how about you come help Tom and me in Aisle One." Meghan shoots me a forlorn look but doesn't protest.

Marlene touches my shoulder. "And you, sweetheart, will you work Aisle Three? They'll tell you what to do. You're tall, so you can help those girls reach the top shelves."

"Sure," I say, a part of me secretly relieved to be working apart from Meghan. Maybe I'm in a weird mood today. Maybe I'm tired. But for some reason, she's starting to get on my nerves, and I have a feeling that two hours in a confined space with her will only lead to arguing.

I turn the corner into Aisle Three. And I probably should have been expecting it—Marlene did say *girls, high school,* and *National Honor Society,* after all—but when Carissa Hayward looks up at me, I am utterly surprised to see her.

THE FOOD PANTRY is busy tonight. Really busy. The clients form a long line that jams up against the counter and snakes out the door. Many of them are young mothers with babies and toddlers. A few couples come in together, holding hands. Some older men shuffle in alone. They bring their own bags and boxes to carry the food home. None of them smell. All of them smile and thank us.

I don't know what I was expecting, but it wasn't quite this. I think of Meghan's dismissive tone. I think of my grandfather before he died, railing against "those lazy bums who take government hand-outs." I wish my grandfather were here to meet these people. It's obvious none of them *want* to be waiting in line for a dented can of tomato soup and a bruised bell pepper. They have no choice. They are hard-working people just trying to make ends meet.

The minutes fly by. We're so busy that I don't even have a chance to think about Carissa. Aisle Three is the produce and perishable foods aisle, and I'm in charge of bringing out more food from the giant refrigerator in the back. Milk, yogurt, lunchmeat, ground turkey, frozen sausage patties. The vegetables we're handing out today are yellow squash, red onion, and bell peppers. Carissa talks to the customers, checking their slips of paper that list any food allergies and how many people are in their household. She asks what foods they prefer and calls out a list to me. I gather the various items and bring them up to the counter. People are excited about the yellow squash—guess they haven't had any here for a while. Some of the vegetables are shriveled and the boxes of milk and meat are soggy with condensation. I never thought about what a gift it is to drive to the grocery store and choose what I want to eat.

Toward the end of the rush, a woman slides her half-filled bags of food down the counter to our aisle. She only looks a few years older than us, but she has a baby on her hip and a toddler in a stroller. Her face is carefully made-up, and her hair is neatly combed into a braid, and she's wearing a sundress. She could fit in perfectly at our high school. If I drove by her on the street, I would think she was a babysitter taking the kids outside to enjoy the last rays of the day's sunlight.

But her eyes give her away. Her eyes are exhausted.

Carissa hands her the vegetables, a carton of milk, a container of yogurt. "How about some lunchmeat?" she asks. "Sausage patties? C'mon, Brad, hurry up."

I grab deli turkey and sausage patties and place them on the counter. The woman smiles at me.

"Thank you," she says, placing the items in her bag. Then she moves along. I want to ask her if she needs help carrying her bags, but I don't know if we're allowed to. And then the next person is sliding down the counter to our aisle, and Carissa's already barking out orders for more food items.

Five minutes later, the young woman comes back in through the exit and approaches our aisle. "Excuse me," she says to Carissa. "I'm sorry, but do you have any ground turkey left? I saw a woman outside with some."

"You already got your two meat items," Carissa says. Her tone is brusque. She turns her attention to the next person in line.

"I can trade one of them back." The woman holds up the lunchmeat in one hand, the sausage in the other. "Please. I would really appreciate it if—"

"Look," Carissa snaps. "We have a whole line of people waiting, and you already had your turn. I'm sorry but you need to take what you got—"

I can't believe Carissa is on a power trip over this. I grab one of the packages of ground turkey and jog up to the counter.

"Here," I tell the woman. Her eyes light up when she sees what I'm handing her. She tries to give me back the sausage patties, but I wave her off. "It's fine, keep it. You can have both."

"Thank you *so much*," she says. I've never seen someone this excited over groceries. She's practically jumping up and down. With one more smile at me, she hurries away, probably trying to get out of there before Carissa intervenes. Which is a wise move.

"That was against the rules," Carissa grumbles. "Clients only get two meat items."

"It's not a big deal. We have plenty. It's almost closing time, anyway."

She whirls away from me, planting a fake smile on her face to assist the next person in line. Two minutes later, she accidentally-on-purpose drops a container of yogurt and it breaks and spills all over the floor. "Whoops!" she says with a pointed look in my direction. It is, of course, my job to clean it up.

Soon after I finish mopping up the yogurt mess, our shift is over, and the pantry doors close for the day. Carissa sweeps the floor while Lindsay packs up the perishable items and I lug the boxes back to the fridge.

Marlene reappears in our aisle. "Thank you kids for helping us this evening," she says. "Come back anytime. We could always use volunteers."

I glimpse Meghan standing behind Marlene. She rolls her eyes at me and mouths, *BOR-ING.* I ignore her.

Carissa shakes Marlene's hand with one of her fake professional smiles. "It was a pleasure to be here," she says. "You are doing such good work. Our community is lucky to have you."

"Thank you, dearie," Marlene says, then excuses herself to go check on the other volunteers.

Which leaves me standing there in the cramped space between Aisle Two and Aisle Three. My ex-girlfriend on my left, my new sort-of girlfriend on my right.

Just last week, I would have killed for a situation like this: me, Brad Hoffman, showing off in front of Carissa with a new girl. But now that it's happening, all I want is to disappear. I am filled with such longing for Rose that my chest hurts. How I wish I were here with her instead.

"Brad, are you ready to go?" Meghan says, looping a finger through my belt loop.

Carissa's eyes flit to Meghan, then to me. She tilts her chin up slightly, increasing the wattage of her fake smile. "Hi," she says, sticking out her hand for Meghan to shake. "I'm Carissa. I don't think we've been introduced."

I clear my throat. "Um, Carissa, this is Meghan. Meghan, Carissa."

Meghan presses her body against mine as she leans over to shake Carissa's hand. "Nice to meet you," she says, but her tone is flat. I can tell she doesn't like Carissa. Once the handshake is over, Meghan slips her hand into mine and squeezes, hard.

"Well, we should probably be going..." I try, but Carissa ignores me.

"I'm Brad's ex-girlfriend," she states. "We were together for a year."

"Ten months," I tell Meghan, who is glaring at Carissa.

"More like eleven. Don't play it down, Brad. We were pretty serious." She leans in close and stage-whispers into my ear, loud enough for Meghan to hear, "Remember? You always said you were *crazy* about me."

I pull away and cough uncomfortably. I can't believe I actually wanted this to happen. I actually *wanted* to run into Carissa when I was out with Meghan. Why? Why did I wish for this? Now that it's happening, I'm literally sweating—from anxiety and also because it's hot and stuffy in this cramped space—and my stomach is in knots.

Meghan's nails dig into my palm like claws. "We'd better go. Right, Brad?" her voice is a high screech. "Bye, *Melissa*."

Carissa doesn't bother to correct her. "Nice to meet you, hon," she says, waving her perfectly manicured fingers. She holds my gaze for a long moment, biting her lip as if about to say something more to me. But before she can, I turn away. Meghan pulls me out the door.

I know what Carissa was trying to do: she wanted me to miss her, yearn for her, want her back. But I don't.

I don't want Meghan either.

Mostly, I feel tired.

"I can't believe that girl," Meghan huffs as we make our way to my car. The tent and broadcasting equipment has already been torn down, on its way back to the station.

"Sorry about that. I didn't know she was going to be here."

"I can't believe you used to date her. What a witch."

"She's not that bad." Carissa has her faults, sure, but I don't like hearing Meghan call her names.

Meghan rolls her eyes and drops my hand. We're silent the rest of the distance to my car.

Driving away from the food pantry, we pass an older woman I recognize as one of the last clients we served. She's walking down the sidewalk in the dark, carrying a grocery bag full of food. It looks like it's painful for her to walk—like her feet hurt, or maybe her knees.

Meghan points out the window. "Look at that lady. I don't think *she* really needs to eat more food. Am I right?" She laughs.

That's the moment I realize that the ugly parts of Meghan remind me a lot of the ugly parts of Carissa.

And the truth is, I don't like Meghan. Not at all.

I pull over to the side of the road, roll down the passenger window, and lean over Meghan, ignoring her protests.

"Excuse me, ma'am?" I call to the older woman struggling with her groceries. "We were just working at the food pantry. Could we give you a ride?"

When I get home, all I want to do is stagger upstairs to my room, slip off my shoes, fall into bed, and sleep till tomorrow. I've been up since five. I had to deal with Carissa. And Meghan did not take it well when I told her I think we're better off as friends. Her face seemed to cinch inward, like a purse being drawn closed, and she wouldn't meet my eyes. "You're such a jerk," she said, storming out of my car before I'd even fully parked. She slammed the door so hard I half-expected the hinges to snap off.

I am not looking forward to work tomorrow. But I'm not thinking about that right now. All I'm thinking about is sleep.

"Brad? Is that you, honey?" my mom calls from the living room.

"Yeah."

"Can you come in here a minute please?"

I groan but make my way down the hall toward her voice. She probably wants to hear about my day. Or maybe she wants me to fold a load of laundry.

But as soon as I walk into the living room, I know something is wrong. My dad is sitting on the couch, a watery smile on his face. He looks pale and tired. My mom's eyes and nose are red—she's obviously been crying.

Crap.

"Come sit down with us," Mom says, patting the space between her and Dad on the couch. "We have something to tell you."

I walk across the room and sit down on the couch, but it seems like I am outside my body, watching myself move. I am numb. *This is it. These are the last moments before my family splits apart.*

"We love you so much, buddy," my dad says, patting my knee, and then his voice chokes up and he can't say anything else. I've never seen my father cry before. He nods at my mother, as if to say, *You tell him.*

Mom grabs my hands in hers. Her palms are cool and dry, like always. That small familiar detail is a comfort, and I cling to it. My heart is beating with adrenaline, and I remember that Friday evening a few weeks ago when I came home and the house was dark and empty. That was the first inkling I had that something was wrong. Ever since then, a part of me has been waiting for this moment. Waiting for the bomb to drop. I know what Mom's going to say —*Brad, your father and I are getting a divorce*—but I still force myself to listen.

"Brad," she says. "Your father..." She takes a deep breath that turns into a sigh.

Dad puts his hands over Mom's so the three of us are holding hands together. He looks at me and gives a little apologetic shrug. "What we're trying to tell you, buddy," he says, "is that I have cancer."

Chapter 24

I stare out the airplane window. The gray buildings and strips of freeway lengthen and expand as we descend into the smog of Los Angeles. Since LAX is so chaotic, the show producers opted to fly me into Burbank, a much smaller, quieter airport. I am a hot mess of emotion: excitement to see my family, anxiety about what they'll think of me, fear that I'll fall back into bad habits during this week at home. I am too full of jumbled emotions to try to sort anything out. Instead, the whole flight I've focused my thoughts on Daniel, replaying our kiss, picturing his sweet smile.

Out my window, the ground rushes up to meet us. The plane's wheels touch the earth and, all of a sudden, I'm home.

And then I'm walking through the terminal toward baggage claim, so full of adrenaline and nerves I'm shaking. My armpits are damp with sweat. I duck into the restroom and splash water on my face. In the mirror, I don't see much difference from the person I was two months ago. Brown hair, brown eyes, round pink cheeks. Will my family be disappointed? Will everyone laugh at me behind forced smiles?

I take a few deep breaths, the way Doris taught me, and continue down the corridor. Baggage claim is through a set of double-doors, in an outdoor alcove close to the parking lot. I adjust my backpack on my shoulders, tighten my ponytail, and the automatic doors open to let me pass through.

It's a gorgeous autumn day. The sunshine is so bright that it takes my eyes a moment to adjust after the dim indoor lighting.

I don't know what I was expecting, but it certainly wasn't this.

A huge crowd of people surrounds the baggage claim area.

They erupt into cheers and applause when they see me. Some of them are holding "WELCOME HOME ROSIE" signs; others are wearing T-shirts emblazoned with my name. Front and center, my parents beam at me with open arms. Carissa waves a balloon and Scotty jumps up and down. My mom is crying. I run to them, tears rushing to my own eyes. *My family.* Their arms enfold me like a blanket.

"Rosie! Look at you!" Carissa says. She pulls me to her and squeezes me fiercely.

"I missed you," I mumble into her hair, surprised at how much I mean it.

Carissa pulls away. "I can fit my arms around you now!" she says, laughing. She winks at a nearby camera.

Of course. The cameras are here, capturing everything. This is nothing more than a big show. I turn away from Carissa and scan the crowd.

I recognize some faces: kids from my homeroom, our neighbors across the street, my parents' friends from their running club. But my gut sinks in disappointment, and I realize I am searching, despite myself, for a certain face. A certain face that isn't here.

✰ ✰ ✰

"Tell. Me. Everything!" Holly says as soon as we're alone in my room. It is both comforting and strange to be back in my own room with the sunflower wallpaper, sitting cross-legged on my bed with my best friend. My room is unchanged, yet so much has changed in the past nine weeks.

"Well..." I begin, savoring the details of this moment—the buzz of anticipation that always comes with sharing stories, Holly's wide eyes, the way she twists a corner of my comforter with her fingers whenever we sit on my bed like this, talking.

"Tell me! Tell me!" Holly says.

I try, and fail, to suppress a smile. "Last night...I...kissed a boy!"

"Oh my gosh!" Holly shrieks, grabbing a pillow and hitting me with it. "Tell me everything!"

And so I do. I tell her about the girls' cabin and the common room and the dining room and the gym; about Leslie and Mark and Doris and Daniel. Mostly, I talk about Daniel. About how sweet he is, and how he called me pretty.

"Of course he did! You *are* pretty, Rose," Holly says.

"Thanks."

"I mean it. You've always been pretty."

I look down and smooth my palms over the bedspread. I never know how to respond when Holly says things like this. I'm not pretty, I know I'm not, but if I deny it she'll only keep insisting I am. But it feels awkward agreeing with her when it is so obviously not the case. I am not pretty. Ask anyone. They'll tell you. I'm sure even my parents would agree that Carissa is the pretty twin.

"So what's going on at school?" I ask. "What drama have I missed?"

"Well, I guess the main thing everyone's been talking about is Carissa and Brad splitting up," Holly says in an offhand way.

At the mention of Brad's name, my heartbeat quickens. "What?"

"Right after you left, Carissa broke up with Brad. You mean she didn't tell you?"

I shake my head. I feel... I'm not quite sure what I feel.

"I assumed you knew," Holly says. "Though I guess it makes sense, you were gone when it happened, and you haven't had contact with anyone while you've been away on the show. I assumed Carissa would have said something. I'm sorry, Rose—I should have told you right away!"

Holly is the only person who ever guessed my feelings for Brad. She can read my face, even when I'm trying to hide my emotions. She said I always lit up when he was around. At first, I tried to laugh it off or change the subject, but she kept bringing it up and bringing it up until there was no way I could deny it anymore.

Over the summer, I finally had a breakdown at Holly's house.

That morning, when Brad came by to get Carissa for a day at the beach, he and I had talked for ten minutes while Carissa was upstairs in her room, getting ready. I'd just started listening to this amazing humor podcast after Brad had mentioned it to me a couple weeks before, and that morning in the kitchen we talked about the latest episode, where the main guy pulled an extremely complicated prank on this prestigious college marching band. It was hilarious.

"I really wish I could listen to more of their stuff," I said. "The archives on their website only go back a couple months."

"I have some of the old episodes saved on my computer," Brad said, his voice rising eagerly. "I'll send them to you."

"Really?"

"Yeah, no problem."

"Thanks. That would be amazing."

We smiled at each other.

Then Carissa came downstairs, dressed in a tiny bikini and sarong, a silver necklace dangling into her cleavage. As soon as she entered the room, all of Brad's attention snapped to her like a magnet. He was immediately, completely captivated by her presence. Carissa, meanwhile, didn't even glance at Brad. She looked bored, as if *she* was the one who'd been kept waiting all this time instead of the other way around.

"What are you guys talking about?" she asked, grabbing a bottle of water from the fridge.

"Nothing important," Brad said, and it was as if he grabbed a kitchen knife from the butcher block and physically sliced through the connection I had felt between us. He draped his arm around Carissa's shoulders. "Ready to go, babe?"

"Yeah," she said. "Bye, Rosie."

"Are you going to the pool?" I couldn't help but ask, following them out into the front hallway.

"No, the beach," Carissa said. She turned to Brad. "Rosie *hates* the beach." She smiled at me as if I was her little scaredy-cat sister, five years old and terrified of drowning. She knew the real reason I didn't like going to the beach. I wasn't scared of the waves. I didn't like going to the pool, either, and pools don't have waves. Carissa knew I hadn't even owned a bathing suit in years. She was putting on a show in front of Brad, building herself up by putting me down. I pictured them getting into Brad's car and driving away, laughing at me. In that moment, I hated my sister, and I hated Brad, too. I hated both of them.

As soon as they left, I hurried over to Holly's house, and by the time I got there I was in tears. "Brad doesn't like me, and he's never going to," I sobbed. "He's my sister's boyfriend. I should not be thinking about him this way, I know that—but I can't help it. And every time I see him, it only makes things worse."

Holly didn't say anything for a while. She just rubbed my back and let me cry. When she finally did talk, after my sobs had turned to sniffles and my ragged breathing calmed down, she didn't say she'd known it all along. She didn't lecture me about how Brad was off limits. She didn't even say anything bad about Carissa. She said, "This really sucks. I'm sorry."

"Thanks." I wiped my nose on a tissue.

"You are amazing, Rose," Holly said. "And someday, you'll find a guy who truly loves you. You don't want some stupid guy who'd choose Carissa over you, anyway."

"Thanks, Hol," I said, hugging her. I went into her bathroom and washed my face, and then we watched a marathon of *Gilmore Girls*. And that was that. We never talked about it again. I think Holly could sense there was nothing more I had to say about the topic. She knows me, and she knew that talking about Brad would only make it harder for me to push away my feelings for him.

And now, all of a sudden, Carissa and Brad are no longer together? I can't wrap my brain around this shift in the universe.

"Carissa broke up with Brad?" I repeat.

Holly nods. "The last week of summer—right after you left."

"Why would she do that?"

"Why do people ever break up? I'm sure it was a mixture of

things. It seemed a long time coming to me. They weren't very good together."

"They weren't?" I'd always thought Carissa and Brad were Buena Vista High's designated Perfect Couple.

"No, they weren't a good fit at all," Holly says, thumping a pillow for emphasis. "Carissa can be so judgmental—she was overshadowing Brad, and savoring it. You know how she gets, Rose."

Yes, I know. More than anyone, I know what it's like to be overshadowed by Carissa.

I remember how she would come downstairs and walk into the kitchen without even saying hi to Brad or looking at him or acknowledging his presence in any way. At the time, it didn't even register as unusual. They weren't having a fight—that's just the way she treated him. I thought all couples were that way. I thought after a certain point, you got used to each other. The butterflies faded. You stopped caring as much.

"I guess she did sometimes seem bored when she was around him," I admit. My insides are jumbled, tumbling, like clothes in a dryer.

"I don't think it was Brad's fault," Holly says. "I think that bored look is Carissa's default expression."

"Was he really shaken up about it?"

Holly shrugs. "I think he was surprised. Everyone at school was. And they had a fight on morning announcements."

"They had a fight? On air?"

"Yeah. She was pushing Brad's buttons, and he kind of exploded at her. Poor guy—it was like he was tricked into it. Carissa can be so manipulative. Anyway, Brad's not doing morning announcements anymore. Now this annoying underclassman has his spot. It's not the same at all."

"Wow." In the couple months I've been gone, so much of what I took to be unchangeable has shifted hugely.

"Yeah," Holly says. "But it doesn't matter, anyway, right?"

"What do you mean?"

"Because you're taken now. He missed his chance."

It's the first time since I confessed my feelings for Brad that Holly has brought them up directly. There is so much I want to tell her, to discuss with her, to comb through with her—but I'm so filled with words, it's impossible to get any words out. There are too many places to start. So I nod.

"Daniel sounds great!" she squeals. "You should bring him to Winter Formal. Your show will be finished taping by then, right? It's not until December."

"Yeah," I say dazedly. "It will all be over by then."

Chapter 25

Brad

The house is dark when I pull into the driveway after my dad's first chemo appointment. Is Mom still at work? It's nearly seven P.M., which is late even for her. The past few weeks, she's been putting in more and more hours at the real-estate office—she's either trying to bring in more money to help cover Dad's medical bills, or trying to escape the sadness enveloping our house, or maybe a combination of both.

Dad unbuckles his seatbelt and opens the car door, trying to give me a cheerful smile, but I can tell he's exhausted. I am too.

You want to know what my day was like? Here, I'll give you the run-down:

1. Alarm Fail.

Just when I think I'm finally getting the hang of this early-rising business, I have a morning like today. When my alarm blared, I felt exhausted—like I only fell asleep five minutes before. My eyes were scratchy sandpaper. I knew there was no way I was making it out the door to go running this morning before school. So I hit snooze, rolled over, and descended back into sleep.

Only I must not have hit snooze. Or my phone has it out for me. Because when I opened my eyes with a weird panicky jolt in my abdomen, the clock read 7:44. Sixteen minutes until the first-period bell.

Chaos: commence.

Mom had already left for work, so I couldn't ask her to write me an excuse note. Dad was sleeping, and there was no way I was waking him up. I threw on a T-shirt, jeans, and sandals, grabbed my backpack, and rushed out the door without even brushing my teeth.

2. The Announcement.

Miraculously, I slipped into first period just as the bell was ringing. Since today is Friday, there weren't morning announcements. *Double miracle,* I thought. *I won't have to listen to Carissa and that annoying guy who took my place.* Mrs. Sussman marked attendance and prepared to launch right into the lesson. But suddenly the intercom crackled and Carissa's voice came on.

"Good morning, Buena Vista High! This is Carissa Hayward, here to wish you a happy Friday and share a brief announcement with all of you. I know we don't normally have morning announcements on Fridays, but I have super special news for you today, so Mr. Marshall gave me the go-ahead."

"Thanks, Mr. M!" the annoying co-host chimed in. I must have groaned, because Leo rolled his eyes at me in solidarity.

"So," Carissa continued, her voice high-pitched and perky as always. "As you all know, my twin sister Rosie is a contestant right now on the TV show *Help Me Lose Weight and Live Again!*"

At the sound of Rose's name, I sat up a little straighter.

"We are all *so* proud of her, and my family just found out this morning that she is coming home for a few days as a surprise visit!"

Now I wasn't tired at all. I felt like I'd downed a Red Bull in one long slug. *Rose? Coming home? Today?* My heart was beating really fast.

"So," Carissa said, "we're organizing a welcome-home party for her at the airport this evening. Her flight gets into Burbank at six-fifteen P.M. We'll be hanging out at the arrivals gate. Everyone is invited! Bring balloons, bring signs, bring your pretty smiles. The TV cameras will be there, too!"

All around me, students buzzed with chatter at the mention of the TV cameras. It was irritating. *Do these people even care about Rose? Or are they using her to try to get on TV?*

"Let's all show Rosie how much we love her!" Carissa exclaimed.

My heart sunk as it dawned on me that I wouldn't be able to go. I was taking my dad to his first chemo appointment that evening after work. There was no way I could bail on him. I told myself that Rose wouldn't even notice or care. Still, there was a giant pit in my stomach when I thought about how I wouldn't be there.

3. Work Fail.

After school, I was able to fit in an hour at the station before driving home to pick up my dad for his chemo appointment. The hospital made me nervous, and I figured work would help me push the nerves away. But it backfired. I was so distracted that I misfiled a bunch of paperwork, realized halfway through, and had to go back and start all over again. My thoughts kept shifting from my dad to Rose, and how much I wished I could be at the airport to welcome her home. I knew a ton of people would be there; it's not like she would notice my absence. But still, it seemed important. For months she'd been at the back of my mind, a comforting presence in my thoughts when comfort was hard to come by. Now I couldn't shake the feeling that I was letting her down.

Thankfully I wasn't working the soundboard, or I probably would have messed up all sorts of cues. Jerry came over as I was getting ready to leave and asked, "You okay?" I must have looked really dazed and tired if even Jerry noticed. I told him it had been a long week and promised I would be on top of my game for the early show tomorrow morning.

To top it all off, Meghan showed up at the station as I was leaving. Things have been awkward between us since the food pantry fiasco, and when I see her I feel tongue-tied and clumsy. She alternates between glaring at me like I've killed her cat and completely ignoring me like I'm invisible. Today was a glare day. I did my best to smile, which made her revert to the invisible tactic, looking away and ignoring me. Delightful.

Which brings us to...

4. Dad's Appointment.

We were running late. Well, *I* was running late, which meant I was late to pick up Dad at home, which meant we were a few minutes late to his appointment. (Why is it that when you're running late, the universe likes to rub it in by making you stop at every single red light?) Dad didn't say anything, but he didn't have to. Being late stresses him out. I felt terrible, piling stress on top of an already awful situation. Like getting chemo isn't stressful enough without your irresponsible son making you late.

The local hospital has a brand-new cancer center, and we were ushered into one of the rooms there. Everything was new and gleaming and pristine. On the one hand, you want your hospital to be clean, but on the other hand there was something unsettling about it. The whole place was *too* clean. It reminded me of a museum. Sterile. Cold. My dad doesn't belong in a museum. He's always been a gritty, suntanned, fresh-air-and-dirt type of guy. It was wrong for him to be in that too-clean room with all those beeping machines. Scary to see that tube running into his muscular arm. Like the world has gone topsy-turvy.

Dad could probably tell I was freaking out, but I tried my best not to show it. At his request, I'd brought *The Da Vinci Code* to read aloud to him, but when I opened it up to the first chapter and began to read, my voice shook. My hands were sweaty and shaky, too. I cleared my throat and tried again, hoping Dad didn't notice. I only got through two pages before I set the book down on my lap and asked if we could watch TV instead. He said that was a good idea, he was having trouble concentrating anyway.

We watched Wheel of Fortune and Jeopardy. The colors seemed garishly bright and all the contestants had happy dumb smiles on their faces. I hated them all. Who cares about winning money or vacations or new cars? None of it matters. Everyone spends their time obsessing about stupid stuff that doesn't even matter in the end. It's infuriating.

All day, I've felt like a different species than everyone else, walking around in a haze. I even feel distant from my dad. I don't want to talk to him about how scared I am—I mean, he's the one who's sick! He's probably a million times more afraid than I am. I need to be the strong one, for him and my mom. That's why I'm not telling anyone about Dad's cancer. I need to be strong, and I won't be strong if I'm crying to Leo about how scared I am.

Finally, Dad's treatment was done and we were allowed to leave. Walking out the hospital doors into the cool evening breeze was like escaping prison.

So, that was my day in a nutshell.

I lock the car and help Dad inside the dark house, where he collapses into his favorite recliner. Then I wander into the kitchen, flicking on all the lights along the way, and dump a can of chicken noodle soup into a pot on the stove. Dad said he isn't hungry, but I know Mom will want him to eat something, and chicken noodle soup seems like the right thing for this situation.

Who am I kidding? I have no idea what you're supposed to make someone for dinner after their first chemo appointment. I wish there were instruction manuals for life.

As I stir the soup, watching bubbles begin to form, the pit in my stomach relaxes a little. I think about Rose and realize she must be home from the airport by now. Which means she's right across town. Which means I could drive ten minutes and see her if I wanted to. Not that I would do that—I'm not a total weirdo—but still, it's comforting to think of her so close.

I wonder when I'll get to see her.

Maybe soon.

Hopefully soon.

Chapter 26

Saturday morning, I wake up early and head to the gym as soon as it opens. I'm hoping the gym won't be crowded at this time of day; I feel self-conscious working out away from camp. Mid-week the cameras will accompany me to the gym to get "at-home footage" of my workout, but for now I don't have to worry about them. I get to work out all by myself, in peace, with no red light blinking in my peripheral vision.

The gym in my hometown is part of a national chain of gyms that has a deal with the *Help Me Lose Weight and Live Again* TV producers. I tell my name to the lady at the front desk, and she types it into her computer, then smiles widely and offers to give me a tour of the facilities.

"It's okay," I tell her. "I'll look around by myself."

She points in the direction of the locker room so I can store my gym bag and car keys. "Welcome home!" she calls after me. "Have a great workout!"

I am relieved to see that I was right—the gym isn't very crowded at eight on a Saturday morning. A group of middle-aged women is midway through an aerobics class in one of the group exercise rooms. Some guys lift weights, a few people run on elliptical machines and ride exercise bikes. But no one pays me much mind.

I step up onto a treadmill facing a large window looking out onto the sidewalk. Across the street is Tony's Taco Shack, by far the best Mexican restaurant in town. I wish I could eat at Tony's while I'm home, but I don't trust myself. Their carnitas tacos are dangerously delicious. Instead, I think of some new foods I've grown to love: a raspberry smoothie, a salmon fillet, a fresh salad.

Across the street, the windows of Tony's Taco Shack glint in the sun, winking at me. According to Mark and Leslie, Tony's carnitas tacos would certainly be in the "bad" column. But the way Mark and Leslie categorize some foods as "good" and others as "bad" doesn't sit quite well with me. Especially when I think about the future and how I want to live my life forever. The rigid system at camp isn't sustainable. I want to be able to savor a carnitas taco piled high with fresh salsa and not feel guilty for eating something "bad."

It's not good or bad. It's just food. Right? That's the whole point —the deeper lesson I'm trying to teach my body and my brain and my heart. Food is meant to fuel my life, not define my life.

I slip on my earbuds and blast my favorite classic tunes playlist. I power-walk on the treadmill for a few minutes, and then boost my pace up to a steady jog. George sings, "Here Comes the Sun." The world falls away. And I run. I run and run and run toward Tony's Taco Shack, which never gets any closer.

✧ ☆ ✧

I'M into my fourth mile, in my running groove, sweat dripping down my face, my ponytail thumping against my back in a steady rhythm, Bob Dylan singing about broken hearts and rolling stones, when out the window I glimpse Brad.

Oh, there goes Brad. He runs by on the sidewalk, wearing sweatpants and a T-shirt with the sleeves cut off.

Then, immediately, my mind rewinds, pauses. *Brad? Wait, was that him?*

No, I tell myself firmly. *Stop it. You're seeing things. That was definitely not Brad. That guy had a buzz cut.*

I turn up my music and try to concentrate on my workout. Daniel is probably at the gym right now too. I wish he were plodding away on the treadmill next to me with his steady pace and focused breathing, holding out a thumbs-up to me every so often, encouraging me to run a little bit farther, a little bit longer.

Here I am alone. No one to encourage me but myself.

Suddenly, I sense a presence on the treadmill to my left—someone standing close, trying to get my attention. I turn, and there he is.

Brad.

He's smiling and saying something, but I can't hear him over my music.

"Brad!" I say, too loudly, forgetting not everyone has music blasting in their ears.

He grins. "Rose!"

I take off my earbuds and push the "down" arrow on my treadmill, slowing to a walking pace, trying to catch my breath. "Hi," I say, using my towel to wipe sweat off my forehead. My chest heaves and my face is hot. I am a giant sweaty tomato.

"I can't believe it's you," Brad says. His hair does look shorter. Much shorter. But when he smiles—his big contagious smile that fills his whole face—he is the same Brad he always was.

"When did you get home?" he asks.

"Yesterday," I huff. Even though I've slowed to a walk, my heart is still thumping very hard and fast in my chest. "It's, like, a test or something, for the show. Trying to get us off track at home."

"Man, it's so great to see you. I can't believe you're here! I saw you, and I was like, *I swear that's Rose, but it can't be her, because she's in Texas…*"

"I thought I saw you, too—through the window—but I didn't think you'd be up this crazy-early on a Saturday."

"Yeah, I've got a whole new routine going on. I've got a radio show!"

"You do? That's fantastic!"

"Thanks! Oh man, it's so cool Rose, you would love the studio—"

My treadmill beeps, cutting him off. I glance down. TEN MINUTES REMAINING flashes across the screen.

"Ah," Brad says, stepping back. "I've hogged enough of your time—I should let you get back to your workout…"

"Oh, no, it's okay, really."

Brad waves me off. "I'm gonna lift some weights," he says. "Will you come find me when you're done? Before you take off?"

"Sure."

"Okay. I'll be over there somewhere." He gestures toward the other side of the gym, walks backward a few steps, then stops. "Oh, and Rose—you look great!"

I blush and wave him off, putting my earbuds back in. I increase the treadmill's speed to a steady running pace. My legs move with renewed energy, and the remaining time flies by.

✧ ✩ ✧

His short hair makes him look older, more composed and responsible. It brings out his features more—his big eyes, strong nose, jawline flecked with stubble. I glance down sharply, aware I've been staring.

"I like your haircut," I say.

"Thanks," Brad replies, running his hand over his head, forward and back, as if surprised to find all his hair gone. "Everyone keeps saying how different I look."

"Welcome to the club!"

"Aw, you're the same Rose to me," he says. I can tell he means it in a good way, but it makes my heart sink.

I've finished my run. Brad and I are stretching on the big blue mats, sunlight slanting in through the floor-to-ceiling windows. Or rather, I'm stretching, and he's leaning back on his elbows, visiting with me. This early on a Saturday morning, we're the only ones in this area of the gym. I extend one leg in front of me and lean forward, stretching my hamstring. One day, I'll be able to touch my toes.

"Wanna get lunch?" Brad asks, pointing out the window. "We could go to Tony's."

I laugh. "Lunch?"

"Tony's is amazing. Have you been there?"

"I have, and yes—their carnitas are the best. But, for one, I'm supposed to be watching what I eat."

Brad smacks his forehead. "Sorry! I'm horrible."

"Plus," I continue, "it's ten in the morning! Tony's isn't open yet."

Brad's face reddens slightly. "Guess it feels later to me. I've been up since five-thirty."

"Five-thirty *A.M.?* On a Saturday?"

"Yeah, I had to work the switchboard for the early morning show at the station," Brad says. He tells me all about it—leaving morning announcements, going to WAVE 104.3 to ask for an internship, learning to work the sound switchboard for the early morning shift, and now having his own show late on Sunday nights.

"I'm calling it Countdown to Midnight," he says. "Cool, right?"

"It's perfect," I tell him. One thing I love about Brad is how honest he is. He never hides anything, he just tells it like it is—and he's always so open about his emotions. He's fearless.

I wish I could tell him all the things I want to tell him. I wish I were braver.

Later, after I've done too many weight circuits and lunges and sit-ups to count, and my whole body feels like one giant, aching muscle, Brad and I walk together out of the gym.

"You are a workout monster," he says. "You were totally kicking my butt on the weight machines."

"I don't know about that," I reply, wiping my face with my towel to hide myself from him for a moment.

"No, it's a fact," Brad says. "You kicked my butt *hard*." He laughs.

"Thanks," I say, forcing myself to laugh, too. What I'm thinking is: *I may be losing weight, but will I ever feel beautiful? I want to be strong...and feminine, too. Can I be both?*

"I recognize this baby," Brad says, patting the hood of the hand-me-down car Carissa and I have shared ever since we got our licenses. "The Green Dragon."

"As ferocious as ever." I unlock the door and toss my gym bag in the back seat. "You want a ride home?" I try to keep my voice casual. This is no big deal. This is just Brad. Carissa's Brad.

He shakes his head. "Thanks, but I've gotta say no—running back home is part of my workout."

"Oh, okay."

A pause. The two of us stand there outside the gym entrance as if we're both waiting for something. Brad runs his hand over his buzzed hair. His face is so open, so friendly and earnest and familiar, that for a moment I think, *Screw it all—who cares that I'm on an extremely rigid diet and it's only* 10:42 *in the morning? Maybe I will go to Tony's Taco Shack, because what if this is it, what if this is the end, what if he never asks me to do anything ever again—*

"So, will you be here tomorrow morning?" Brad asks.

"Um. Yes."

"Okay, me too! I'll see you then."

"See you tomorrow."

He grins, waves, and jogs away. I plop down into the driver's seat and watch him through the windshield. He turns the corner without looking back, disappearing from my sight. Already, the morning seems like a dream.

Brad's already at the gym when I get there the next day. He's on a treadmill facing the window, his sweatshirt and water bottle on the treadmill next to his. He bobs up and down a lot when he runs, almost as if he is dancing rather than working out. A dark spot of sweat soaks through the back of his T-shirt, between his shoulder blades. Seems he's been here a while already, yet he's still running at a fast pace. He looks strong. I wonder what I look like when I run. Quickly, I push the thought away.

"Good morning," I say, stepping up on the treadmill beside him. I lift up the sleeve of his sweatshirt. "Treadmill hog."

"I put it there," Brad says, breathing hard, "to save this treadmill for *you!*"

"Oh. Well in that case, thank you."

"You're welcome." Brad slows to a walk, grabbing his sweatshirt and draping it over his own treadmill. I hand him his water bottle, and he squeezes some water into his mouth. He starts to return the bottle to his treadmill's cup holder, but suddenly aims the nozzle at me and squirts. Droplets splash across my neck.

"Hey!" I laugh. "No fair! My water bottle isn't a squeeze top!"

"Sorry," Brad says, grinning. "Inspiration struck, and I went with it."

"Well, beware. I'll pour mine on your head when you least expect it."

"Touché, Miss Hayward. Touché."

He says it in a joking voice, but I'm remembering how he would sometimes call Carissa "Miss Hayward" too. Suddenly this all seems awkward and forced and I'm questioning everything. *What am I doing here working out with Brad? What is this between us?* As much as I try to fool myself, deep down I know we were never *real* friends—just friends by proximity. More like acquaintances. He's just a guy who used to date my sister. Who is probably still in love with my sister. *The whole time he's with me, he's probably thinking of Carissa,* I remind myself. *None of this means anything.*

I concentrate on fiddling with my treadmill's control keypad, pushing the up arrows to get to a brisk walking pace.

"So is this what it's like working out in Texas?" Brad asks.

"Pretty much. A treadmill's a treadmill, you know? But it's nice not to have any cameras around, recording every detail. I can take a long water break and no one cares."

"I didn't even think about the cameras. I mean, it seems obvious now, but it didn't register. That must be strange."

"It is. You forget about them after a while, though."

"I'm surprised they didn't follow you out here. Don't they need footage of this, too?"

"Oh yes, and they're getting it. They'll be here to film me working out tomorrow."

"I'll make sure not to squirt any water on you then."

"Just you try. I'll be ready."

"Them's fightin' words. You better watch your back." Brad smiles and shoots me a wink.

And suddenly, I'm not thinking about Carissa anymore.

"You should come bowling Wednesday night," I hear myself saying. "It's for the show—they've planned this big party for the cameras to film. You know, with my tons and tons of friends. To show what a fun time I'm having now that I've lost a little bit of weight."

My tone comes out sharper than intended, and Brad catches my eye. "Are you not having a good time, being back home?" he asks, concern pinching his brow.

"No, no—I am. It's just...strange, I guess."

"How so?"

I don't know quite what I'm trying to say, and I'm not sure I want to be talking to Brad about all of this. He has no idea what it's like. Daniel's the person I should be talking to. Daniel will understand exactly what I mean. "Just—you know—the cameras and stuff. Having them here."

"Yeah, that must be weird," Brad says, but something in the way his expression shifts makes me feel like I've let him down. Like he knows there's more to it than that, more that I wanted to say, but I didn't trust him to hear it.

And after he told me all about his life the past couple months. He trusted me.

"You should come Wednesday night," I insist. "Bowling. It would be nice to have you there." I study the control panel of my treadmill and press the "down" arrow twice—not because I'm tired, but because I want something to do with my hands.

I hear Brad's steady breathing, the rhythmic pounding of his running shoes. For a few moments, I think that maybe he's not going to answer. Maybe he doesn't want to come bowling and is trying to drop the subject.

Then he says, his voice casual: "Will Carissa be there?"

My heart sinks.

"Yes." My voice sounds tight and small. I take a sip of water to regain composure. I blink a few times. Then I force myself to glance at Brad with a smile. "Yes, Carissa will be there," I say again, trying to pound the reality of this situation into my brain. *Carissa is the one Brad cares about. Not me.* I increase my pace to a jog, then to a run.

"Sure, I'll probably stop by," Brad says.

The conversation veers off to other topics, like his radio show and the school football team and a hilarious thing Ostertank did in class this week. I laugh when I'm supposed to, but I'm not really listening. My feet pound on the treadmill in a steady rhythm, and in my mind each footstep echoes a syllable of my sister's name, *Ca-riss-a, Ca-riss-a, Ca-riss-a,* until I can't take it anymore. I press the red emergency button and my treadmill jolts to a stop.

Brad slows his treadmill down to a walking pace. "Are you all right?" he asks.

"I'm not feeling well," I pant, stepping off the treadmill. "My stomach hurts. I'll see you later, okay?"

I head for the locker room without daring to glance back. Is he watching me walk away? Or has he already put his headphones in and restarted his workout?

I don't want to know. I can't bear any more disappointment.

Chapter 27

Brad

I am stoked that Rose invited me to her bowling party. I mean, I know it's not *that* big a deal—there will be lots of people there. With all the cameras and hoopla, and Rose at the center of it all, I doubt I'll actually get to spend any real time with her. Not like here at the gym, talking, just the two of us.

Still, I'm happy she invited me. Even though I completely suck at bowling.

The thing is, I really don't want to see Carissa. With Rose busy at the center of the party, not only will I not get to spend any real time with her, but even worse I could be stuck making awkward conversation with Carissa the whole night. It used to be she ignored me in the school hallways, but lately she's been giving me these sympathetic smiles. Not a real smile. The head-pat version of a smile. Like she feels *so sorry* for me.

I don't know if I can stand an entire night sucking at bowling and having to deal with head-pat smiles from Carissa, who in all likelihood will be sneaking off to make out with Ryan behind the pinball machine.

Not that I care anymore. I mean, I don't particularly want to watch my ex-girlfriend making out with someone else. But any lingering pain from our break-up isn't related to Carissa. It's more like aftershocks from the way everything fell apart—so sudden, like the ceiling of my life collapsed on top of me. You think your life is stable and then, in a moment, everything changes.

Actually, it's not even about Carissa anymore. What I'm thinking about now is my dad, the giant of my life, looking so vulnerable with his pale shaved head. The chemo dripping into his veins. The sterile hospital smell. Coming home from school to find him sleeping in his recliner, a blanket pulled up to his chin even though it's warm inside the house.

My point is that Carissa can make out with Ryan behind the pinball machine all she wants. She can make out with whatever guy she wants to. It's none of my business (something she told me repeatedly in the weeks following our break-up).

It's funny how annoying a person can get once you fall out of love with them. How did I never notice the way Carissa sometimes cleans dirt out from under her fingernails instead of looking you in the eyes when you're trying to talk to her? Or the way she will interrupt group conversation with shrieks of laughter about an inside joke that not everyone understands? Or the way she's always reapplying her lip gloss and licking it off when she talks, and then reapplying it again?

These are the thoughts that are ricocheting around my brain after Rose invites me to her bowling party and in the next breath says that Carissa will be there. I can't place her tone—it almost seems like she is winking at me, emphasizing Carissa being there. Is she hinting at something? Does she want me and Carissa to get back together? Maybe that's what this is all about. Maybe Rose isn't interested in hanging out with *me* at all. Maybe she merely wants to put me in the same room as Carissa. Maybe she hasn't heard the full scoop yet about Carissa and Ryan. Maybe she's trying to be nice.

I remember how excited I was yesterday, when I groggily walked into the gym, same morning routine as any Saturday, and spotted Rose on one of the treadmills facing the big windows. I thought, *Oh, there's Rose*, like it was no big deal. Like it was completely normal to see her there. That's the thing—being around Rose does feel normal, in a good way. Like I can be myself without having to worry about putting on an act. I feel comfortable with her.

Okay, maybe not *completely* comfortable. I get a shivery excitement whenever I see Rose, that special kind of nervous energy when you're crushing on someone.

Because, yeah.

I'm crushing on her.

Big-time.

Yesterday morning, when I glimpsed her bouncing ponytail for the first time in two months, it was achingly clear how much I like her. No longer was it something I could avoid or ignore.

I like Rose. I *really* like her.

As soon as I saw her, butterflies spawned furiously in my stomach. I was wide awake. Giddy. Usually when I get to the gym I head straight for the weight machines because I've already done my cardio workout by running to the gym from my house. But when I saw Rose, I made a beeline straight for the treadmills. I didn't care I'd already run three miles. I needed to be near her.

My heart was beating like crazy as I jogged over and stepped onto the treadmill beside her. "Hey, stranger," I said, in what I hoped was a suave voice.

She didn't hear me; it was only then I noticed she had earbuds in. She was staring straight ahead, focused on her run. *Maybe I should leave her alone.* I tried to back quietly off the treadmill, but I half-stumbled and frantically waved my arms to regain my balance. And of course, that was when Rose turned and noticed me.

"Brad!" she said loudly. Her smile gave me hope.

"Rose!"

She took her earbuds out and pushed the "down" arrow on the treadmill, slowing to a walking pace. "Hi," she said. Her cheeks were flushed from running. Even working out, she is radiant.

"I can't believe it's you," I said. That was all my brain could think to say. I could feel this stupid grin spreading across my face.

"It's me," she said.

"When did you get home?" I asked, even though I knew she had arrived the day before. I didn't want her to think I hadn't cared enough to be part of her welcome-home surprise mob at the airport. And I didn't want to get into my reason for having to miss out. It would be better if she thought I didn't know.

We spent the rest of the time at the gym talking and catching up.

When we made plans to meet up at the gym again today, I felt like I'd won the lottery.

It's so easy to talk to Rose. Even when she's talking about being on a television show, she still seems down-to-earth. I've never met anyone else like her. She is always herself in any situation.

I want to be that way, too. I want to just *be Brad.*

I'm still working on it.

✧ ☆ ✧

RIGHT NOW ROSE and I are talking about books or Spanish class or some silly mindless topic that somehow seems interesting when I'm talking about it with her—I've never known anyone who can make the minutiae of life seem so interesting—when all of a sudden her treadmill is stopped and she's standing there, panting, her face pale.

"Are you all right?" I ask, punching at the down arrows on my own treadmill.

"I'm not feeling well," she says. She steps down off the treadmill. "My stomach hurts. I'll see you later, okay?"

And then she's walking away, toward the exit, not even bothering to take her water bottle or towel with her. I'm still marching mechanically forward on my treadmill, mind whirring, wanting to call after her or ask if there's anything I can do, but it all happened so fast. She seemed fine a moment ago, and then she was practically doubled over in pain. What if she has the stomach flu? Or food poisoning? Or what if it's something more serious—like, what if her appendix is about to burst? That happened to a kid in my third-grade class, Teddy Thompson, and he was in the hospital for nearly a week.

I hate to think of Rose in pain. There must be something I can do to help. Like drive her home—yeah, of course, I can make sure she gets home safely. She definitely shouldn't be driving herself home.

I leap off my treadmill, grab Rose's towel and water bottle, and sprint for the exit.

Outside, the sun has risen and the light seems bright after the dim coolness of the gym. The faint breeze smells of the ocean. I look out onto the mostly empty parking lot, searching for Rose's car. I don't see it. Maybe she already left?

There's a metal bench next to the door, empty. A protein bar wrapper scuttles on the concrete beside the trash can. I bend down and pick it up, throw it firmly into the garbage, and sit down on the bench. I don't feel up to going back inside. I am tired. Really tired.

Across the way, a plastic bag billows with air, caught in the limbs of a scraggly tree. I could spend all year picking up trash from the bushes and trees and sidewalks and there would always be more. People are always going to litter.

Sometimes, no matter how far I've come, it seems like nothing has changed at all. Like I'm always running on a treadmill—moving forward, but not really going anywhere. Sometimes, it all seems pointless.

The gym door opens with a squeak and bangs shut. I glance over. Rose.

"Hi," she says, looking surprised to see me. "What are you doing?"

I stand up and step toward her. I want to reach out and touch her arm, her shoulder, but instead I hold out her towel and water bottle. "You forgot these."

"Oh, yeah—thanks." She takes them from me and keeps walking.

"Hey, wait up," I say, following her. "Are you okay?"

"Yeah, I'm fine."

"Let me drive you home."

"Oh, Brad." She stops, faces me. Her eyes are red-rimmed and her cheeks are white. "That's not necessary."

"Yes it is. You're not feeling well. You look pale."

"You're just used to seeing me all red-faced from working out," she says, attempting a smile.

Still, I can tell something is wrong. She doesn't seem like herself.

"Please, Rose," I say. "Let me drive you home."

"You're in the middle of your workout."

"I'm done now."

"Won't it be out of your way?"

I hold out my hand. "Give me the keys, Hayward."

She reaches into her workout bag, pulls out a tangle of keys, and hands them to me. I can't tell if she is pleased or embarrassed. "You really don't have to do this," she says. "I'll be fine."

"I know. I want to." I follow her around the corner where she's parked the Green Dragon on the street. "Parallel parking this bad boy —impressive!" I joke, but she barely cracks a smile.

I walk around the car and slide into the driver's seat. Carissa never let me drive this car. "You're not the best driver," she'd say, citing the one time I dinged a lamppost in a parking lot the week I got my learner's permit. Carissa has an incredibly sharp memory for the mistakes of other people.

But this morning, the Green Dragon is not Carissa's car. And it's not Carissa I'm picturing behind the wheel. I think of Rose's body warming this seat, her legs working these pedals, and my whole body thrums. I try to clear my head, focus my thoughts on my actions: here is the gearshift, here is the steering wheel. Tilt the rear-view mirror; check that the parking brake is off. When I turn the key in the ignition, one of my favorite indie bands blasts from the speakers.

"You know Blind Pilot? I love this song!" I drum my thumbs on the steering wheel and pull out into the street.

"So good, right?" she says, smiling. Then, like a curtain falling down, her face gets serious. "Brad, why are you being so nice to me?"

I turn down the music. "Why am I being so nice to you?"

She nods, meeting my eyes.

"Rose, I..." I claw for words like a dog futilely clawing for grip on ice. "We're friends, aren't we?"

"Yeah."

"Well, that's what friends do, isn't it? Watch out for each other?"

She nods again, but her eyes seem far away. What is she thinking? Was that question some sort of test, and I failed?

We *are* friends, aren't we?

"I like you," I add, and quickly turn up the music again, to cover up any awkward silence. When I glance over a few moments later, she's singing along to "Three Rounds and a Sound." Her voice is uninhibited and beautiful.

We drive along like that for a few minutes, enjoying the music. Way too soon, we're arriving at her street. I make the turn slowly, lifting my foot from the gas pedal so the car moves at a crawl. I want to keep driving around with her like this all day.

"Brad," Rose says. "Can I ask you a question?"

I force my voice to remain casual. "Of course."

"Is Carissa...um...never mind." She looks down at her lap, her hair partially obscuring her face.

"No, go on. What about Carissa?"

Rose sighs. "Was she the reason you weren't at my welcome-home thing? At the airport?"

Crap. So she did notice I wasn't there.

I disappointed her. I let her down.

The truth spills out of me in a rush. "Listen—I'm sorry I wasn't there, Rose. I totally wanted to be there. I meant to tell you yesterday. My dad...well, he's sick. He has cancer."

"Oh, Brad." Rose puts her hand on my arm. Her eyes are wide. "I'm so sorry. I had no idea."

"Nobody does. I haven't told anyone, not even Leo. My dad doesn't like being the center of attention. He doesn't want people to worry about him. Anyway, Friday was his first chemo appointment, so I went with him. My mom would have cried the whole time, which wouldn't be good for anyone. So I promised I would go with my dad and read to him while he is, you know. Getting his treatment."

"Wow, that's really..." Rose shakes her head. It looks like she might cry. She clears her throat. "I'm sorry, I don't even know what to say. I'm just so sorry, Brad. Do you know... I mean, is the prognosis...?"

"The doctors caught the cancer early, so that's good. He'll have chemo and radiation, and hopefully that will get it all."

I swallow. It's too terrifying to think about the possibility of the treatments not working. I try to push my dad out of my mind.

Then I realize something Rose said. "Wait—why would Carissa being there make a difference?"

Rose tucks a strand of hair behind her ear. Is she blushing? "I don't know. I thought, maybe you wanted to avoid her, or something?"

"No, it's not like that. I promise, I would have been there if I could."

Rose doesn't reply. She's probably thinking about my dad. I want to change topics. "Okay," I say. "Now it's my turn to ask you a question."

"Shoot."

"Have you had your appendix out?"

She laughs. "That's random! And actually, yeah, I have. Seventh grade. Mine almost burst, and Carissa was scared for months that hers was going to burst too. I forgot about that till now. Why do you ask?"

"You said your stomach hurt, and that was the first thing I thought about. I'm always worried about my appendix bursting."

"Well, you don't have to worry about me," Rose says.

I pull into her driveway and park. "So you'll be okay for your bowling party on Wednesday? Is it still on?"

"Yes—well, I pretty much have to be okay. The camera crew is already on a plane out here. I can't flake on everyone." She grabs her duffel bag off the floor, looking up at me through her long lashes. "Do you think you'll be able to come?"

"I don't know. I'm a terrible bowler."

"Me too," she says.

"No way—I doubt you're terrible at anything."

"That's either very sweet, or very sarcastic."

"Me, sarcastic? Never!" I smile into her friendly eyes. How is it possible to simultaneously feel so nervous and so comfortable around someone? "If I come on Wednesday, you have to promise me one thing."

"What?"

There are so many things I want to say. *That I'll get to talk to you. That you genuinely like my company. That you'll hang out with me later.* Instead, I say, "That there'll be a special lane with bumpers, for you and me."

She grins. "I think I can manage that."

"Okay. Good."

"Then you'll come?"

"I wouldn't miss it."

She opens the door and climbs out. I get out too and toss her the keys.

"Oh, Brad—I forgot this was my car. How are you going to get home?"

"I'll run. It's not too far."

She bites her lip. "Are you sure? I feel bad."

"Don't. I wanted to run a little longer anyway. You focus on feeling better, and I'll see you soon."

"See you soon," she says, waving from the front walkway. "And thanks!"

I take off down the street toward my house, sprinting, invincible. I'm so keyed up; I feel like I could run a whole marathon.

If Rose was waiting for me at the finish line, I feel like I could do anything.

Chapter 28

Rose

Carissa is way more excited about this whole bowling party thing than I am.

"Finally, you're back!" she exclaims when I walk through the front door.

I wave her an absent-minded hello, still in a daze over the news about Brad's dad. I've only met him a few times. He's a tall, burly guy who seems invincible. He asked questions about my life like he actually cared to know the answers. I can't even imagine how Brad must be feeling. What an idiot I was, bringing up my welcome-home thing at the airport like I'm the center of the universe. Who am I turning into, my sister?

I head into the kitchen for some water. Carissa follows.

"Hurry, take a shower, and then we're going shopping!" She claps and smiles her genuine Carissa smile, the smile that melts hearts, the smile that gets her anything and everything she wants.

I swallow a big gulp of water. "What exactly are we shopping for?" I have never liked shopping. Carissa knows this.

"A new outfit! For you to wear on Wednesday!" She bounces from one foot to the other, sashaying her hips in a little dance. "You're gonna look *so* gorgeous! I'll do your make-up too!"

"I told Holly I'd hang out with her today."

"Invite her too!" Carissa says. "It'll be fun!"

Invite Holly? Is she serious? I wipe half-dried sweat from my brow and study my twin sister's face for a hint of sarcasm but find nothing. She smiles at me, earnest and happy. Who is this person? Has she really changed this much in the two months I've been gone? Or am I seeing her differently, now that I've changed?

Or maybe this is all an act Carissa's putting on, trying to get in my good graces before the cameras arrive.

I text Holly and she agrees to meet us at the mall in an hour. Then I trudge upstairs to take a shower.

When I emerge from the bathroom, Carissa is sitting cross-legged on my bed. *Infinite Jest* rests heavily in her lap. She's reading the inside cover flap.

She looks up. "This is a thick book, even for you," she says. "Is it good?"

"I'm only about half-way through, but everyone says it's David Foster Wallace's masterpiece." I pull on jeans, feeling ugly and flabby as I wiggle them on in front of my tiny sister. They're loose on me, though—I need to wear a belt to keep them up. Carissa gave me one the first day I got home. It's brown faux leather with a silver butterfly buckle.

"I think Brad's reading this," Carissa says. She turns it over in her hands and studies the cover.

"He's reading *Infinite Jest*?"

"Yeah—I mean, not that I care."

"I didn't know he liked to read."

"He doesn't. He's trying on this whole new persona, to win me back. It's kind of pathetic."

My heart tightens. I lean over and rub the towel vigorously over my hair, avoiding her gaze. "Do you guys talk much anymore?"

"Not really. He got fired from morning announcements, and now he disappears at lunch. I don't know where he goes."

"Fired?" I flip back my hair and stand upright. "He told me he quit."

Carissa's eyes widen. "When did you see him?"

"We ran into each other at the gym."

"Why didn't you mention it earlier?"

"I didn't think it was a big deal." I run a hairbrush through my hair. "Is it a big deal?"

"No," Carissa says, smoothing her own hair flat with her hands. "I just didn't know you guys talk."

"We don't—we ran into each other."

In the bathroom mirror, I watch as Carissa stretches out her legs, leans forward, and touches her toes. I can't imagine what it's like to be her—to bend and move so effortlessly. "Rosie, I asked you a question," she says.

"What? Sorry, I didn't hear you."

"Did. Brad. Ask. About. Me?"

More than anything, I want to tell her "No." I want to erase what really happened, shove those words back into Brad's mouth, and pretend that he hadn't mentioned my sister at all. That he never thinks about her anymore. That he's totally, completely over her.

But I don't want to pretend anymore. I'm on a new path in my life—getting healthy, gaining strength, pushing my limits. I don't want to lie. Not to myself. Not to other people. And that includes my perfect twin sister.

So I say, "Yeah. He did."

"Really?" She rolls her eyes, like *How lame*, but I can tell she's pleased. It makes my stomach hurt anew.

"I invited him to the bowling thing, and he asked if you would be there."

"You invited him?!" she squeals. "Why?"

I shrug. "I didn't think you'd mind. You're bringing Ryan, aren't you?"

"No, he's busy that day." She sighs. "I don't know—we'll probably end things soon."

"What? I thought you really liked him. You broke up with Brad over him, right?"

"Breaking up with Brad had nothing to do with Ryan and everything to do with Brad being an unmotivated slob I was embarrassed to be around."

"Wow. That's harsh."

"I'm only being honest. But it's fine you invited him. No big deal." She places *Infinite Jest* back on my nightstand and vaults off my bed. "I just don't want you to be humiliated if he hijacks your big event and makes a scene like he did at Matt's party. It was so humiliating. Like, *Seriously, Brad, get a grip.*"

"Well, you guys were together a long time."

She waves her hand in the air, as if swatting away a moth. "Enough about him. Knowing Brad, he probably won't even show up. C'mon, let's find you some cute clothes!"

I follow Carissa downstairs, surprised at the excitement fluttering in my belly. I can't remember the last time the mall actually seemed appealing. Maybe not since Mom schlepped us there to sit on Santa's lap as kids.

As I buckle my seatbelt, trying to picture myself in a cute skirt, or a flattering flowy top, I realize who it is I want to look good for. *Daniel,* I think. *I'll text Daniel a photo.* But if I'm being honest with myself, that's not the face that first popped into my mind.

In spite of everything, the truth is that I'm genuinely excited to see Brad on Wednesday. Even if he is only there for my perfect twin sister.

THE LAST TIME I came to this bowling alley was when Carissa and I had our birthday party here in sixth grade. Mom is dead-set against hosting two separate birthday parties for us, so Carissa and I have always celebrated our birthday together. Who gets to pick the activity alternates every year. In fifth grade, I chose to see a movie at the old-fashioned movie theater two towns over, where waiters zoom down the aisles before the movie begins, serving you popcorn and root beer floats. Carissa drank her root beer float too quickly and ruined the beginning of the movie with her loud-whispered dramatic complaining about her brain freeze. I think she just wanted to complain about something, to remind me that this was not the outing *she* would have chosen for our birthday party if she had been able to choose.

Sixth grade was her turn, and she chose bowling. It came as a surprise, since Carissa had never expressed interest in bowling before. I did not like bowling. I felt so exposed walking out onto the bowling lane with everyone watching. I was awkward as I lifted my arm behind me and then swung the ball toward the pins. Some people can make bowling look graceful. Holly is a very elegant bowler, the ball rolling gently off her fingertips, barely making a sound as it whizzes down the lane. Even if she doesn't knock down many pins, she still looks like she knows what she's doing. At my sixth-grade birthday party, not only did I bowl gutter ball after gutter ball, but more than once the bowling ball got stuck on my fingers, dropping with a loud *thud* onto the lane.

Today, the bowling alley is more crowded than I've ever seen it. The welcome-home group from the airport has expanded to encompass even more people from high school who I only sort-of know and girls from my fourth-grade dance class who I haven't talked to in years. Adding to the chaos is the film crew busily setting up lights and mics and dragging thick cords around the floor, searching for outlets.

Fortunately, I've been able to lay low so far: everyone seems content to stay in their little social pods at their respective bowling lanes. The assistant producer interviewed me on camera when I first arrived, so I'm hoping he'll leave me alone for a while.

I'm wearing the new flowy dress Carissa and Holly helped me pick out, belted at the waist. I like the heart-shaped neckline and the way the skirt swishes against my legs. This dress makes me want to twirl.

What I didn't think about was how the dress would look paired with bowling shoes.

"I look like a clown playing dress-up," I tell Holly.

"Everyone looks like a clown in bowling shoes," Holly says, cinching hers on tight. "If you're a clown, you are a beautiful clown."

She catches sight of something behind me and her expression abruptly shifts to surprise.

"What?" I turn toward the bank of glass doors glinting in the late afternoon sunlight, and there he is.

Brad.

"I can't believe Carissa would do this," Holly whispers. "Seriously—she's trying to hijack your party as a stage for her own drama? I know she's your sister, but that is not okay."

I bite my lip. "Actually, Hol... Carissa didn't invite him. I did."

"*You* invited him?"

"Yes."

"Why?"

I try to keep my voice casual, to stop a smile from spreading across my face. There he is. Brad. He came. "I ran into him at the gym," I explain. "It was a spur-of-the-moment thing."

"You aren't usually one for spur-of-the-moment." Holly narrows her eyes at me. I've never been able to hide things from her. She smiles and says, "Well, you'd better go over and say hi. He looks a little overwhelmed."

It's true. This whole scene is overwhelming. The cameras, the crew, the noise, the lights.

I stand up, smooth my dress with damp palms, and take a few steps in Brad's direction. Carried toward him, as if I'm riding a wave. Any moment now he'll glance in my direction and see me. He'll see me and smile and walk across the room to me.

Just then, one of the glass doors opens, and in struts Carissa. She's carrying a giant tray of veggies and dip and looks flawless as ever. The whole room—including Brad—turns to gaze at her. Time holds its breath. If this is a romance movie, Carissa (*not me, not me, how could I have thought it was me?*) is the heroine. She is the one who ends up with the guy. I am merely the catalyst, a small footnote in the plotline. My purpose is only to bring them together again.

Chapter 29

I haven't been to the bowling alley in a long time. Since middle school, probably, when it was the fad to have your birthday party here and sneak off to make out in the tiny space behind the pinball machine in the arcade room. I'm not really a bowling guy. There are only so many jokes you can make about throwing gutter balls before it gets old and you can't keep pretending you're still doing it for laughs.

I yank open one of the glass-paned doors, that dark glass that's impossible to see through, and step inside. The place looks the same as I remember, except the formerly beige walls are now bright turquoise and dozens of sequined cut-out stars hang down from the ceiling. I don't know if the stars are always there, or if they've been put up specifically for Rose's big celebration. Cameras and cords and lights are everywhere.

I pause on the threadbare carpet in the entryway, looking for Rose. I am completely out of place. What if she was joking when she invited me? What if she didn't expect me to actually come? If she sees me and looks surprised—not the good surprised, the weirded-out surprised—and gives me a fake smile or a forced hug, I'm going to want to die.

I spot Mr. and Mrs. Hayward over by Lane 5, also looking a bit bewildered in the midst of all the cords and cameras and scurrying. And there's Scotty, doing some sort of kick dance across the carpet. I always liked Scotty. Carissa often got annoyed by his silly antics and persistent questions, but I enjoy talking to him. He's real smart for a little kid, and he always laughed at my lame jokes, even when Rose had to explain an especially bad pun to him because he didn't understand the double-meaning.

I scan the room. *Rose, Rose, Rose...where are you?*

The door opens behind me and slams closed. I turn, and there she is.

Carissa.

She is carrying the hugest food platter I've ever seen. It looks like a garden in her arms, a round silver platter heaped with a rainbow of cut-up fruit and vegetables. Her brow furrows in concentration as the platter wobbles unsteadily. The thing looks *heavy*. Instinctively, I step forward to help her.

"Brad!" she says, relief in her voice.

I reach over and take the handles from her.

"Thanks," she says, letting me shift the weight into my arms.

The platter is unwieldy—the kind of thing I'd stagger under a couple months ago, but I've been going to the gym so often that it's not really a problem now.

She flashes her disarming Carissa smile at me. Her hair is beginning to grow out, curling under her ears. She's wearing a low-cut T-shirt, tight jeans, and heavy eye make-up. It looks like someone drew circles around her eyes with purple marker. Did she wear this much make-up when we were together? It's possible. It's only been a few months, but when I think back on that time it's like I'm looking through one of those fish-eye lenses. Like everything was distorted back then.

When I made my Brad Hoffman Self-Improvement Plan two months ago, I expected to change. I wanted to change. That's the point of making goals, right? To change yourself. What I didn't expect was that my feelings for Carissa would change, too. She seems like an entirely different person than the girl I was so in love with. I can't tell if she actually *is* different now, or if I'm the one who has changed. Maybe a little of both.

"Follow me," Carissa says, making her way across the carpeted entryway. "There's a table over here where they want all the food."

I follow her down a couple steps into the bowling area, with the shiny bright lanes and solemn rows of bowling balls waiting to be chosen. The producers have rented out the entire bowling alley for today. I recognize some people from school. Carissa's gang is here—my old friends—Danny, Tim, Stacey, Mel, and Lindsay. Leo had to work, so he couldn't make it.

I haven't been hanging out with the group at lunch anymore. I'm usually so tired from my early morning runs and work at the radio station that I take a nap in my car during lunch. I have class with Danny and Tim, but we've been assigned seats across the room and we don't get a chance to talk very much. They're standing in a clump by Lane 6, laughing, slipping bowling balls on and off their fingers and pretending to throw them at each other.

They don't see me. I don't want them to. I am filled with dread at the thought of having to go over and make small talk and listen to the same old jokes, the same crude wisecracks. It's strange. I used to think they were hilarious. I used to make those wisecracks myself.

I glance away and focus on following Carissa's sashaying walk to a table at the far end of the room, by Lane 1.

My arms ache by the time I set the platter down beside a stack of paper plates and napkins—the fancy kind of napkins, thickly expensive, folded into thirds. There are bright cups filled with forks and spoons, and confetti strewn festively across the tablecloth.

"Thanks so much," Carissa says again. She leans close as she says it, touching my arm.

This is the first time she's touched me in any way since our break-up. It catches me by surprise, and I shift away slightly. "This looks really nice," I say for something to say, gesturing at the table.

"Yeah, it does, huh?" Carissa says. "Rose did most of it."

I remember when all I wanted was to be alone with Carissa like this. I imagined so many different scenarios with the two of us, off together somewhere, leaning in close and talking. I planned out what I would say. I rehearsed speeches to win her back. Only now that I'm here with her, in the far end of this dimly lit bowling alley, and she's standing very close and touching my arm... I can't think of anything to say.

Instead, my brain is flooded with memories. Wrapping my arms around her, holding her hand, leaning over and kissing her. Kissing her and kissing her again, like it was nothing. I remember when she used to touch my arm all the time—squeezing it to emphasize a point she was making, hiding behind it during a scary part of a movie, gently grazing it with her fingertips as we sat together on the quad at lunch.

I reach even further back in my memories, to when Carissa and I first began doing morning announcements together. I thought she was beautiful, but in a cold way. I never thought she would go for a guy like me. Or maybe I didn't think she was my type of girl. As we got to know each other, my attitude changed. I saw her moments of warmth and wittiness. I was swept away by her confidence and grace and style.

But lately, more and more, I'm thinking that maybe my first instincts were right all along. She never was the girl for me.

Carissa didn't know me in middle school, during my gawky, growth-spurt, braces-wearing period. My parents decided to move to a new house the summer before my freshman year of high school, which meant we changed school districts and I went to a different high school than all my friends from elementary and middle school. At the time, I was upset—I felt behind the friendship curve. Everyone else had years of shared memories and experiences that I missed out on.

But I met Leo at the bus stop the first week of school, and we quickly became inseparable. As far as girls were concerned, I came to see that maybe it was a good thing I didn't know any of these people from middle school, because it also meant that nobody knew my middle-school self. Nobody had a memory of me with food stuck in my braces; nobody knew about the horrible bowl haircut my mom gave me up till seventh grade. Even as kids, people put labels on you and hold on fiercely to those labels. It doesn't matter if you grow and change and take on new parts of your identity. It's nearly impossible to get people to see who you really are. So, going into high school, I was actually one of the lucky ones. I got to start with a clean slate.

If Carissa had known me back in middle school, I wonder if she ever would have dated me. Maybe I would have been branded with an "uncool" label that, no matter what, I would never have been able to unstick.

But everyone goes through awkward phases, right? I'm sure even Carissa has memories from middle school she wishes she could erase. What if we *had* known each other in middle school? What if I had been invited to Carissa and Rose's birthday party back then? Would I have been the one Carissa took behind the pinball machine?

I doubt it.

I imagine my middle-school self, with the braces and the bowl haircut, wearing a Star Wars T-shirt. I wanted so much to belong. I wanted so much to have a girlfriend. To kiss a girl in the shadowy light of the arcade, behind the pinball machine.

But if I had been invited to their birthday party in middle school, I can guess how it would have unfolded. I would have spent the whole party talking to Rose. She wouldn't have thought I was hopelessly uncool when I rolled gutter ball after gutter ball. I bet we would have laughed about it together. We would have tried bowling zany throws simply for the fun of it.

I scan the rows of bowling lanes, one after another after another, like an assembly line. I don't see any bumpers set up.

Rose, where are you?

"So, you got this okay?" I ask Carissa, nodding at the veggie platter.

She looks surprised. "Are you taking off?"

"Gonna explore for a bit. I'll see you later."

I walk away from Carissa, toward the arcade room. I want to see this spot behind the pinball machine that I've heard so much about.

Chapter 30

Rose

As soon as Carissa enters the room, Brad turns and sees her. He immediately hurries over to help her carry the ginormous veggie platter the producers have ordered for the party.

My instinct is to run away. This is *my* party, but I'd rather be anywhere else in the world than standing here watching Brad and my sister get back together. *Hide!* my brain screams, even though this is a bowling alley and there aren't many good hiding places. *Anywhere! Get away!*

I can't bear to glance back at Holly—can't bear to see her stricken, sympathetic expression. I didn't realize how high my hopes had risen until suddenly they came crashing down. And what was I so hopeful about, anyway? It wasn't only about seeing Brad. Because I've seen Brad. I've talked with him, run with him, stretched with him at the gym. We're...friends.

I guess my hopes had more to do with seeing him here, now, in my new dress, in my new self, in front of the cameras and all these people.

But why? What was I hoping to prove? I don't know. All I know is that I feel like a complete fool. My face is hot and my hands are sweaty.

I head for the restrooms, next to the snack bar in the back of the bowling alley, but just as I get into view of the welcoming WOMEN sign, Carissa's friend Lindsay pulls open the door and disappears inside.

Crap. I don't want to get stuck talking to anyone, least of all Lindsay. Before I went on *How to Lose Weight and Live Again*, she used to ignore me even if we were the only two people in the room—

even if it was New Year's Eve and we were sitting in my house on the same couch, both wearing plastic tiaras and eating the puppy chow I'd made that afternoon. She could not deign to waste a word on my existence.

But now, in the two times I've had to interact with her since I've been home, she has fallen all over herself trying to be nice to me. I don't know why. Maybe she's worried I'll say something mean about her on TV? Or maybe now that I'm on a TV show, I'm worthy of her conversation? Still, it's an obviously fake, surface-level niceness. I don't want to be stuck making small talk with her in the restroom.

The snack bar beckons. I wish I could drown out my thoughts by devouring a nachos supreme or corn dog platter. But I know that wouldn't make me feel any better. Actually, it would make me feel a million times worse. And the last thing I need right now is a camera catching me stuffing my face with junk food.

I keep walking.

I remember when Carissa and I had our sixth-grade birthday party here. It seems like so much has changed since then, but deep down, it really hasn't.

I didn't even want to invite all these people. These aren't my friends. Three months ago, they wouldn't have even said "hi" to me in the halls. But now they're here, all of Carissa's popular posse, kids I've had classes with since freshman year, random people from school —all of them immaculately dressed, ready for their close-ups on national TV.

The producers wanted to show me at home, surrounded by friends, happy in my new healthy lifestyle. And I let myself get swept up in the giddy hopefulness of planning. I let myself think that maybe these people could be my friends, and maybe I would be happy at the center of everything. But I realize now that it's all a lie. This isn't real, it's staged. Fake. Hollow.

Across from the snack bar is the arcade room. I dash through the doorway into the dimly lit cave. Screens flash at me, begging to be played. The coin slots glow. There's a racecar game, Tetris, PacMan, an air hockey table, and, over in the corner, a pinball machine. The Who, the same one that was here in sixth grade.

There's a wedge of space between the wall and the pinball machine. I want to cram inside it and disappear, but I know I can't. The space is much too small for me to fit.

Or is it?

I move closer, turn my body sideways, and slide my hip between the wall and the pinball machine. Slowly, slowly, I slide myself farther and farther in. It's a snug fit, my body pressing against the metal lip of the pinball machine, but it's not unpleasant. It actually feels comfortingly snug. Like a cocoon. Safe and hidden away from everything.

I slide all the way over to the far wall. I lean my forehead against the back of the pinball machine, close my eyes, and try to focus on my breathing. I try to push Brad's face out of my thoughts, but it's impossible. All I can think about is him. Here at my party. With Carissa. How he turned and saw her come into the room. How he instantly ran over to help her.

How I'm such an idiot to think it would ever be otherwise.

And Daniel—what about Daniel? I try to summon his face, but it's blurry. I try to remember the feel of his lips kissing mine, but my lips are cracked and dry and the memory seems removed, more like a movie I saw or a book I read. Not something that actually happened to me.

I squeeze my eyes more tightly shut.

I'm not sure how many minutes have passed when I hear footsteps come into the arcade room. I wonder if it's my mom or Holly, or maybe one of the camera crew looking for me. How embarrassing if the cameras find me here, hiding behind the pinball machine at what is supposed to be my own celebration. I scrunch further back behind the bulk of the machine, as far as I can go, willing myself to become invisible.

Maybe it's just a kid who wants to play a game. Maybe it's Scotty. I try to peek around the pinball machine, but I can't see much.

The footsteps come closer.

What will I say if someone finds me here? What can I possibly say to explain myself?

"Rose?"

In the dim light, I make out Brad's face.

Of course. Out of everyone, of course it's Brad who's found me.

"Hi," I say, because I don't know what else to say.

"Hi," he says. "Can I join you?"

"There's not much room."

"I can squeeze," he says.

Before I can say anything else, he's scooting in between the wall and the pinball machine, and then I feel the warmth of his body next to mine. Our arms touch, all the way down to our hands. I want so badly to grab his hand, to lace my fingers through his. But I don't.

For a few moments, there's only the sound of our breathing. Then Brad asks, "What are you doing back here?"

"I could ask you the same question."

"It's pretty crazy out there. So many people running around, cameras everywhere. I wanted to go somewhere quiet for a few minutes," he says.

"Me too."

"What made you think of going behind the pinball machine?" Brad asks with a teasing innuendo in his voice I don't understand.

"What?" I ask. "What's that tone for?"

"Nothing, just—something I heard. About what people do back here."

My face grows hot. "Back here? What are you talking about?"

"Someone once told me that people came back here to...you know..."

Gross gross gross. My whole body feels hot and icky and I swear there's a spider web in my hair.

"Kiss," Brad says softly. His face is very close to mine.

But my brain can't focus on how I'm crammed together with Brad in a tiny space, in the dark, our arms touching. I can barely even register what he's saying. Because I can't stop thinking about the spider web I swear is in my hair, and about spiders crawling all over my skin. Who knows what creatures are scuttling around back here? Who knows what's been done back here, behind this pinball machine, in the dark of the arcade room?

"I didn't know that," I tell Brad, breathing slowly, trying to remain calm. "Who told you that?"

Brad hesitates, and suddenly my interest sharpens. "Who told you that?" I ask again.

"I don't really remember," he says. "It might have been Carissa, actually."

Our sixth-grade bowling party clicks into focus. Is that why Carissa chose to come bowling? So she could make out with Cody Turner behind the pinball machine? It all makes sense now. I think of my sixth-grade self, hopelessly fumbling to throw a bowling ball straight down the lane. I was so clueless—I thought bowling was the point.

It seems I'm always missing the point of things.

"I didn't think about where I was going," I tell Brad. "I just wanted to hide."

"Hide? But this is your party! All of this, it's all for you."

"Not really," I say. "It's for show. I don't really know any of these people."

"You know me," Brad says, which for some reason makes me want to cry. Do I know him? Does he even care to know me, the *real* me? Or is all of this a silly, meaningless game to him?

I nudge my shoulder against his. "I need to get out of here."

"What?" he whispers.

"I need to get out of here. I'm getting claustrophobic."

"Oh. Okay." He scoots out into the room, and I follow.

After the close darkness of that small space, the world seems bright. I blink to adjust my eyes to the light. Brad stands a few feet away, watching me. There's no one else here. I look up at the ceiling, stretching my arms above my head, rolling my neck back and forth. It's a relief to be able to move my limbs.

"Are you okay?" Brad asks.

"I'm fine." I shake out my hair, dust invisible cobwebs off my shoulders. "But I should probably get out there. I mean, they might be looking for me. The camera crew. They probably want to start filming soon."

"Yeah, you're right," Brad says, following me out of the arcade room. I'm walking faster than normal. I want to get away from him. I want space to sort out my feelings. The last thing I need is to have a meltdown here, in front of all these people.

Brad matches his pace to mine. "Hey, Rose," he says. "Is there a bumper lane set up?"

"A bumper lane?"

"Yeah, for you and me." He smiles, and I remember our conversation at the gym the other morning. It seems like years ago. "I only came because you promised me we could bowl together, Hayward. With bumpers."

Across the room, I spot Holly sitting by herself at Lane 5. She looks lonely, and I feel terrible for abandoning her. Not only tonight, but for the past two months. She's been so understanding about it all —and she's the one who helped Carissa sign me up for *Help Me Lose Weight And Live Again* in the first place—but I realize what a terrifying decision that must have been for her. Knowingly volunteering to go half of senior year without her best friend. That's some serious sacrifice. And it must mean she was seriously worried about me and my health.

More and more, it's becoming apparent that I was the only one *not* worried. I guess that says something. Even though I didn't realize it at the time, I guess I did need to make a change.

Holly glances up, sees me, and waves. A coy smile twists her lips as she notices Brad right behind me.

Next door in Lane 6, ignoring Holly as usual, Carissa and her friends are making a scene, shrieking with laughter as they dance to a pop song that's blasting over the loudspeakers.

"Are you sure you don't want to bowl with *them?*" I ask Brad, pointing.

He glances over, then turns back to me with an exaggerated shudder. "No," he says. "Please don't make me."

"I thought...maybe you'd want to bowl with Carissa." A fist grips my heart, squeezing, squeezing.

Brad shakes his head. "I promised I'd bowl with you. You're the one who invited me, not Carissa."

It's not exactly the enthusiastic response I was hoping for, but I guess it'll have to do. Even if he only came as part of some big plot to win Carissa back, at least for now Brad is here with me. And for the next three hours, or however long this bowling party lasts, I'm going to focus on having a good time. With my friends. That's the point of this whole charade, isn't it?

Chapter 31

"I thought...maybe you'd want to bowl with Carissa," Rose says, and I deflate.

So is that the whole reason she invited me? We just had a total moment of connection in the arcade room. Real, genuine connection. It was like something that happens in a movie, not in real life. Not *my* life, at least. When I slid behind the pinball machine and saw her there, I was both surprised and not surprised. Like some part of me had known all along she would be there. And she seemed both surprised and not surprised to see me—almost like she had been waiting for me without knowing it, too. The only thing she said was, "Hi." Her eyes looked huge in the dark. It was all I could do not to lean over and kiss her, right there.

She could probably tell what I was thinking, and it freaked her out. That's why all of a sudden she couldn't wait to get out from behind the pinball machine. That's why she race-walked out of the arcade room. She only wanted me here for Carissa. She probably thinks she's doing me a big favor, trying to help me get back together with her sister.

But how do I tell her that's not what I want? Whenever I try to think of ways to come out and say it, I sound like a jerk.

Rose, I know you're trying to get me back together with Carissa, but it's never gonna happen.

Rose, I'm sorry, but your sister isn't really my type.

Rose, I don't want Carissa. I want...

My heart is a lemon crammed into a juicer.

Rose looks at me, waiting, her eyes unreadable.

I shake my head, fumbling for words. "I promised I'd bowl with you," I finally spit out. "You're the one who invited me, not Carissa."

Even to my own ears, it sounds lame. Really lame.

Rose, I just want to be close to you. I know we haven't spent that much time together, but sometimes I feel like you're the only one who's real.

Rose smiles, but disappointment lurks in her eyes. "Okay," she says. "Lane 5—Holly's already there. I'll be there in a minute, after I go talk to someone about bumpers."

"Oh, do you want me to—I can help—" I stammer, but she's already walking off in the direction of the front desk. So I head over to Holly, who's sitting by herself with a full rack of bowling balls at Lane 5. Carissa and my old group of friends are dancing and laughing and generally trying to call attention to themselves the next lane over. Great. This is going to make it hard to avoid them.

"Hey Holly," I say, trying to act casual, like the two of us hang out all the time. It's true I've never had a full conversation with Holly before, but she seems nice. Carissa's never liked her for some reason. She and Lindsay and Mel used to make fun of Holly's clothes. Back then, when Carissa and I were dating, I never even questioned it. Why? Who *was* that Brad? He seems like a totally different person, like an old friend I've lost touch with and don't even miss.

"Hi, Brad," Holly says, scooting over to make room for me, even though there are three empty seats beside her. "Where's Rose going?"

"Oh, uh, she's going to ask them to put bumpers on this lane. Is that okay with you?"

"Are you kidding? I love bumpers. They make bowling way more fun."

I sit next to her, a seat between us, and stretch my legs out onto the bowling ball rack, trying to look relaxed. Maybe if I appear that way, I'll start to feel that way.

"I remember at Rose's sixth-grade bowling party," Holly continues, "we all felt so grown up. Or at least, we wanted to act like grown-ups. So we insisted that we didn't need bumpers. Only *babies* need bumpers. I remember Carissa saying that." She smiles ruefully. "Rose and I were on this very lane, Lane 5. I remember because five is Rose's lucky number."

"It is?"

"Yeah. She kept saying that our luck was going to change. But it never did. The two of us bowled gutter ball after gutter ball. If we knocked one pin down, it was cause for celebration." Holly laughs, shaking her head. She has a nice laugh—open, genuine, like Rose's laugh. "We tried hard, though."

"That's all that matters, right?" I say, sounding like some lame motivational video. Holly is spared from having to respond because Rose sits down on Holly's other side.

"Bumpers are on their way!" she declares, triumphant.

Sure enough, an attendant comes over and steps carefully onto the lane's side rails, reaches down to unlock something, then yanks up the bumpers as if by magic.

"Thank you!" Rose calls. Then she leans across Holly's lap, addressing both of us: "Ready for your close-up?"

I stare at her blankly, and Holly looks equally uncomprehending. Rose nods at a cameraman to our right, only a hundred feet away, red light blinking.

"Show's starting, huh?" Holly says softly. "I don't know how you do this all the time."

"You get used to it," Rose replies.

"I didn't even notice him," I say, glancing around. Now that I'm looking, cameras are everywhere. Behind us, panning the room. Up by the shoe counter. Overlooking the bowling lanes. The cameraman to our right begins walking closer, focused on us.

"Act like you're having fun!" Rose whispers, smiling a wide fake smile.

"I am," I say. "I'm with you."

I don't know if Rose hears me, but Holly catches my eye. Embarrassed, I stand up and reach for a bowling ball, fitting my fingers into the holes. "C'mon! Let's show these bumpers who's boss."

I stride quickly down the lane—one, two, three, release. The bowling ball flies off my fingers, landing with a loud *thump* partway down the lane. It careens toward the pins in a crazed zigzag between the bumpers. And then...*boom*...the pins fall. I watch as the last one standing wobbles, wobbles, wobbles, then finally falls.

"Woo hoo, strike!" Holly yells.

"Strike, strike, strike!" Rose chants. "Go Brad!"

I turn and bow. As I'm walking back to my seat, Carissa strides over from the neighboring lane and intercepts me.

"You know that wasn't really a strike, Hoffman," she says, tapping her index finger against my chest and smiling up at me. "It doesn't count. You used bumpers."

"It does *so* count."

"No it doesn't! It's cheating." She smiles wider, her hand on my arm.

"This is Rose's party, and she says it's a strike. Right, Rose?" I call.

Rose nods. "Right!"

"See? It's officially declared a strike." I turn away and head over to Rose and Holly.

But some part of me wants to see the expression on Carissa's face. I can't help it. I glance behind me. Carissa catches me looking and sticks out her tongue.

This is so weird. Carissa hasn't said a word to me in months. And now she's...what? Flirting with me? Or putting on a show for the cameras? Yeah, that's probably it. She loves being part of the drama.

I sit down next to Rose, my knee brushing against hers, but she stands up abruptly. "My turn," she says.

"Get a strike!" Holly says.

"Strike, schmike. The real challenge is if I can bounce the ball against the bumpers more times than Brad did."

Holly laughs. "Your ball did hit the bumpers like a zillion times," she says to me.

"What can I say? It's a talent." I grin and try to catch Rose's eye, but she walks up to the lane without looking at me.

☆ ☆ ☆

Later, Holly goes to the bathroom, leaving me alone with Rose. I spot my opportunity and seize it. "Hey, can I ask you something?"

"Sure," she says, looking through the bowling balls for hers, spinning them around and sliding her fingers in and out of the holes. "Why did we all have to choose bowling balls that are the same color?" she says, picking one up and hefting it from one hand to the other. "I can't tell if this is yours or mine."

"It doesn't really matter. Use mine if you want."

"But my fingers might stick." She slides her fingers in and lets her arm fall to her side, then bends her arm at the elbow and brings the ball up again, like she's lifting weights. "I'm pretty sure this is mine."

"Good."

"Yeah, I think it is."

"Good." I glance back toward the bathroom for Holly. I don't see her. "Listen, Rose," I say. My voice is croaky. I swallow. "Are you free this weekend?"

She freezes and looks at me, surprise evident on her face.

I hurry on, my heart pounding. "Because, you know, I was thinking maybe, if you wanted, you could come on my radio show." I try to muster my most winning smile. "You'd be my first guest."

"Oh, Brad, that's really nice of you to ask," she says. I brace myself for the *But*—and, yep, it comes: "But so you know, I can't talk about *How to Lose Weight and Live Again*. At least, not yet. They have a nondisclosure agreement until it airs."

I smile with relief. I wasn't even thinking about the TV show. "That's okay. I just think we'd be good together on-air. We used to talk about it, remember?"

She nods. "I remember."

"Okay. So, Sunday at eleven. I'll come pick you up around ten-thirty."

"That sounds great."

Then she hefts the bowling bowl, strides up to the lane, and with one strong fluid arm motion, releases the ball right down the center. We both watch the ball career forward, certain and sure, as if being drawn by a magnet. It slams into the front pin. The rest of the pins fall down in a fan behind it.

"Striiiiiike!" I shout.

Rose turns, beaming. She dances back over to me, raising her arms in an adorable way. I want to dance with her. I want to twirl her around and pull her into my arms for a slow dance.

I should ask her to the Winter Formal. Will she be done with the show by then? Would she want to go with me? Does she even like dances?

She plops down in the plastic seat next to me. "Beat that, Hoffman."

"I don't think I can. I mean, you didn't even need the bumpers!"

"Bumpers are for babies," she says, her voice playful. But her smile doesn't quite reach her eyes. I've heard that phrase before, but I can't remember where.

It isn't until later that evening that I remember Holly's story about Rose and Carissa's sixth-grade birthday party. *Bumpers are for babies.* I think of sixth-grade Rose, rolling gutter balls. And I think of Rose today, parroting her sister's words. And something inside me breaks a little.

Chapter 32

"Well, that was a success," Carissa says, boxing up the last of the veggie tray into plastic containers to take home with us.

"You look so pretty in that dress, Rosie," Mom says, kissing my cheek. "Did you have a nice time?"

"Yeah," I tell her, chewing a baby carrot. "I did." And it's true—I can't remember the last time I had so much fun being silly and laughing and acting like a kid. I think of Brad turning around and throwing the bowling ball through his legs, the round surprise of his eyes when the ball sailed over the bumpers and onto the next lane over. "I meant to do that," he said, as Holly and I howled with laughter. Remembering it now, I smile to myself, shaking my head.

"That was nice of Brad to come," my mom continues, wiping Scotty's face with a napkin. Scotty squirms and turns his face away. "Come on, sweetheart, hold still—you have ranch dressing all over."

Carissa looks my way and rolls her eyes. "Brad's such a ham," she says. "He was totally playing it up for the cameras today. Trying to be the funny guy."

I toss the rest of my carrot in the trash and lift up a box. "Ready to go?"

Walking out to our car, my family trailing behind me, I try not to think about Carissa and Brad, but I can't help it. The look on his face when she first walked in and he rushed over to help her carry the veggie platter. The way she touched his arm and teased him about the bumpers. The way he turned back to look at her as he walked away. They may technically be broken up, but they sure seemed friendly enough today.

And yet...when Brad asked me, "Are you free this weekend?" my first thought had been that he was asking me out. It pains me to think of it now. In that moment, my heart leapt and time seemed to slow to a standstill. Could he read it on my face? Could he tell what I was thinking? I remember how he rushed to continue, to explain: he was inviting me to be a guest on his radio show. Rose Hayward: Reality Show Contestant. Interesting Guest #1 for Brad Hoffman's Radio Comedy Hour.

I'll call him Sunday morning, claim a sore throat or a stomachache. *I'm so sorry, Brad, but I can't make it tonight. Maybe next time.*

When we get home, I check my phone. One missed call. Daniel. I dial his number, wanting more than anything to hear his voice, his laughter—something to tether me back to the world at camp, which seems so very far away at the moment. I've only been home for five days, but I feel like I'm losing myself, slipping back to the person I used to be. Not physically; my exercise and eating are right on track. But emotionally, I am a jumbled, pathetic mess. So far from the strong, confident person I am at camp.

The phone rings and rings, and then Daniel's voicemail clicks on. I leave him a rambling message about bowling and workouts and ask him to call me back when he's free.

A minute later, my phone beeps with a text message. But not from Daniel. From Brad.

BRAD: Thanks for inviting me today. I had a lot of fun. See you Sunday for the Brosie Showsie!

The Brosie Showsie. I can't believe he even remembers that silly name I came up with so long ago.

Crap. There's no way I can bail out on him now.

✩ ☆ ✩

Brad arrives at 10:30 on the dot. I expect him to honk, but he sends me a text.

BRAD: I'm here.

My parents and Scotty are already in bed. Carissa is at a friend's house working on Winter Formal decorations. Earlier she'd asked my opinion on color themes, showing me swatches carefully arranged on a square of black foam board: rose and burnished gold, or forest green and eggshell?

"They both look great," I said, uninterested.

"But if you *had* to choose between one or the other," she insisted.

"Um... I like forest green and eggshell."

"Oh." She sniffed and whipped the swatches away, disappointed. "Well, I think rose and burnished gold is better. Softer, more romantic."

"Okay. Go with that, then."

"We probably will," she said. "I've gotta run. See you." And she was off.

I'm glad she's not here to give me a hard time about hanging out with Brad—or, worse, flirt with him like she did at the bowling alley.

I text Brad a quick reply that I'll be right down. Then I give myself one last look-over in my bedroom mirror. My hair dried with a slight curl to it after my shower this morning—a different look than usual, but I like it. My cheeks are a little flushed and my eyes look extra big, probably due more to nerves than to the eyeliner I applied, then wiped off because I didn't want to try too hard, then lightly applied again. I'm telling myself I want to look nice for my first radio interview, that it has nothing to do with Brad, even though I am kidding myself. He's the only one who's going to see me.

I take a deep breath, grab my purse, and creep softly down the darkened stairs to the front door. Opening it carefully, I jump back with a shriek.

"Sorry!" Brad says sheepishly. "I didn't mean to scare you."

I lean against the doorframe, trying to calm my racing pulse. "I—I thought you were waiting in your car—"

"Well, um, I came up to the door to get you, but then I thought I better not knock because your family is probably asleep and I don't want to wake them up or anything, so that's why I texted..."

I close the door and lock it behind me, then walk with Brad across the front lawn toward his car parked at the curb.

"That's sweet of you," I say. "Coming up to the front door."

"Oh, it's nothing," Brad says. "You look really nice, by the way."

"Thanks," I say, a warm blush flooding my cheeks. I'm wearing a silky floral shirt I bought last year on a shopping excursion with Holly, but then never had the courage to actually wear because it's sleeveless and I've always been self-conscious about my arms, worried they'll jiggle when I gesture as I talk. But I do love this shirt—the color, the fabric, the polka-dots of daisies—and when I was getting ready tonight it called out to me. It fits me much looser than it used to, but I wrapped one of Carissa's belts around my waist the way she taught me when we were getting ready for bowling.

Funny how much has changed in such a short time. Carissa is giving me fashion advice. I have a boyfriend. Brad is single.

Brad is single.

I have a boyfriend.

I cross my arms over my chest and attempt to steer the conversation back to a joking banter. "I had no idea people did that anymore," I say. "Walk up to the front door."

"What else would you have me do? Smoke signals?"

"I don't know, maybe honk."

"Honk? What kind of a guy do you think I am?"

"It's nothing on you. I thought all guys did that." I'm thinking of Ryan coming to pick up Carissa the other night. The impatient *beep beep* of his horn, the loud idling of his engine. Now that I think about it, I guess Brad never did honk for Carissa when they were dating. He would always come inside to wait for her, and that was when he and I would talk.

"I promise I'll never honk, Rose Hayward," Brad says. "I'll always come up to the front door to get you."

"Thank you, Brad. You gentleman you." I make my tone light like his, but inside I am giddy with nervous energy and a vivid ache of hope.

"Let me show you something else," Brad says, stepping a little bit ahead of me. "This will knock your socks off."

He reaches out and opens the car door for me. "After you, madam," he says with a flourish of his arm.

I put my hand to my forehead as if I am about to faint. "Who are you? Superman?"

Brad winks. "You figured me out," he says. "Just don't tell anyone."

"As long as you don't tell anyone my secret," I say, sliding into the passenger seat.

"What's that?" he asks, looking down at me.

"I'm really the Incredible Hulk."

He bursts out laughing, and I realize that making Brad Hoffman laugh might be my favorite feeling in the world.

Chapter 33
Brad

I unlock the door to the radio studio and flick on the lights. Rose is a warm presence behind me, making me abuzz with nervous energy. I have to concentrate on what I'm doing to keep from knocking things over.

"Ta da!" I fling out my arms in what I hope is a funny and not hokey way. "Where the magic happens!"

"Wow," she says, looking around appreciatively. I like that she actually spends a few moments taking in the room—not only the control panel of buttons and switches or the microphones and headphones we'll use on-air, but also the less-noticeable details like The Beatles' *Abbey Road* poster on the wall, the Golden Mic trophy that Jerry got a few years ago from the Chamber of Commerce, the box of green tea and chipped yellow mugs on a side table.

"Want something to drink?" I ask her. "Coffee? Coke? Water?"

"Water is fine. Or—actually, if it's not too much trouble, could I have some of that green tea?" She points to the table.

"Sure! No problem. I'll make a cup for myself, too, as a matter of fact."

As a matter of fact. I sound like my dad.

"Need some help?" she asks.

"That would be great." I don't actually need help—how hard is it to microwave water and plop in a couple tea bags?—but I'm simply happy to be near her for as long as I can. She follows me into the staff room with the fridge and microwave.

"I'm surprised by how nervous I am," Rose admits as I pour water into the mugs.

"Oh, you shouldn't be. This is nothing compared to those TV

cameras you're used to." I mean this to be comforting, but Rose looks chagrined, so I keep talking: "Really, you're gonna be great!"

"Thanks," she says, giving me a smile I'm not sure is real. "For as long as I've dreamed about being on the radio, this is my first time in a studio. It is *so* cool."

"Right?" I set the mugs in the microwave and turn it on. "Most people don't get it. Leo thinks radio is a dying art form."

"What? That's ridiculous!"

"I told him, what do you think those sports podcasts you listen to are?"

Rose laughs. We stand there in silence for a few moments, watching the microwave whir.

"You know something?" I say. "I get nervous before every show."

"Really?"

"Yeah." I never admit to anyone I'm nervous, but there's something about Rose that makes me want to tell her everything. "On my first solo show, I was a nervous wreck. My throat was so full of lumps I was worried I wouldn't be able to talk at all. I kept swallowing and swallowing and ended up playing a whole bunch of music. I barely said three words on-air. But as the weeks went on, it got better."

The microwave beeps and I open the door. We slide out our mugs and dip our tea bags into the steaming water.

"It must be hard, being on-air all by yourself," Rose says. "I'd worry my mind would go blank and I'd run out of things to say."

"The trick is to relax and pretend you're having a conversation with someone. Have someone in mind you're talking to." I realize that these past weeks, when I've gone on-air in the humming darkness of the studio, Rose is the one I've been talking to in my mind. She's both the person I most want to impress, and somehow also the person I can most be myself around. How can I be so nervous and yet also so comfortable around her? I take a sip of my tea without thinking and burn my tongue.

Rose must notice me wince. "You okay?"

"Be careful, it's hot."

We make our way back to the studio. I thought it might feel cramped to have another person here with me, but being with Rose seems normal. Like she's here every week.

I pull out Rose's chair for her and she sets down her tea with a flourish.

"Thank you, Superman," she says, smiling.

I duck across the room to the control panel and get the switches ready to go, pretending to study the instruction sheet even though I could do this in my sleep, so as to hide the goofy grin I am sure is on my face.

"It's 10:57," I tell Rose. "We go live in three minutes." I sit down and show her how to tighten the headset and adjust the microphone.

"And one last thing, if you're nervous?" I add. "Remember I average about two-and-a-half listeners who are probably asleep with the radio on. So the main thing is to have fun."

She nods, her eyes serious.

I cue the intro music and hit play. Holding up my hand, I use my fingers to count down the seconds. "Three, two, one..."

Chapter 34

Rose

"Three, two, one... Welcome to your Countdown to Midnight on WAVE 104.3!" Brad says into his microphone. "Tonight I am very pleased to present to you a special edition of the show, called the Brosie Showsie!"

I can't believe he's actually using that silly name. He not only remembered it, but he likes it enough to use it live on the air. Though he could be kidding around. Maybe he thinks it's a stupid name and he's using it as a joke.

"This is your host Brad Hoffman, and I am honored to be here with my special guest, Rose Hayward!"

"Hi," I say, leaning in close to the microphone. My voice sounds high-pitched, a nervous squeak. I swallow and try to remember what Brad said. *The trick is to relax and pretend you're having a conversation with someone.* I try to imagine Brad without his headphones on, without a microphone in front of him—me and Brad, somewhere other than a radio studio, talking, nobody listening to us. Just me and Brad.

The thought doesn't make me any less nervous.

It's a good kind of nervous, though. The stomach-dropping, toes-wiggling kind.

"So, Rose," Brad begins. "I have a question for you."

"Okay."

"It's a question I'm sure all my listeners are *dying* to hear the answer to..."

He lets the silence stretch for a beat or two, building anticipation, and a flood of disappointment courses through me. He is going to ask about *Help Me Lose Weight and Live Again,* even though I specifically told him I'm not allowed to talk about it. I remember what he said right before we went on-air: "I average about two-and-a-half listeners." The pit in my stomach grows. I know he's going to act like it's not a big deal, that I can talk about the show right now, I won't get in trouble, nobody will even be listening.

But it *is* a big deal. To me it is. I try to decide what I should do when he asks the inevitable. Should I storm out? Wait till a commercial break and then leave? I can call Holly for a ride home.

"The question is..." Brad says.

I brace myself for a question about what it's like to be on reality TV, or perhaps he'll press me for behind-the-scenes details about the show. Gossip, hook-ups, fights between contestants and trainers.

"...Are you a dog person, or a cat person?"

I laugh in relief.

"What are you laughing about?" Brad says. "It's a serious question!"

"Boy, that's a tough one. I think I'd have to say...a dog person. What about you?"

"Not yet, not yet. I'll tell you in a minute. Okay then, what if I throw horses into the mix?"

"Still dogs."

"Gerbils? Hamsters?"

"Nope. Kinda freaked me out as a kid, to be honest."

"Fish?"

"C'mon, dogs are way better than fish."

"Is that your final answer?"

"Yes. Dogs, hands down."

"Ding ding ding! We have a winner!" Brad says. "As my two-and-a-half listeners know, I am also a dog person all the way."

"Phew! Good thing we're compatible."

"I guess we can continue with the rest of the show now," Brad says. He winks and gives me a thumbs up, and I know it's going to be a fun night.

☆ ☆ ☆

THE NEXT FIFTY-FIVE minutes fly by, and all of a sudden Brad is wrapping up the show. "So long, farewell, and I'll catch you next Sunday night!" he says. "And special thanks to our guest, Rose Hayward, for being with us. I'll say it right here, right now, in front of all you listeners out there: this girl is one in a million!"

With that, he flips a button on the switchboard to fade out into the closing music. Then he takes off his headphones and smiles at me. "Well? What'd you think?"

I take off my headphones, too. "That was amazing! I had so much fun."

"I did too. The time flew by even faster than usual." He leans forward and pushes some more buttons on the extremely complicated-looking switchboard.

"That was really nice," I say. "What you said at the end."

Brad looks up at me, right into my eyes. "It's the truth," he says simply.

If this were a scene in a movie, I would swear we are having A Moment. The cheesy romantic music would swell in the background, and time would have that weighted feeling that lets you know something important is happening.

But this isn't a movie, this is real life. And not Carissa's real life. *My* real life.

I look into his eyes, anticipation fluttering in my chest.

But nothing happens.

Brad returns his attention to the switchboard—getting the automated song playlists cued up for the next few hours of airtime until the early morning DJs come in for their show.

I pick up our empty tea mugs and carry them to the little sink in the staff room. I rinse them out in super-hot water, trying to quell that ache in the pit of my stomach. What am I disappointed about? I was on the radio! With Brad! Chatting for a full hour with no awkward pauses or uncomfortable silences, no, none of that, just the two of us laughing and joking and interjecting like we do this all the time, like it was nothing out of the ordinary. I should be ecstatic right now!

But I'm not. I'm sinking down into the hollow emptiness the old me would try to push away by gorging on an entire pan of brownies. I want to sit down on the floor and hold my knees and rest my head in my arms and sit there for a while with my eyes closed.

So, after I dry the mugs on a duck-patterned dishtowel, that's exactly what I do.

After a few minutes, I hear Brad's footsteps. "Rose?" he says, alarm in his voice. In two seconds he's kneeling beside me, his hand on my arm. "Are you okay?"

I lift my head and force a smile. "Yeah, just tired."

"C'mon," he says. "I'll drive you home."

The ride is quiet, like maybe we've talked ourselves out. It's a nice quiet, though. Comfortable. Brad drives with one hand on the steering wheel, the other arm resting out his open window. A midnight breeze trickles into the car, playing with my hair, making me feel more awake. More at peace with things.

It's a good feeling. Closure.

Brad pulls up to the curb beside my sleeping house. The Green Dragon is parked in the driveway, and I wonder if seeing the car pains Brad. Does it make him think of Carissa? Or of me?

"Hey," he says, cutting the engine. "I know you're not allowed to talk on the phone or text or anything when you're at camp, but can you get snail-mail? Like, if I sent you letters, would you get them?"

"Yeah, letters are allowed." I am caught off guard, but in a pleasant way. Brad is full of surprises. I never thought he'd care enough to write me.

Although it's one thing to ask for an address—it's quite another to follow through. I don't actually believe he'll write me any letters. I imagine myself sitting up hopefully in my seat every week when mail is passed out, only to be disappointed again and again.

That's the thing about surprises: sometimes they only lead to letdowns.

"Well, here." Brad reaches across my lap and opens the glove compartment, pulling out a pad of sticky notes and a pen. He smells of laundry detergent and his hair nearly brushes my cheek. My stomach shivers. "Can you give me your address?"

"Sure." I carefully write it out on the pad of paper and hand it to him.

"Thanks." He peels off the sticky note with my address, studies it, then slides it into his wallet.

I unbuckle my seatbelt and it pulls up the hem of my top, exposing a thin strip of my stomach. I quickly tug my shirt down and yank the sides of my cardigan tighter to cover as much of myself as possible.

"Wait till the next time you see me," I say, trying to make my voice light. "When I come home in December, I'll be a brand new me."

Brad scrunches his eyebrows. "Don't say that. I like this Rose. I like the way you are now."

"You're sweet to say that."

"Not sweet. Just telling it like it is."

"Thanks. But I mean on the outside. I'll still be me, only thinner. Prettier."

Brad is quiet, studying my face. I look down and fumble on the floor for my purse. My stomach turns in knots. *He doesn't see you that way,* I remind myself. *To him, you're just Carissa Hayward's sister. The friendly fat girl. The reality TV celebrity. Nothing more.*

Brad clears his throat. "Don't change too much, okay?"

Something in his tone catches me by surprise. A tenderness.

I look up into his eyes. The car is a warm, safe cocoon. I've dreamt about this moment hundreds of times, and it is exactly the way I always imagined it would be: the radio turned so low it's a nearly inaudible hum, dewy light from a streetlamp slanting gently through the windshield, and Brad's face, so close I can count the freckles on his nose.

"Rose," Brad says.

My heart is beating so rapidly, I worry he's able to hear it.

"I—"

Suddenly, my cell phone rings.

"Should you get that?" he asks.

I wish more than anything I had left my phone on vibrate after the show.

"It's okay, you can get it," Brad insists, sitting back in his seat.

Whatever that was between us is gone now. I yank my purse onto my lap and pull out my lit-up phone.

DANIEL blinks up at me from the caller ID.

Daniel. Shame burns in my chest. I said I would call him tonight, but I completely forgot. Ever since Brad picked me up, I haven't thought of Daniel once.

"Everything okay?" Brad asks.

"Oh, it's uh—it's Carissa," I lie, as the phone stops ringing and clicks over to voicemail. "She's probably wondering where I am. What time is it?"

"Twelve-thirty-two," Brad reads from the dashboard clock.

"Oh, wow, it's late. I should probably go."

"And you're heading back to Texas tomorrow?"

"Yep, my flight leaves in the morning."

"What time?"

"Nine."

"That's early."

"Yeah."

My cell phone beeps, signaling a new voicemail. Is Montana one hour or two hours different from California time? I can't remember. Either way, it's the middle of the night where Daniel is.

"So, how's Carissa doing?" Brad says abruptly.

My stomach tightens. So that's why he wanted to hang out with me—to find out about Carissa. He's still in love with her. Obviously. How could I have thought otherwise, even for a moment?

"You know better than me," I say, opening the car door. "You see her more than I do."

"I don't see her very much anymore," Brad says.

"Well, she seems fine. The same as always. She's busy planning the Winter Formal."

"Isn't that not till December?"

"You know Carissa. Never too early to get organized."

I climb out of the car and push the door shut.

Brad rolls down the passenger window. "I had a lot of fun tonight, Rose."

"Me too. I guess I'll see you around."

"For sure. Have a safe trip tomorrow."

"I will. Bye, Brad."

I give a small wave, then head up the path to my front door.

"Rose!" Brad calls.

I stop and turn toward him. Hope blossoms in my chest.

"Next time you're home," he says, "will you come on my radio show again?"

My heart sinks. That's probably the real reason he invited me on his show tonight. He's buttering me up for when I come home for good, and *Help Me Lose Weight and Live Again* premieres on national television, and suddenly I'm a reality TV star. He wants to use me to impress his boss and boost his ratings.

"Maybe," I say, because I can't think of a better response. Then I turn and flee into my house without looking back, angry at the tears burning my eyes.

It doesn't matter that Brad is smart and funny and handsome and easy to talk to.

It doesn't matter that merely sitting next to him makes my pulse quicken.

It doesn't matter that he gets my obscure references to terrible song lyrics and he's the only other high schooler I know reading *Infinite Jest.*

It doesn't matter that I feel differently about him than any other guy I've ever met, even Daniel.

None of it matters, because Brad is in love with Carissa. And, no matter how much weight I lose, I'll never be Carissa.

Chapter 35

Brad

Rose shuts my car door and turns to walk away. I am desperate to keep talking, to say something that will keep her with me a moment longer. Thinking about the distance between Texas and California makes panic rise in my throat. Six whole weeks she'll be gone filming the rest of the TV show. It seems an eternity. Especially when I think about my upcoming week: going with my dad to his chemo treatment, watching his tired eyes as I read aloud from his favorite Dan Brown novel.

For a couple hours tonight, I completely forgot to be worried. Like worry is one of those weight vests, and I was able to take it off for a little while. Because of Rose.

If she were with me, everything would seem more bearable.

"Wait, Rose!" I call out through the passenger window.

She turns. The openness on her face gives me a glimmer of hope. *Maybe we did have A Moment, right before her phone rang. Maybe— just maybe—she wanted to kiss me, too.*

I fumble for something half-normal to say to her. What I want to say is, *Please don't go*. But I can't say that. I know she has to go.

"Next time you're home," I ask, "will you come on my radio show again?"

Something passes across her face. Her smile shifts, tightens. It must have been the wrong thing to say, but I don't know why.

"Maybe," she says. Her voice sounds tired and distant. Then she turns and continues up the walkway.

I want to climb out of the driver's seat and run across the lawn and grab her hand. But I'm scared. I don't know what I would do after I reached her. My heart sinks as I watch her disappear inside the dark house.

When I get home, I take my wallet from the back pocket of my jeans and slip out the note with her camp address. Looking at the yellow square of paper with Rose's loopy cursive scrawled across it makes the anxiety inside me die down a little. Here is something tangible, proof of the connection I felt between us the past few days.

I drift to sleep writing a letter to her in my mind. I dream that I'm in the middle of a churning ocean, gripping a life preserver, frantically waving my arms and scanning the horizon for a boat or the shore. I wake up before anyone comes to my rescue.

☆ ☆ ☆

THE NEXT DAY, Leo is waiting beside my locker after second period. "Brad!" he calls, waving. I jog over and we bump fists in greeting. Ever since my dad's cancer diagnosis, I've felt weird around Leo—I still haven't told him, and normally I tell him everything.

"I never see you these days," Leo says. "You been busy at the station?"

"Yeah, working a lot. And trying to stay on top of school stuff. You know how it is." I grab my math textbook and shut my locker with a bang.

"What are you doing this afternoon? Want to head over to Tony's for some carnitas?"

"Sorry, man, I can't—I'm busy."

"I thought you were off Mondays."

"I am, but I'm volunteering at the food pantry today."

Leo gives me a look like, *Who are you?* But he says, "That's cool. I didn't know you did that."

"It's a recent thing."

"Doesn't Carissa volunteer there?" He raises his eyebrows like, *I see what you're trying to do, Hoffman.*

I shake my head, *It's not like that.* "I don't think she goes very often," I tell him. "I've only seen her once. Besides, I'm over her."

Leo looks skeptical.

"Seriously, I am. I don't care what she does or who she's with. I've moved on."

"Yeah you have," Leo says, giving me a high five. The bell rings and we head down the hall toward the senior building. "Hey," he continues, "I heard Mel's having a Halloween party. You should come. Carissa will be there, but since you're over her now..."

"Sure, sounds fun."

"Awesome! Maybe we could do a costume together. Something hilarious, like Dumb and Dumber, what do you think?" Before I can respond, Leo turns and punches my arm. "DUDE! You know that cute girl from the station? What's her name?"

"Meghan."

"Yeah, Meghan. You should invite her to the party. That would really tick Carissa off." He laughs.

I laugh too. "Thanks, but no. Meghan and me, not gonna happen."

"What? I thought you said you were over Carissa."

"I am! But I'm over Meghan too, all right?"

Leo shakes his head. "Brad, Brad, Brad."

"What?"

"What is going on with you lately? How am I so behind on your life?"

"You're not behind. There's not much to tell," I say, even though that is a blatant lie.

Leo looks at me, one eyebrow raised, and that's when I know it's time. I need to tell him about my dad.

But just then, Stacey runs up and loops her arm through Leo's, kissing him on the cheek. "Hey, baby!" she squeals. She smiles at me. "Hi, Brad."

"Hi." So, I guess these two are "on" again. I swallow down the lump in my throat. I'll tell Leo some other time.

The three of us head to Ostertank's room. Before class starts, everyone is talking about Rose's party at the bowling alley.

"Did you see that cute dress Rosie was wearing? Carissa picked it out for her. She's got the *best* fashion sense."

"Rosie looked like a *completely* different person!"

"I would not have even *recognized* her."

"I know, you can actually see her cheekbones now!" Ashley says, giggling. I must glare at her, because she says, "What, Brad? It's a *compliment.*"

"I don't think she's changed that much," I mutter.

"C'mon, Brad, be nice," Stacey hisses as Ostertank walks into the classroom and shuts the door. "Just because Rosie is Carissa's sister doesn't mean you can't be happy for her."

"That's not—I wasn't—"

But I don't get to explain myself because Ostertank is passing out a pop quiz. "Anyone who talks gets a zero!" she yells.

I sigh, shoving my book under my desk. Sometimes it's like I'm not in sync with the rest of the world.

✧ ☆ ✧

It's a relief to walk through the doors of the food pantry, set down my backpack, and get to work restocking shelves. Today we got a shipment of instant mashed potatoes and bags of rice, and I spend my first half hour unloading the giant boxes and stacking the goods as neatly as possible on the shelves. Then I sort through two giant bags of potatoes, throwing out the rotten ones. I let my mind wander, and of course my thoughts skitter around my dad.

I feel like a bad son admitting this, but I'm dreading going with him to chemo tomorrow. My mom said it means so much to him that I go, and I'm trying to look at it as a gift—a chance to step up and be there for the man who has always been there for me.

But the truth is, his chemo appointments freak me out. I don't like the sterile hospital hallways and the blue-walled chemo room with paintings of the ocean that you can tell are supposed to be calming, but aren't, not to me. They only make me think of drowning.

I don't like the dripping of the drugs or the blinking lights of the machines. I don't like not knowing what any of the machines do. I don't like how helpless I feel in that room. My dad a weary shell beside me, trying to appear strong even though he is exhausted, and all I can do is turn the page of that stupid Dan Brown novel and keep reading, willing my voice not to shake.

I've started writing a letter about all of this to Rose, but I don't know if I'll mail it. Sometimes when I start writing to her, it's like the letter morphs into my personal journal and I word-vomit on the page, writing writing writing without really even thinking.

I probably won't mail the letter. I'll think of something else to write her, something more funny and upbeat.

"Brad! Could you help up front?" Marlene calls. "We have clients!"

"Coming!" I set down the crate of sorted potatoes and head toward the front counter, yanking off my slimy latex gloves and pulling on some clean ones.

Technically, the food pantry is closed on Monday afternoons; it's supposed to be our time to restock, unpack, and get ready for the week. But Marlene has such a big heart that she can't bear to turn anyone away. If a client knocks on the door and Marlene is here to answer it, they will be welcomed inside and served no matter what hour of what day it is.

"Can you work Aisle Three?" Marlene asks. "Jewell's got Aisle Two."

"Sure." I wave to Jewell, the tiny old lady with the bowl haircut who barely looks strong enough to lift a carton of eggs. Good thing Marlene's got her working the baked goods aisle—nothing too heavy there.

Marlene works Aisle One, helping the clients get signed in and asking about their dietary needs. It appears to be a family: a man, a woman, and two little girls, maybe four or five years old, in matching dresses and pigtails. The man smiles a lot and the woman keeps saying, "Thank you, thank you so much." The girls peer over the counter with round eyes.

When they get to me, I offer as much yogurt, cheese, and meat as we're allowed to give. The woman carefully packs everything in a reusable bag they brought. "What do you say?" she asks the girls.

"Thank you," they chime in unison.

"You're more than welcome." I wave goodbye as they head outside with their mom. The man finishes packing up the produce into a big box they brought along.

"This is our first time here," he says to me. "I never thought we'd have to come to a food pantry. But life is a roller coaster. You never know, my man. You never know."

I nod, unsure what to say.

"My mom used to repeat this saying," the man continues. "Whenever we'd walk by a homeless man? She'd say, 'There by the grace of God go I.' And then she'd give him some food or money. I never really understood that until now. I got laid off from my job a few months ago, and I'm having a hard time finding a new one. Nobody's hiring these days. My wife works, but only part-time, and her paycheck barely covers our mortgage. We blew through our savings when little Macie, that's our daughter—she got sick and needed emergency surgery. So, here we are." He sighs, but it turns into a smile. "We are really grateful for what you do here."

"It's not a big deal."

"Yes it is. What's your name, my man?"

"Brad."

"I'm John." He shakes my hand. "And I'm a lucky man, let me tell you."

The word is out of my mouth before I can think to stop it. "Lucky?"

John smiles. "Yes indeed. I am the luckiest guy in the world to be married to that amazing woman out there. She's my best friend. Always looking on the bright side, always supporting me." He hefts the box off the counter. "This is only temporary. I know we'll get back on our feet. And everything's better when you're going through life with your best friend. You know?"

"Yeah," I tell him. "I think I do."

When I get home that night, I fold up my long letter to Rose. Then I slide it in an envelope, carefully write out her camp address, and put on two stamps, to be safe. It's a pretty thick letter.

And I don't change my mind. The next morning, when I head out for my run, I drop it into the mailbox.

The rest of the day, even during my dad's chemo treatment, I feel lighter.

I don't tell my dad about the letter, or about my feelings for Rose —but it's as if he knows. Maybe he can read something on my face or in my body language. At one point, as I pause between chapters, he reaches over and pats my hand.

"No regrets, son," he says. "All you get to take with you at the end are the memories you made with the people you care about."

"Dad, I...don't talk like that. It's not the end."

"Oh, I know that. I'll be around for a while yet, don't worry. I'm just saying—people and love are what matter in this life. That's what I've learned from all of this."

"I love you, Dad."

"I love you too, son."

He smiles, and when I look at him I don't see a gaunt, sick, exhausted shell of a man. I see my father. The same strong, wise person who raised me. The same man he always has been. And for the first time since I learned about his cancer diagnosis, I don't feel afraid. I feel grateful to be in this hospital room with him.

In a few moments, I will clear my throat and begin reading the next chapter aloud. But for now, I sit here holding my dad's hand, the two of us gazing out the window at the sunlight slanting through the tree branches and the blue sky far above.

Chapter 36

Rose

My alarm blares much too early. Even though I was only home for a week, my body fully adjusted to California time, so it seems like it is two hours earlier—four A.M. instead of six A.M. I groan, roll over, and set the alarm for five more minutes. Right as I'm drifting off, it blares again. Darn it.

I slog out of bed, throw on my workout clothes. My head is clogged with dreams...what did I dream about? Something nice. I remember excited butterflies filling my stomach. The best kind of butterflies.

As I leave the girls' cabin, the cool morning air hits my face like a splash of water. My eyes blink awake. I breathe in deeply. As tired as I am this morning, I am also relieved. After being away, coming back to camp is a gift. The oak trees, the dining commons, the gym—I'm surprised by how much I missed my life here.

When I'm at camp, I am proud of the person I'm becoming. I'm moving forward. Every pound I lose, every mile I run, every weight I lift, is tangible proof of a changed me. A better me.

Here at camp, life is simple. My days are organized by a strict routine. Breakfast, then work-out in the gym; lunch, then a hike on the trails around the grounds, then evening gym time; dinner, then relaxation in the common room with Daniel. We usually do a jigsaw puzzle, watch a movie, or just talk. Everything is easy with Daniel. Calm.

As I approach the guys' cabin, Daniel comes up the path. "Hey, Rosie!" he shouts, running up and wrapping his arms around me in a bear hug. "I missed you!"

"I missed you too," I say, hugging him back. After a few moments, he pulls away and looks at me. His smile is infectious; I can't help but smile too.

"How was home?" I ask.

"My workouts were off without you there." He grabs my hand. "How'd you sleep last night?"

I look into his eyes, make a point to notice how kind they are. "I slept like a rock," I say as we walk together to the dining commons for breakfast. "How about you?"

As the words leave my mouth, I suddenly remember my dream—a flash of it, like a memory. Brad holding my hand. Laughing, his arm around my waist, drawing me to him. Leaning me against a wall, kissing me gently.

I slip my hand out of Daniel's and wipe it on my T-shirt. "Sorry," I say. "Sweaty palms."

Daniel begins talking about his lumpy mattress, the way he always feels a small hard rock under his back no matter how many times he shifts positions or how he tries to angle his body across the bed.

"But I wasn't even tired this morning," he says, holding the door open for me. We walk together into the dining commons. "I was so excited to see you."

"Me too."

"Rosie! Daniel!" Doris shouts from across the room, waving us over to her table. She hugs us both like she hasn't seen us in years.

Daniel sits at the table with Doris, but I remain standing, still processing my dream. "Want me to get you a banana?" I ask.

"Sure, thanks babe," Daniel says, turning away to talk with Doris.

I walk in a daze toward the fruit table, trying to push Brad's face from my mind. It was only a dream, yet the memory of his kiss is so vivid. Thinking about it makes me blush. And I hate myself for it.

At home, things were the opposite of simple. Emotions and yearnings rushed back that I've been trying for months to stamp out.

It doesn't matter that I'm changing, growing braver and stronger every day. When I'm standing next to Carissa, I still feel inferior. The fat twin. The ugly twin. The just-a-friend twin.

I know Brad only sees me as a friend (he made that pretty obvious)...yet, even back at camp, I can't quite rid myself of him. He should not have any ownership over this place, but even miles and miles away, on a secluded ranch in Texas, memories of him seep into my daily life. I think about him everywhere: when I run on the treadmill, when I stretch my legs, when my favorite Beatles song comes on my headphones. "Here Comes the Sun."

The truth is, I miss him. I miss him like someone has taken an ice-cream scoop to my stomach and dug out a triple-scoop cone.

And it doesn't get easier. A week passes, and every morning Brad is what I think about when I first open my eyes. Two weeks pass. My stomach churns anxiously. Every night I close my eyes and try to think of Daniel, but Brad's face seeps into my dreams. Brad's laugh echoes in my ears. Brad, touching my arm, running beside me on the treadmill, looking at me seriously as I talk, his brow crinkled, as if what I'm saying truly matters. As if I truly matter to him.

My yearning for Brad is made worse by my guilt about it. Not only is Brad thousands of miles away, not only is he my twin sister's ex-boyfriend, and not only is he still mooning over said twin sister—none of it should matter, because I already have a boyfriend.

☆ ☆ ☆

My least favorite part of being on the show is the personal interviews. At some point during the week—particularly after traumatic emotional events, like weigh-in night, or after evening work-outs when you're really tired and wanting nothing more than dinner and your bed—that's when they like to grab you.

"Hey, Rosie," I'll hear, and my heart drops with dread every time. I'll turn, and there he'll be, Camera-Man Dave, camera squatting on his shoulder like an ugly bird with blinking red eyes. "Can I talk to you for a minute?" He'll always ask like it's a question, but it's really not. You can't say no to individual interviews. It's one of our "obligations to the show." That's how Britta phrased it when going over the contracts we signed the first day.

"How you doing?" Camera-Man Dave asks now, intercepting me as I duck out of the gym.

I want to ask him, *How does it look like I'm doing?* I'm dripping with sweat, aching from muscle exhaustion, and stumbling around on four hours of sleep because I've been tossing and turning every night the past week, unable to shut off my brain from obsessing about Daniel and Brad and what to do or what not to do.

Trainer Mark exits the gym, waves to us with a big fake smile, and strides over to join the conversation. It's like he has a radar for when I most want to be alone, and those are the times he chooses to strike.

"Rosie!" he bellows, placing his sweaty palm on my bare arm. *Gross.* "How was your trip home?"

"Fine." I force a smile. The more cheerful I act, the quicker this is likely to go. "It was really great, actually."

"Fantastic. Dave showed me some of the footage earlier—looked like your family was very happy to see you. Especially your sister."

"Yep. We've never been apart for this long, so. You know."

"And your friends. What was it like to see them again?"

My smile broadens as I think of Holly. And Brad. "It was wonderful. They make me feel like, however much I've changed on the outside, I'm still the same person inside."

Mark nods, but something sparks in his eyes. "Interesting how you said *they*. Earlier you'd mentioned how you only have *one* real friend at home. Molly, is it?"

"Holly," I correct him, my stomach knotting uncomfortably as I sense where this is going. But I don't know how to stop him.

"Yes, Holly, excuse me. But now you said *they*. Who is this other person you're referring to? Could it be the young man you were spotted with? Is there a romance brewing, perhaps?" He smiles in a teasing way, but to me he looks like a snake. I don't trust him. And I don't want to talk about Brad.

"Oh, no—that's just a friend." I try to prop up the corners of my smile. But my distrust and annoyance must show on my face, because Mark only leans in closer.

"Don't sell yourself short, Rosie. Look at me."

Grudgingly, I meet his eyes.

He jabs his finger at me. "You. Deserve. Love." His tone is so patronizing, I want to turn on my heel and storm away.

The words come out before I can stop them. "Oh, you don't have to worry about me. I do have someone special."

He waves away my words. "Are you talking about your fellow camper Daniel Waldon? Oh, everyone knows about your *special* friendship."

I gape at him, heart hammering. Daniel and I have purposefully been discreet. We don't want a ton of attention when the show airs. Relationships are hard enough without all that extra expectation and public scrutiny.

Mark laughs. "Sorry, were you trying to keep that under the radar? Whoops!" The snake smile. "Nothing goes unnoticed around here, Rosie."

I swallow, trying to calm down. I look past Trainer Mark and Camera-Man Dave, out at the trees and dusty horizon. Still, I can sense the camera lens zoomed in on my face.

I want so badly to take off running.

"Anyway," Mark continues in a sing-song voice. "That's why I was surprised to see you canoodling with Mr. California Surfer when you were back home."

"I told you. We're. Just. Friends."

Mark holds up his hands. "Calm down, Rosie. All I'm saying is, prepare yourself. You deserve love. And The New You is going to be *gorgeous*—I guarantee suitors will be lining up at your door!" He winks.

I need to take a shower.

No, I need to see Daniel.

No, I need to be alone.

"Can I go now?" I ask Camera-Man Dave. He doesn't say anything, but Mark steps aside. I take that as permission and flee.

☆ ☆ ☆

AFTER DINNER we get to call home for five minutes. I try my mom's cell.

Carissa answers. "Hello?"

"Hey, it's me. I only have five minutes."

She immediately launches into a monologue about how stressed she is and how Ryan is annoying her and how Brad has been acting all weird lately.

"Wait, what?" At the mention of Brad's name, my attention perks up.

"I don't know what happened," she sniffles. "Brad's acting like he's totally over me."

"What do you mean?"

"I mean he's *over* me! He's into someone else!"

"He is? Who?"

"I don't know."

"Then why do you think he's into someone else?"

"Because of Mel's Halloween party."

"He came with someone?" My heart pounds.

"No, no—he was all by himself. But he talked to me and Ryan and seemed totally cool with it. He wasn't jealous *at all*, Rosie! He and Ryan even talked sports."

Relief washes over me, and I can't help but hope: maybe it is true. Maybe he *is* finally over Carissa.

"Caris, is Mom there? I can only talk for two more minutes before they cut me off."

"No, she's at the grocery store. I'm the only one home. But listen, Rosie, I need you to help me with something."

I can't remember Carissa ever asking me for help with anything.

"You need *my* help? With what?"

"Well, Brad's working at that radio station all the time. I never see him anymore. I bet he thinks he has no chance at ever getting back together with me, so he's given up."

"Are you saying—"

Carissa cuts me off. "You and Brad are friends, right? Or, at least, friendly."

My stomach hurts. "I guess so."

"So you can put in a good word for me. You know, hint that he still has a chance to win me back."

"How can I do that? It's not like I talk to him."

You have one minute remaining, says the computerized phone voice.

"Don't you guys write letters?" Carissa says.

I bite my cheek. "Who told you that?"

"Stacey did. Brad told Leo, Leo told Stacey. It's just letters, Rosie, it's not a big deal. So you'll help me out?"

"Um..."

"Because I've decided I want him back. His transformation worked. Like, at the Halloween party, he was wearing the lamest costume but he still looked cute. You'll never believe what he dressed up as."

"What?"

"A pinball machine. He made these flipper-things out of cardboard that he wore on his hands, and on the back of his shirt he taped little bits of paper and gum wrappers—like, what you would find behind a pinball machine, I guess."

My voice sounds higher than normal. "That's clever."

"It was weird. He was wearing a T-shirt of some band—"

"The Who?"

"I don't know, some band."

"No, I mean was the band The Who?"

Carissa's voice brightens. "Oh—yeah, actually, I think that's it. How'd you know?"

"That's the pinball machine at the bowling alley."

"Oh my gosh," Carissa says. "Remember our sixth-grade birthday party? When I made out with Cody Turner behind that pin—"

Her voice cuts off, replaced by the hollow buzzing of the dial tone.

I'm left with my own thoughts of that pinball machine. Remembering what it was like, pressed up in that small space next to Brad. Our arms touching. The smell of his shampoo.

There's a knock on my door, and then Daniel comes in. I try to shake thoughts of Brad away.

"Hey," Daniel says. "Did you get to talk to your mom?"

"No, she was at the store. I talked to Carissa."

He raises his eyebrows. "Did y'all have a nice chat?"

"Yeah," I say, making room for him beside me on the bed. "We did."

Daniel sits down, rests his hand on my thigh. As he tells me about his brief conversation with his mom, I try to listen. I should be giving him all my attention. I should be a good girlfriend. But my thoughts keep flitting back to Brad. Does he think about that afternoon, wedged in together behind the pinball machine? Maybe so. Why else would he dress up as a pinball machine for Halloween? Specifically, *that* pinball machine.

Our pinball machine.

Daniel squeezes my knee. "You must have had a good talk with your sister," he says. "You look really happy."

Chapter 37
Brad

Hi Rose,

Hope you're getting settled back in at camp. Hope this letter finds its way to you. And hope you can read my handwriting! I'll try to write neatly.

I can't remember the last time I wrote a letter. I almost forgot how to address an envelope—where you're supposed to write the return address, where to put the stamp. Is that embarrassing to admit? Should I scratch out that last sentence?

Oh well. I'm gonna keep it in there. I don't feel like I need to try to be "cool" around you. Like, I can just be myself, weirdness and all.

That's such a gift. You have no idea.

I wonder what you're doing right this moment. What are your favorite parts of your day? What are your least favorite parts?

My least favorite hour is probably third period, right now. I'm sitting here in Ostertank's class, trying to discreetly write this letter to you while she's lecturing about some old dead poet. It's hard to even understand what she's saying with the perpetual cough drop in her mouth.

See what you're missing? Haha. I'm sure you can't wait to come home again.

Oof. The dinosaur is looking at me. I should probably go.

-Brad

Hi Rose,

Good morning! I'm writing to you from the radio station at 5:46 a.m. Fourteen minutes until the early-morning show starts. I've already got everything cued up and ready, so I decided to make myself some tea. I'm using the same mug you used when you were here.

Is it weird that I remember what mug you used?

(It's the one with the lizard wearing a birthday hat.)

Anyway. There's a really pretty sunrise this morning. The whole sky is covered with bright pink clouds. Wish you were here to see it.

(Though I hope you are peacefully sleeping right now in your warm, cozy bed. If I remember correctly, you and I are both night owls. It's tough to try to become an early bird when you're a natural night owl.)

-Brad

✧ ✩ ✧

Dear Rose,

Is it okay that I'm sending you a package instead of a normal letter? I'm crossing my fingers this makes it to you all right.

Enclosed you will find:

- *A workout playlist I made for you. It's on a flash drive because I don't think I can share it with you online, since you aren't allowed to use your phone or computer. I'm hoping one of the producers will do me a solid and put it on your iPod, so you can listen while you kick butt on the treadmill. (And I hope you like it!)*
- *A terrible drawing I made for you of Tony's Taco Shack, with the not-so-subtle hope we can actually go out for those carnitas tacos when you come home.*
- *This hilarious cartoon that immediately made me think of you. Since you can't use the Internet there, I printed it out for you.*

- *A piece of sea glass I found at the beach the other day during a run. Here's a little piece of home for you. Don't forget about us!*

I'm sure you're doing amazing. Keep it up, Incredible Hulk.
-Brad

HEY ROSE,

Today was a tough day. I'm worried about my dad. He's been feeling more and more sick with every week of treatment. Today he couldn't keep much of anything down. I tried making him eggs, toast, chicken soup, and grilled cheese. He didn't want any of it.

He's been incredibly optimistic through all of this. Always talking about how lucky he is that the doctors caught the cancer early. Making plans for the future with utmost certainty that he'll be back to his old self in no time.

I hope he's right.

I can't imagine life without my dad.

Sorry to unload on you like this. I should probably rip up this downer of a letter instead of sending it you. The last thing you need is stress from me.

No one else but you knows about my dad. I haven't even told Leo. It never seems like the right time.

Anyway. It's nice to be able to "talk" to you like this even when you're far away. Thanks for listening. Thanks for always being there. Thanks for being you.

You're pretty great, you know that?
-Brad

HEY ROSE,

Thought of you at the radio station last night. It seemed weirdly empty without you there. I felt like I was talking to myself, when I wanted to be talking to you.

Chapter 38

Rose

The weekly weigh-in is over, but my insides remain twisted in anxious knots. My weight loss is on track, but I don't feel relieved. I don't feel happy. I feel...sad. And guilty. And confused.

The words from Brad's latest letter flit constantly through my mind. *I felt like I was talking to myself, when I wanted to be talking to you.* It sounds like he misses me. Doesn't it?

As soon as I finish reading his letter, I'm aching for another letter from him. When mail is passed out each Monday, anticipation thrums through me. The sight of his handwriting makes my heart swoop.

Stop it, I tell myself. *Calm down.*

I know Daniel is the one I should be giddy about.

And I am. Sort of. It's confusing.

Brad is only a friend, I repeat to myself like a mantra. *Brad is only a friend.*

But I know that isn't exactly true.

The past few weeks I've been living on autopilot. I am a machine going through the motions of my daily work-outs, pounding away on the treadmill, straining through weight reps, enjoying the pain. Craving the pain. Because at least pain is a distraction.

Daniel is always around, saving me spots at meals, holding my hand as we go on hikes in the afternoon. Twice, I've heard him tapping on my window at night, but I've pretended to be asleep. When I'm with him, I feel guilty. He is so nice to me.

I don't deserve him.

For the first time ever, food is unappealing. My stomach is constantly in knots of anxiety. Food tastes bland, the textures all wrong. Slimy and gritty and too soft. I force myself to swallow bites of protein bars. I drink a lot of water, trying to wash away my uncertainty.

I know how I *should* feel: grateful. Lucky. Happy.

But I don't.

On Sunday night, after dinner, I can't take it anymore. I am suffocating. I tell Daniel I have a headache and retreat to my room, but after two minutes of lying facedown on my scratchy bedspread, I roll over and stand back up.

I'm going to explode if I stay still for another second. I don't like when my body is still because that means my mind has a chance to quiet down. When my mind is quiet, the thoughts rush in. And it's painful. I don't like thinking about the freckles on Brad's nose that night he drove me home, or the minty toothpaste smell of Daniel's breath as he leaned toward me for our first kiss. I don't like thinking about Brad telling me not to change too much, or Daniel telling me that I'm the sweetest girl he's ever met.

I slip out of my room and head straight for the gym. It'll be empty now, right after dinner—everyone will be relaxing or celebrating today's weigh-in. I want to be alone. I want my mind to be filled with nothing but the pounding of my sneakers as I run.

I push the treadmill speed arrow up and up. The belt gains speed until I'm sprinting. My chest is tight and my legs are wobbly. My stomach churns. I keep running. Faster, faster. As if I could run straight out of this twisted situation I've managed to get myself into.

My legs ache. My stomach heaves. I'm slightly dizzy.

I press the down arrow until the treadmill slows to a stop. My body crumples. I rest my head on my knees and let the tears come.

I'm not sure how much time has passed—five minutes? Ten?—when the door to the gym squeaks open and footsteps sound.

"Rosie?" Doris calls. "Is that you?"

I try to quiet my crying but can't catch my breath. My nose is clogged and my eyes are swollen. I use the sleeve of my shirt to wipe my hot cheeks.

Doris hurries over. "Sweetheart, what happened? What's wrong?" She kneels next to me, placing her hand gently on my shoulder. The comforting weight of her hand reminds me of something my dad used to do, a touch on my shoulder as I crouched over the kitchen table doing homework or sat on the couch watching television before bed, a gesture of reassurance that said *I'm here, I love you, good night.* Maybe it's that gesture that makes me do what I do next.

I open my mouth, and I tell Doris everything.

After I finish, she looks at me with serious eyes. "Well, Rosie, I think you need to ask yourself a question. And then you need to answer it honestly."

"Okay," I say nervously.

"Do you like Brad because you genuinely *like* him? Or do you just want something that's Carissa's?"

Tears catch in my throat. "I don't know." And it's true. I don't.

Doris rubs my back, tucks a strand of hair behind my ear. "Daniel is a great guy," she says. "And I can tell he cares about you. Why not give yourself a chance to have something that is yours completely?"

I nod, wiping tears from my face. Doris is right. Daniel is wonderful. He doesn't play games. He tells me how he feels about me. Brad, on the other hand, is a mystery. As impossible as it is to push him out of my thoughts right now, it will only get worse the longer whatever this is goes on. He is nothing more than a giant time-bomb ticking away: *heartbreak, heartbreak, heartbreak.*

I've been trying to convince myself that he has feelings for me, and I've been pushing away all evidence that he doesn't. Now the evidence comes rushing back. The way his attention was always drawn to Carissa like a magnet, interrupting any conversation he was having with me. How he flirted with Carissa at my bowling party. He even asked about her in our last conversation after the radio show.

I realize his letters are nothing but a friendly gesture—and probably only because he sees me as a gateway to my sister. Just like Bobby Mayers asking me to that stupid dance all those years ago.

Brad doesn't want me. He wants Carissa.

It's always been Carissa.

Later that night, alone in my room, I take out a plain white envelope from the top desk drawer. Usually, I don't respond to Brad's letters. I just can't let myself go there. The one time I did—after he opened up about his dad—I mailed him a silly hand-drawn comic, where he was Superman and I was the Incredible Hulk, and together we saved the world by throwing wild gutterballs at the evil villains. I mailed it to the return address he puts on his letters—his home address.

But I don't want to do the same with this note. I don't want him to know it's from me. (Although he might. Is my handwriting recognizable?)

The last note Brad sent me was written out on WAVE 104.3 stationery. I grab it out of my suitcase, where I keep all his letters. The station's logo and address are printed in blue ink at the top of the page.

Perfect. I'll send this to him at the radio station.

I tear out a fresh sheet of paper from my notebook. I'm surprised by how easy it is—my handwriting flows neatly across the page as if writing this letter is no big deal at all.

Dear Brad,

Carissa told me she doesn't have real feelings for Ryan. If you ask her to the Winter Formal, I bet she'll say yes.

Sincerely,

Your Fairy Godmother

Chapter 39

Brad

I'm at my locker, hurrying to get my books for class, when I sense a presence beside me.

"Brad."

I turn. Carissa tucks a strand of hair behind her ear and smiles at me, her dangly earrings winking in the sunlight. "Can I talk to you?"

I'm surprised to see her, but I try to act nonchalant. "Sure." I shove my locker closed. "I'm kind of in a hurry, though."

"That's okay, I can walk with you toward the English wing," she says, again catching me off guard—I didn't think she knew my class schedule. Maybe it was a lucky guess.

"What's up?" I ask, falling into step beside her. She's wearing a skirt I've always liked, bright blue with a slit up one side. The sunlight catches the highlights in her hair.

"Well, it's about the Winter Formal," she says.

"Do you need people to help set up the decorations?"

"No, I—"

"I might have to work that night, but I bet I can get the radio station to donate some door prizes. Or at least I could give a shout-out to everyone on air. Maybe somehow the radio could be hooked up to the speakers and we could set a time that I could come on and say, *This one goes out to all the dancing fools at the Buena Vista High Winter Formaaaaal!* That would be cool, huh?"

"Yeah," Carissa says, looking flustered. "I mean, maybe. But listen. This isn't about— the reason I wanted to talk to you was—well, Brad, I was wondering if you wanted to go with me."

"Go with you where?"

"To the Winter Formal. You know, as my date."

I stop in my tracks. "As your *date*?"

"Yes. Why is that so hard to grasp?"

"Well, for one, what about the past three months? What about that guy, Ryan? Last I heard you two were together."

Carissa waves her hand dismissively. "Oh, that's nothing. Old news."

"Sure didn't seem like 'nothing' at Matt's party."

"That was *months* ago."

Despite myself, I'm getting worked up. Carissa's always been able to do this to me. When she argues, she acts like things that happened in the past don't count for squat. "How do I know you won't ditch me at the dance for some other guy?"

Carissa sighs as if I'm the unreasonable one. "Fine, be that way." She steps away from me, then turns back. "I know Rosie will be disappointed, though."

At the mention of Rose's name, my stomach flips. "Rose? Won't she still be in Texas?"

"No, taping ends the week before the dance. I know it would make her really happy if the four of us went together. She thinks of you as a friend, Brad."

"She *is* my friend."

"That's what I'm saying. She'll be bummed if you don't go to the dance. She actually seems excited about the whole thing."

All of a sudden, something clicks in my brain. "Wait, what do you mean *the four of us*? Who's she going with? Holly?"

"No. She's bringing along that guy she's dating, from the show. I forget his name right now. David? Drew?"

The words hang in the air between us.

That guy she's dating, from the show.

That guy. She's dating. From the show.

That guy she's dating.

"I didn't know Rose was dating someone." I feel dazed.

Carissa snaps her fingers. "Daniel! That's his name. Daniel. Yeah, they've been dating a while. Since before she came home to visit. It's pretty cute, actually. Who would have thought, our little Rosie in love!"

Since before she came home to visit. Which means all that time we spent together, when I thought there were sparks between us, she had a boyfriend.

Disappointment cuts through me like a laser.

"Okay, fine," I hear myself saying. I force my attention back to Carissa. "I'd love to go to the dance with you."

Carissa's face brightens. "You would?"

"Sure. As long as you actually want to go with me."

"Of course I do, Brad. I've missed you. I've missed us." She links her arm through mine and leans her head on my shoulder.

Her hair smells like coconut, and her skin is warm against mine. This is exactly what I used to dream about. Carissa Hayward said she misses me. Carissa Hayward wants me back.

But as I meet her beaming smile with a forced smile of my own, my stomach churns. And as Carissa presses her lips against my cheek, Rose's face flashes across my mind.

Chapter 40

Carissa answers mom's phone again when I call.

"Rosie, exciting news!" she says. "Brad and I are going to the Winter Formal together!"

"You are?" My stomach drops. I only sent my letter yesterday. There's no way Brad has received it yet. "That's...great. Wow."

Even though this is what I expected to happen—what I *wanted* to happen—when I wrote Brad that note, I still feel like the breath has been punched out of me.

He didn't need my nudge. He asked Carissa all on his own.

I guess there was still a part of me, even after everything, that hoped it wouldn't happen. A part of me clung to the possibility that I'd read everything wrong and Brad didn't have feelings for Carissa anymore. A part of me thought maybe—just maybe—what I felt between us that day behind the pinball machine, and that night in Brad's car, was actually *something*. Something real.

Carissa's going on and on about how great the dance is going to be. "We can get a limo with everyone, or just the four of us," she says. "What do you think?"

I must have missed something. "Um, what do you mean, the four of us?"

"Me, Brad, you, and Daniel," she says matter-of-factly.

"Wait—me? And Daniel? Why don't you go with your friends like always?"

"Stacey is being super irritating lately. She got into Stanford and now she's acting all stuck-up."

"Stanford? She heard back already?" I sent in my online

applications for the UC schools, but we're not supposed to hear admissions decisions until the spring.

"She applied Early Decision," Carissa explains. "Whatever. She's a snob. Besides, you're my sister. My *twin* sister. We've always promised we'd go to a dance together, and it's almost our last chance."

We promised no such thing. I remember when Brad asked Carissa to Homecoming and she flounced out the door like a princess, barely even glancing at me. She's never wanted to be around me in public before, much less at a school dance. There must be an ulterior motive. Does she want more face-time on TV?

"You know, Caris, the show's going to be over by then. The cameras won't be filming at the dance."

"I know. So that means you can come, right? You'll be home."

I sigh. I'm tired and overwhelmed and I don't have the energy to argue with her anymore. "Dances aren't really my cup of tea."

"C'mon, Rosie. You just never had anyone to go with before. The Winter Formal will be the perfect opportunity to show everyone the new you!"

What *new me*? "I'm the same person I've always been, Carissa."

"Don't say that, sis. Don't get down on yourself. You've lost so much weight! We can go shopping again and find you a killer dress!"

In all our lives, I can't remember Carissa ever calling me "sis" before. She must be really happy. And for some reason, she really wants me to go to this dance. I know her heart is in the right place. Still, I can't help but wonder...would she have wanted to go to Winter Formal with the old me?

I don't think so. I can't imagine her wanting to get a limo for the two of us and our dates.

"The thing is, Rosie..." she says, then hesitates.

"What?"

"Brad seems to think you guys are friends."

At Brad's name, I zoom back into the conversation. "He said that?"

"Well, yeah," Carissa laughs. "Why do you sound surprised?"

"No, we are. We're friends."

"He's hoping the four of us can go to the dance together. I mean, you're pretty much the person we have to thank for us getting back together."

"Oh, don't say that."

"It's true! Your letter is what gave Brad the courage to ask me."

I don't tell her I only sent the letter yesterday.

Carissa lowers her voice conspiratorially. "It's amazing, Rosie," she says. "Breaking up with him was the best thing I ever did. He's a totally different person now."

The computerized voice cuts in. *You have two minutes remaining.* I can't wait for this phone call to be over.

"He's super motivated and responsible and passionate about things. He's got this great job at the radio station—he marched in there himself and convinced them to give him a chance, can you believe it? I never knew he had it in him."

"I did," I say softly.

"And he's strong now, too, Rosie! His arm muscles are like...*whew*! All because he was trying to win me back. He made all these changes in his life. Isn't that the sweetest thing you've ever heard?"

"That is pretty sweet." I want to leap onto a treadmill and run and run and run until I collapse.

"And now it's like he's a completely new person," Carissa says.

You have one minute remaining.

"Listen, Caris, the machine's going to cut me off in a minute—"

"Oh, okay, I should let you go. But promise me you'll come to the Winter Formal?"

A memory flashes into my mind: Holly sitting by herself at Lane 5, waiting for me.

"Only if Holly can come with us, too."

I expect Carissa to sigh or put up a fight. Instead, she laughs.

"That's what Brad told me!" she says. "When we were talking

about getting a limo. He said, 'Don't forget about Holly.' Man, you guys must have really bonded at that bowling part—"

You have thirty seconds remaining.

"Seriously, Carissa, I've gotta go!"

"Right, right. But you'll come? I can buy tickets for you and Daniel?"

I think back to the bowling party, how Holly and Brad and I threw our bowling balls down the lane backwards and upside down. *Brad seems to think you guys are friends.* I remember Brad's unharnessed, contagious laughter as his bowling ball careened wildly against the bumpers, zigzagging toward the pins. *He's hoping the four of us can go to the dance together.*

"Okay, fine," I tell Carissa. "I'll come."

The line goes dead.

✧ ☆ ✧

THE REMAINING days pass by in a blur. Suddenly, here we are, filing into the gym for our final weigh-in, on our final night at camp.

Tomorrow morning we will all board the bus back to the airport. Daniel is flying to L.A. with me so we can go to the Winter Formal together. I'm grateful I don't have to say goodbye to him yet.

I think about the girl I was sixteen weeks ago, sitting alone at the back of the bus. Embarrassed, self-conscious, angry. I wanted to shrivel up and disappear. I felt completely alone in the world.

That seems like a lifetime ago.

I'm not even nervous as I step onto the scale. I've spent hours upon hours in the gym, training as hard as I could. I know I've done my best. And that's all any of us can do, isn't it?

I look out at the others—so much more energetic and vibrant than we were at our first weigh-in all those weeks ago. Even grumpy Tony smiles at me. My heart swells with love for everyone.

Doris shouts, "You go, girl!"

Daniel gives me a thumbs-up.

When the numbers on the scale stop whirring… I can't believe my eyes.

I am actually a pound heavier than I was last week.

Doris gasps.

Daniel hangs his head.

Britta Michaelson's megawatt smile falters. "Oh no, Rosiiiieee!" she exclaims. "I am very disappointed to say that you have actually *gained* weight this week. That means you can no longer win this competition."

Brad's voice fills my mind. *Don't change too much, okay?*

Instead of being filled with disappointment or shame, like I always expected to feel if I gained weight here at camp, I feel…*free.*

I shrug. "Oh well. It's just a number on a scale."

Trainer Mark crosses his arms. "What do you mean, *just* a number on a scale? That scale says a lot about you, Rosie."

"No it doesn't. A number on a scale doesn't define me. It never did."

Trainer Leslie narrows her eyes. "Rosie, it pains me to hear these excuses. Now is not the time to quit. This is a signal to buckle down and work even harder. You can reach your goal weight. You *need* to keep going."

"My goal weight is an arbitrary number that *you* chose for me on this show. Maybe my weight right now is where my body wants to be."

"But—" Leslie tries to interrupt.

I don't let her. "I refuse to live my life obsessing over calories and restricting myself on rigid diets. I'm tired of hating my body. I'm tired of punishing my body." I look at Mark and Leslie. "Don't get me wrong—you've done a lot to help me over the last four months. I'm grateful for all that I've learned and accomplished here. But it's not right, the way you act like our bodies are the enemy to fight against, and hunger is a monster to be controlled."

Mark runs his hand through his coiffed hair. Leslie jabs her finger at me. "Don't let your guard down, Rosie. You'll gain all that weight back again. You'll be right back where you started."

"But that's the thing—I'm not the same person I was when I started on this journey. Or actually, maybe I am. Maybe our time here has been less about transforming ourselves into something new, and more about learning who we truly are deep down inside."

Tony nods, encouraging me to continue.

"I've learned about my strength. About my determination. About all the pain I was trying to push away instead of facing it straight on. Now, I refuse to let fear rule my life. And that includes being terrified of gaining the weight back."

"Well, I'm sure your positive attitude will bounce back once the disappointment wears off," Britta says in an upbeat voice, as if she hasn't heard a single word I've said.

I roll my eyes at her. Instead of looking at the cameras, I address my fellow contestants. My friends.

"Here's my plan going forward. I'm choosing to treat my body with kindness. I'm choosing to eat food that nourishes me...and also food that I want to eat simply because it's delicious. A cupcake isn't evil, y'all!"

Daniel smiles.

"I'm choosing to lift weights because doing so makes me feel strong. I'm choosing to run because running helps me clear my head. If there's a day I don't exercise, that's okay! If there's a meal where I eat a bit too much and feel a bit too full, that's okay too! I'm human. I'm learning. I'm in a lifelong relationship with my body, and I want it to be a *healthy* relationship based in love."

Mark and Leslie gape at me.

Britta sputters, "That's not—I mean, it's not—"

"What I'm trying to say is: I understand that I can't win the competition anymore. But I think I'm still a winner. In the way that really matters."

I look once more at the numbers on the scale, and pump my fist in the air.

The other contestants erupt into cheers. Doris applauds like she's at a Broadway show. Daniel lets out a loud wolf whistle.

I jog down off the scale to my place beside Daniel, who picks me up and whirls me around.

For the first time in as long as I can remember, I am completely at peace in my own skin. There is no one in the world I would rather be.

Not even Carissa.

Chapter 41

This time, I make sure I'm there at the airport when Rose arrives back home. I blast The Beatles and the Rolling Stones during the drive there, singing along and trying to dispel my nerves. I can't help thinking about how different everything was four months ago when I drove to the airport with the rest of Carissa's family to see Rose off on her flight to Texas. I remember giving her a hug and telling her, "Don't forget about me." I'd meant to say "us"—"Don't forget about us!"—but for some reason "me" came out instead.

But now I think my subconscious knew exactly what it was saying. It was *me* I was talking about. Only me. I knew deep down that Rose was the one I should be with. The one who understood me, who laughed *with* me instead of *at* me, who I felt comfortable with even when I was being a complete dork.

"Don't forget about me!" I knew she wouldn't. Rose is the last person who would get a big ego. Even being a star on national TV couldn't change that.

But I guess, in a way, she did forget about me. She has a boyfriend. I already know I'm gonna hate the guy.

I park, grab the bouquet from the passenger seat, and jog across the street to the terminal. I don't know if Rose likes sunflowers, but I wanted to bring her something to welcome her back home, and the cheerful yellow petals reminded me of her.

When I round the corner into the arrivals area, I stop in my tracks. Hundreds of people spill out into the corridor, waving banners and holding balloons. Some people are even wearing T-shirts printed with Rose's beautiful face. In the middle of the mess I glimpse three cameras, capturing it all for TV.

I'm glancing around for one of those arrivals information screens when the crowd noise surges. I look over.

There she is.

Rose.

She strides into baggage claim, her radiant smile lighting up the drab airport. The crowd cheers and applauds. Next to me, a couple of middle-aged ladies gasp and exclaim how amazing she looks. "She's a different person after losing all that weight!" To me, she looks like the same Rose, only happier. I want so badly to push my way through the crowd and enfold her in a giant hug.

Rose stops and puts a hand on her chest, clearly taken aback by this huge mob of people shouting her name. I watch her eyes search the crowd, and then she must see her parents and Carissa and Scotty because she waves. I call out her name, too, even though there's no way she can hear me. No way she can see me, all the way back here. The sunflowers are heavy in my sweaty hand.

Rose reaches back and ushers a guy forward beside her. He lifts up their joined hands in celebration. The crowd erupts with more cheers. This must be *the guy*. I immediately size him up: medium build, medium height, short-cropped hair, wide smile. It pains me to admit it, but he looks like a nice guy. Friendly. Genuine. He says something in Rose's ear and she laughs. Great, he must be funny, too.

The crowd presses around me. I need air. I need space. I escape to the bathroom, still holding the stupid flowers. I set them down on one of the sinks and stand there looking at myself in the mirror.

My haircut has grown out. My arms are a little more muscular from working out at the gym. Maybe I have smidges of dark circles under my eyes from all those sunrise runs and early mornings at the radio station. But otherwise I look exactly the same as I did when Carissa broke up with me four months ago.

Am I the same person I was then?

Do I want to be?

In my pocket, my phone buzzes. I pull it out. *CARISSA*. She hasn't called me in forever. Why is she calling now?

"Hello?"

"Brad!" I can barely hear her voice over the background noise of the crowd. "Are you here?"

"Where?" I ask, buying time.

"At the airport! Our little Rosie's back home!"

I'm not in the mood to see Carissa right now. Should I lie and sneak out before anyone knows the difference?

"Rosie! It's Brad, on the phone!" There's a garble of noise. The next thing I know, Rose's voice is in my ear.

"Hello?" she says. "Brad?"

"Hey!" I know there's no way I can lie to Rose. At the sound of her voice, I'm filled with eagerness to see her. Even if it's only from a distance. I grab the sunflowers. "I'm here at the airport. Look at this crowd. You really are famous, Miss Hayward!"

"Thanks. Ahh, this is unbelievable! I can't wait to see you."

In the mirror, I catch my own smile. "You too. I had to miss your last homecoming, there was no way I'd miss this one."

"Sorry, I can't really hear you. Are you still here?"

"Yeah, I'm here."

"Will you wait out front? Don't leave yet, okay?"

"Okay," I tell her, but there's more noise and garbled voices, and then Carissa comes back on.

"Brad, wait there!! I'm coming!!" she shouts before the connection ends.

Adrenaline back in full force, I book it out of the restroom and slip out of the terminal with the beginning-to-disperse crowd. I wait on the sidewalk right outside the sliding glass doors, pacing in nervous circles. Trying to think of the perfect thing to say when I see Rose and hand her the flowers. I hope it's not too weird, with her boyfriend here. I didn't really factor him into the equation. Maybe I'll keep it simple and just say, *Welcome home.* Or would *Congratulations* be better? Can I say, *These made me think of you*, or is that too much?

It seems like I wait forever. I lean against the wall. I stand up and pace around some more.

Finally, the doors whoosh open and two camera guys come out, walking backward, camera lights blinking. The whole Hayward clan follows close behind, plus Holly and a couple of Carissa's friends who I know for a fact have never been nice to Rose. Whatever. Rose walks between her parents, who both have their arms around her. Her mom is crying. Scotty is skipping. Holly is deep in conversation with *the guy*. Carissa, Stacey, and Mel are laughing about something.

Rose is the first to spot me. Our eyes meet and it is magnetic. I take a few steps forward, the sunflowers behind my back, feeling shy and speechless. Which is weird, because I'm never speechless. Rose disengages from her parents and heads in my direction.

"Hi," she says.

"Hi." I look into her honey brown eyes, as kind and open as ever. "Welcome home."

"Thanks."

"Brad!" Carissa screeches, running over. "I knew you'd come! Doesn't Rosie look amazing?? Can you believe how much she's changed?"

"You're beautiful," I tell Rose, but I'm mumbling, and my words are overpowered by Carissa's shout when she sees the flowers I'm holding.

"Brad! You didn't have to get me flowers!" Before I can explain, she wraps her arms around me and kisses me. In front of everyone.

In front of Rose.

I remember when kissing Carissa Hayward felt like I'd won a huge prize. Like I'd managed not to screw anything up that day, and my reward was being allowed to kiss this gorgeous girl. But right now, everything feels wrong. There is a giant pit in my stomach, and Carissa's lips are slick and oily, and I just want to rewind this, rewind everything. I want a do-over. I want to explain.

I pull away, dizzy. I try to meet Rose's eyes, but she's turned away, looking at Holly and *the guy*.

"Brad and I are back together!" Carissa announces to everyone. Her parents beam at us. Scotty does a ninja kick. Carissa thrusts the flowers at Stacey and Mel. "See, you guys? I told you he's changed! The old Brad would *never* have brought me flowers for no reason!"

I clear my throat to say something, but I have no idea what to say.

The guy walks over and slips his arm around Rose's waist. He reaches out his hand for me to shake. "Hey man, I'm Daniel. I've heard a lot about you."

"I'm Brad. Nice to meet you." Even his handshake is friendly—not too firm, not too soft. This guy wins the freaking Goldilocks' Bears Award for everything.

"You wanna come over?" Carissa asks, fiddling with my belt loop. "I can ride home with you."

Rose still won't look at me.

"Uh, you know, I can't. Sorry. I have work." I need to get back to my car, alone, as quickly as possible. I need to figure out what to do.

"Thanks for coming," Rose says. She's smiling at me, but the smile doesn't reach her eyes. "I know you're busy and everything."

"Oh, I wouldn't have missed it." I swallow. There's so much I want to say to her, but not here, not now. The best I can come up with is, "See you at the gym tomorrow morning?"

"Yep," Rose says. "Daniel and I will be there right when it opens."

"You betcha!" Daniel says. He gives me a thumbs-up. As much as I want to hate him, I can't.

"See you soon, Brad!" Carissa calls after me. "We're gonna have the best time at Winter Formal!"

Somehow, I doubt it.

Chapter 42

I can't believe I actually agreed to go to this dance. We haven't even left the house and I'm already nervous. Everyone is coming over for photos, and then we're taking a limo together to the Hotel Del Mar, where the high school has rented out the ballroom for the dance. I told Carissa it was fine if her friends came in the limo with us, but I guess Leo and Stacey broke up a few weeks ago, and now there's tension in the group. Mel and Stacey are going to the dance with some football jocks, so they're taking other transportation. Carissa said the football team is renting a bus. I thought she was joking; now I'm not so sure.

So now Leo and Holly are going to the dance together, and they're both coming with us in the limo. Plus Brad and Carissa. And me and Daniel. All squeezed together in the limo like a big happy family. Yippee.

I'm not the only one who's stressed out; Carissa has seemed anxious all day. She's probably worried about whether the juniors on the Winter Formal committee can handle putting up the decorations properly. My sister likes being in charge almost as much as she likes being the center of attention—in other words, a lot. I feel bad for these poor juniors who have probably been dealing with her micro-manage-y texts all day.

To be fair, the Winter Formal is a slightly bigger deal than I expected. It's a whole event: dinner, dessert, dancing. I told Carissa I only signed on for dancing, not an entire meal. She laughed and rolled her eyes. I wasn't completely joking, though. I'm nervous that everyone is going to be scrutinizing—and judging—what I eat.

Holly and I get ready together in my room. Carissa's secluded herself in the downstairs bathroom, probably preparing to make a big entrance. Holly is wearing an elegant wrap dress with beaded black flowers scattered across the fabric. Its gorgeous dark blue color brings out the blue in her eyes.

"You look stunning," I say. "That shade of blue is Daniel's favorite color."

"Really?"

"Yeah. Random piece of information, sorry—all I meant is that he's going to love your dress. And I know Leo will, too." I always ramble when I'm nervous.

Holly smiles at herself in the mirror, but then she bites her lip and turns away.

"What's wrong?" I ask.

"Oh, nothing—I just—can I use your bathroom?"

"Of course. Are you feeling okay?"

"Yeah, I'm fine. A little nervous, I guess."

"Leo is so lucky to be going with you!"

Holly waves my words away, but I grab her hand.

"I mean it. And I'm lucky, too. Thank you so much for coming to the dance. I really couldn't do this without you."

Holly nods, looking me in the eyes. "I'm always here for you," she says, her voice serious. "You're my best friend." She releases my hand and heads into the bathroom. "Now change into your dress!" she calls over her shoulder.

My dress was a gift from the show producers—sent *before* my big speech during final weigh-in. I doubt they'll be sending any gifts now. I wonder how much of my speech, if any, will even make it past the cutting-room floor.

That's okay. I didn't give that speech for the world to hear. Those were words I needed to say for *myself*.

I untie my cozy bathrobe, slip it off, and step into the dress. I wiggle it up over my hips and slide the straps up onto my shoulders. All that's left is to zip up the side zipper, tie the sash in a bow in the back, smooth down the front...and look up into the mirror.

"Whoa," Holly says from behind me. "Rose. That dress is *amazing.* You look so beautiful."

The dress is made from a shimmery, light purple fabric that reminds me of fairies or princesses. It hugs my curves in all the right places. Impulsively, I spin around, and the skirt twirls like something out of a movie.

Holly steps up next to me. Our reflections gaze back at us: a tall, curly-haired princess in a midnight blue dress, and a slightly shorter, dark-haired fairy in lavender.

"You've always been beautiful," Holly says. "It just took you a while to see it." She points at the mirror. "Same beautiful hair, same beautiful eyes, same beautiful smile...where's that beautiful smile? ... There it is. Same beautiful spirit."

I lay my head on her shoulder. "Thanks."

After a few moments, I blink away the tears from my eyes and we get started on make-up.

✧ ✩ ✧

THE DOORBELL RINGS, and a couple minutes later there's a knock on my bedroom door.

"You girls ready?" Daniel says through the door. "I've been instructed to bring you both downstairs for pictures."

"Just a sec!"

Holly and I grab our clutches and slip on our shoes, and then I open the door with a flourish. "Ta da!"

"Wow," Daniel says, his eyes wide. "You ladies are breathtaking."

"Looking good yourself," I tell him, slipping my arm through his.

When we come downstairs, my parents are already taking pictures in the front hallway of Carissa and Brad, standing close together. Carissa looks perfect as ever in a short, red strapless number. And Brad is her prince. It's like last year's Prom all over again. A surge of panic rises up in my throat. *Why am I doing this?*

I didn't know that Brad and Carissa were back together until yesterday at the airport. I guess I should have expected it, since they're going to Winter Formal together. But somehow I didn't compute that they're officially a couple again until that big kiss yesterday. It killed me, seeing that. You'd think I'd be used to it by now. But it made me feel like a complete idiot—like the connection I've felt with Brad these past few months was only pretend. Our friendship was merely a side effect of Brad trying to get Carissa back. He even brought her flowers. Sunflowers! My favorite flowers, ever since Carissa stole roses from me as her favorite flower in seventh grade.

The point is, as much as things have changed, some things are unchangeable. Brad has made it very clear that he is still in love with my sister. My sister is still the complete opposite of me.

Plus, I have a boyfriend now.

Case closed. Right?

Right.

I squeeze Daniel's arm. "I'm so glad you're here," I whisper.

"What?" he says loudly.

That's when Brad looks up and sees us on the stair landing. His eyes meet mine, and sparks explode inside me. I look down, pushing them away. But I can sense his eyes still on me. Does he think I'm pretty?

Not that it matters.

"Look at you girls!" my mom exclaims as we continue down the stairs. "And you too, Daniel, very handsome. Let's take a group shot! Holly, dear, why don't you go stand over there by Leonard? C'mon, Rosie and Daniel, squeeze in there right next to Brad, that's it. A little more. Good. Everyone say cheese!"

I'm standing so close to Brad, I can smell his spicy cologne. I can sense him breathing in and out.

"Smile!" my mom says.

The fabric of his suit jacket brushes against my bare arm.

"C'mon, Rosie—a real smile!" my dad says.

I lift up the corners of my smile as best I can, trying to steer my thoughts toward Daniel. And Holly. My real friends.

"One more! Rosie blinked in the last one. Smile, everyone!"

I can already tell this is going to be a long night.

Finally, we are released from posing for photos.

"You kids be safe!" my mom says as we make our way out the door.

"Have a blast!" my dad chimes in.

"Oh, don't worry, we will," Carissa says, her arm looped through Brad's. "It's going to be the best night ever!"

Somehow, I doubt it.

Chapter 43
Brad

Carissa, Mel, and Stacey are whispering together, analyzing what every girl is wearing and gossiping about who came with who. Leo is over at another table, talking to his tennis teammates. Holly and Daniel are laughing together about some obscure TV show they both watch.

I stand up from the table. "I'm gonna get more punch. Do you want some?" I ask Rose.

"I'll come with you," she says, and my heart leaps.

She smells like vanilla, and her purple dress shimmers against her golden skin. I can't believe how lucky Daniel is to be here with her.

As we walk across the room to the punch table, Rose asks about my radio show. I tell her about last week, when I got my first caller and was so excited I nearly fell out of my chair—but it was some guy with the wrong number trying to order a pizza. Rose laughs so hard she snorts, which makes me laugh too.

"Stop laughing at me," she says, lightly smacking my arm. "That's so embarrassing."

"It's not embarrassing."

"Yes it is! And it's your fault. You're the only one who makes me snort."

"Well, it's adorable," I say, filling up a glass with red punch. I hand it to her and begin filling up my own.

A couple girls I don't know come up and fawn over Rose. "Oh my gosh, you look *so* great! How much weight did you lose?" one asks.

"What was it like to be on TV?" the other says. "Did you get to meet Mark Stone?"

"Oh my gosh! He's so hot! What's he like in real life?"

Rose answers their questions graciously, but I notice her right eye twitch.

"Hey," I interject. "Sorry, ladies. Rose, can you help me with something?"

"Sure," she says, looking surprised.

The girls smile and nod their goodbyes, then flutter away.

All of a sudden, the lights in the room dim and music thumps from the speakers. Strobe lights flash around the dance floor.

"I guess the dancing's started," I say.

"Yeah." Rose doesn't sound particularly enthused.

"Don't you like to dance?"

"Not really. I always feel self-conscious. This is the first dance I've been to."

"Why didn't you come with us to Prom last year?" I ask.

Rose gives me this *look*. "I wasn't exactly invited," she says quietly.

I am a total idiot. "I'm sure you're a great dancer."

She shrugs. "Anyway. What do you need my help with?"

"Oh. Nothing. I was trying to rescue you from those vulture girls. Also, my ego was getting a little bruised hearing you all talk about how hot that trainer guy, Mark, is. Especially when you've got me right here." I flex my nonexistent biceps. Well, not so nonexistent as they used to be, but still pretty meager compared to the football players, and definitely compared to a professional trainer like Mark Stone.

Rose laughs and squeezes my arm. "Pretty good," she says. "You're definitely not as scrawny as you used to be."

"Hey! Let's see you, then."

She grins and flexes her bicep for me—and, wow, she's got muscle. I don't even have to pretend to be impressed. I place my fingers on her smooth skin.

"Okay," I say. "You've got me beat."

"That's right. You better be nice to me, or I'll beat you up." Is she flirting with me? *Stop it,* I tell myself. *Don't get your hopes up.* She has a boyfriend. We've always teased each other like this.

"You actually *can* help me with something," I tell her as we make our way back to our dinner table. "You can come on the dance floor and help me decide if I do a better robot or lawnmower."

"What about the shopping cart?" she says. "Or, pretty much my only dance move: raising the roof."

"Don't knock raising the roof. That's respectable." We arrive back at our table, and it's empty. Pretty much all the tables around us are empty, too.

"I guess everyone's out dancing," Rose says.

"Well, let's go then." I hold out my hand.

Her smile fades. "I told you, I'm not a big dancer."

"C'mon. It'll be fun."

"No, you can go. I'll come later." She takes a sip of her punch. She does this cute thing where she drinks from the straw at the side of her mouth.

"What?" she says. I guess I'm staring.

"Will you save a dance for me?" I ask.

Rose's eye does the twitchy thing again. She opens her mouth as if she's going to say something, then decides against it. Instead, she sits down at the table.

I sit down beside her. "Did I say something wrong?"

"No, no. Of course not. I'd love to dance with you later."

"Promise?"

"Promise."

We sit there in silence for a few moments, drinking our punch, looking out at the dance floor. I spot Carissa freak-dancing with Stacey, both of them belting out the lyrics. Some rap song. I don't know it.

"School dances would be a lot better if they played The Beatles," I announce.

Rose smiles at me. "Agreed. Or the Rolling Stones."

"Or James Taylor."

"James Taylor is my favorite! Back in middle school Carissa used to swoon over Harry Styles while I'd be in my room daydreaming to James Taylor."

"What's your favorite James Taylor song?" I ask.

"Oh, I don't know. He has so many good ones."

"C'mon, you've gotta have a favorite."

Rose rests her chin on her hand. "Probably 'Something in the Way She Moves.' I always thought it sounded so nice—to be loved like that."

"Yeah, I know that song. That's a good one." I hum the first few bars, but I don't know if Rose can hear me over the pulsing beat of the rap music.

Rose gazes out at the dance floor. Is she searching for Daniel? Does she want me to stop talking her ear off? I sit back in my chair. I love talking with her, but I don't want to be obnoxious.

Then Rose murmurs something I can't hear.

"What?" I lean closer.

"I said, I don't know what she's talking about."

"Who?"

Rose points out at the dance floor. "My sister. She keeps going on and on about how much you've changed. She's wrong. You're, like, the only person here who hasn't changed."

"What do you mean?"

"You and Holly are the only two people who treat me the same. Like I'm still the same person I was before the show."

"You *are* the same person."

Rose looks down and doesn't say anything.

"Hey. You *are* the same person. You're still Rose. You're still funny and smart and beautiful—"

Her eyes well up with tears. "Look, you can cut the crap, okay?"

"What? I'm being honest."

"You didn't think I was beautiful before."

"Yes, you were."

"Save it, Brad. You never gave me one thought before all this happened."

I stare at her, words crammed up inside me. Too many words to get a single one out.

She shakes her head. "I really thought you were different, but you're not—you're the same as everyone else. Saying how beautiful I am now, like it's a big surprise."

She turns away, setting her half-finished glass of punch down on the table.

"Rose, wait!" I touch her arm.

She won't meet my eyes. "I should go find my boyfriend."

The word *boyfriend* is a blade in my gut. Before I can think of something else to say, something to keep her with me, to apologize for whatever it is I said wrong, she's left the table, threading her way through the crowd of bodies on the dance floor. I watch the back of her dark hair slip away from me, until she's disappeared into the crowd and I can't distinguish her from anyone else.

Chapter 44

I push my way through the crowd of dancing bodies, searching for Daniel, tears stinging my eyes. I know Brad didn't mean to hurt my feelings. I could see the surprise and apology on his face when I stormed away. It's not his fault that being here has made me an emotional wreck. I guess seeing him and Carissa back together is harder than I thought it would be. I guess I'm not as over him as I thought I was.

Will I ever be able to let go of my feelings for him? Is it possible to reconfigure your desires, to take the emotional pull you feel toward one person and redirect it toward someone else? Because I want so badly not to be feeling this way about Brad.

Oh, Holly—where are you? In the flashing strobe lights, everyone is a ghost. Being in this mob of people is disorienting. I can't even remember which direction I came from—where the punch table is, where our dinner table is. I plunge forward in the direction that feels right.

I part through the last of the crowd and there, in front of me, is Daniel. He's talking with Holly, and his face is radiant. He's never looked at me that way.

Holly is laughing, her eyes on his. She looks so incredibly happy. I've never seen her laughing with a guy like this.

She likes him, I realize with a jolt. *She is majorly crushing on him.*

Daniel is glowing. He touches her bare shoulder.

He likes her, too.

Something about it makes sense. Maybe all along, I felt so comfortable with Daniel because his essence reminded me of Holly. Deep down, maybe I knew I was bringing him here to meet her.

I'm only standing ten feet away, but neither of them is aware of my existence. They are the only two people in the world.

I turn and flee before either of them spots me.

Holly is looking at Daniel the way he deserves to be looked at.

The way I should be looking at him.

The way I look at Brad.

Outside, I make my way through the rose garden, my pinchy-toed shoes crunching on the gravel path. I'm uncomfortable and wobbly walking in heels, so after a few steps I slip them off and walk barefoot. The night air is cool on my bare shoulders and arms, a relief after the stifling dance floor. I sit down on the ledge of a fountain and dip my toes in the water.

I'm not sure how long I sit there, watching the water trickle down and down, trying to empty my mind.

"Rosie?"

I look over.

Daniel. Alone. I give a little wave and pull my feet out of the fountain, turning around to face him. The gravel sticks to the wet soles of my feet.

"Are you okay?" he says, sitting down beside me on the fountain ledge. "What are you doing out here all by yourself?"

"Oh, just getting away for a minute. It's so hot in there."

"Well, I'm glad I found you. I missed you." Daniel sits down beside me.

No you didn't, I want to tell him. *It's okay. You don't have to pretend.* I tug at my dress. "Everyone's staring at me."

"They're staring because you look amazing."

"Thanks. But I don't know. It's strange."

"What's strange?"

"All this attention. I'm not used to it."

"Maybe you *should* get used to it."

"It seems fake. I don't trust it." Except for Holly, everyone at school used to act like I was invisible. And now they're walking across the room to say hi to me. The whole night has been surreal, and not in a good way. Not the way I imagined it would be.

I want Daniel to understand. Maybe he can help me feel like myself again, rather than a strange imposter in a sequined gown. "So many people have told me how pretty I am now. It's weird."

"It's not weird," Daniel says. "You earned it. I knew you'd blow them all away."

I'm at the Winter Formal with my boyfriend who is sweet and handsome. I'm wearing a glamorous dress that zips up all the way without me having to suck in my breath, and everyone keeps gushing over how beautiful I look. So I should be happy, right? I should be overjoyed right now.

But instead, there is a wrenching hollowness in my gut, and as Daniel squeezes my hand, I have to concentrate very hard to keep from crying.

"Did you think I was pretty before?" I ask. "When you first met me. Did you think I was pretty then?"

"Of course I did."

"As pretty as I am now?"

"Well, c'mon Rosie—look at you. You've worked so hard and lost so much weight." He cups my chin with his palm, tilts my face up so my eyes meet his. "The Rosie I met the first day at camp is like the Daniel I was back then. When I looked at you, I saw the person you could become. I saw the potential buried inside you, like you saw the potential inside of me."

I think of the Daniel I met that day on the gingham-striped couch in the common room. The round red cheeks are gone. He has a fresh haircut. But his green eyes are the same. And his smile—his smile was as contagious then as it is now.

But I don't say any of that. Instead, I stare at the flecks of gold in his green eyes and say, "Like, before I was an ugly duckling...and now I'm a swan?"

"Well, you were never ugly," Daniel says. "But, yeah, I guess you could put it that way. You've transformed, Rosie. You're definitely a swan now." He brushes a strand of hair from my forehead. "A beautiful swan."

The fountain gurgles softly behind us, and the stars wink down from above. I want to feel giddy butterflies when Daniel squeezes my hand. I want to feel the world condense to only the two of us when he kisses me. Because Daniel is a wonderful guy. He is kind and thoughtful. He makes me laugh. He's been there for me these past four months, struggling through workouts together, buoying me up with his optimism and shouts of encouragement.

He is the one who *should* understand me best. He is the person I *should* be with. Who I *should* want to be with.

But, try as I might, I don't love Daniel. And I don't think I ever will.

Or, that's not quite right, because I do love him—but as a friend. I am not *in love* with him.

I pull my hand away. "Daniel, I need to tell you something."

And I let the truth spill out.

Chapter 45

Carissa keeps trying to get me to dance, but I'm not in the mood. The dance floor is crammed with sweaty people, and the DJ is playing some techno crap that is giving me a headache. I'm a horrible dancer with no rhythm, and around Carissa I am self-conscious and clumsy. She dances up against me. Her hair tickles my face. She grabs my hands and puts them on her hips.

I feel sick. I keep thinking of the hurt and anger on Rose's face. *Look, you can cut the crap, okay?*

She's right. I am full of crap. The truth? It's not that I don't want to dance. It's that I don't want to dance with Carissa. If Rose wanted to dance, I would dance with her all night.

"I'm gonna get some air," I tell Carissa.

"What?" she shouts, holding onto my hand.

I pull away and point toward our table. She follows me off the dance floor.

"Seriously, Brad, what is your problem tonight?" she says when we're far enough away from the booming speakers to hear each other.

"What do you mean?" I say, even though I know exactly what she means.

"You're on some other planet. You don't even look at me, you don't seem to notice me. I thought this would be like when we went to Homecoming and Prom. I thought we were back together."

I run my hand over my hair. I really don't want to do this here, in the middle of the Winter Formal, but I'm tired of lying. I'm tired of pretending. I'm tired of trying to be someone I'm not, trying to make myself feel the way I used to, when the truth is that I don't. Not anymore.

Rose's words echo in my head. *Look, you can cut the crap, okay?*

"The thing is, Carissa..."

I force myself to meet her eyes. And I'm surprised what I find there. Her eyes are hopeful. Vulnerable. Like her mask has slipped off and I can see the person underneath. For the first time in a long time, I glimpse that girl I met last year in the school office, when we did morning announcements side-by-side.

I owe it to that girl to be honest.

"I think you're incredible," I tell her. "And I'll always treasure the memories we have. But...my feelings have changed."

The mask drops back down. Her expression hardens. "What are you saying, Brad?"

I swallow. "I think we're better off as friends."

"Are you kidding me?" she shrieks. "Are you seriously giving me the *just friends speech* right now? Get away from me! Get away!"

"Carissa, I'm sorry—"

"Don't. Even." She leans in, pointing her finger inches from my face. "You know the only reason I went to this dance with you is because I felt sorry for you. And now you try to break up with me in front of everyone to humiliate me and get your stupid revenge. I never should have trusted you, Brad Hoffman. You are a loser. You haven't changed one bit. You'll always be a loser!" She's shouting now. Are those tears in her eyes? She whirls away from me and storms toward the bathrooms.

I watch her go with a swirling mix of sadness and guilt and relief. So this is what it feels like to do the right thing, even when it's hard.

Maybe this is what Carissa felt when she broke up with me at the Dairy Queen. That day seems like eons ago. In my initial shock, I couldn't see our break-up as anything more than a terrible mistake. But I understand now that Carissa was only trying to be honest. With herself, and with me. It's obvious that Carissa and I are not right for each other. She simply realized it before I did.

That summer day, when it felt like she ruined my life, maybe Carissa was simply trying to do the right thing even when it was hard.

I make my way back to our group's dinner table, strewn with half-eaten slices of cake and lipgloss-imprinted coffee cups. Holly sits by herself, gazing out at the dance floor. I still don't know her all that well. It's hard to read her expression. Is she upset about something? Sad? Just tired?

"Where's Leo?" I ask, sitting down beside her.

"Oh, he's out there somewhere, dancing with Stacey." She gives me a little half-smile.

Leo, really? You abandoned your date at the dance for another girl? Much less a snarkfest like Stacey?

"Leo's an idiot." I stand up and reach for Holly's hand. "C'mon, do you want to dance with me?"

She shakes her head, waves me back down into my seat. "Thanks, that's sweet of you, but I'm okay. Leo's nice and all, but he and I never really had a love connection. I'm only here because Rose needed me."

"Same," I murmur.

Holly rolls her eyes. "Look, Brad, I know you and Rose have become friends, but that makes it even weirder when you try to act like there's nothing going on between you and Carissa. The whole school knows you're back together. You're not at this dance for Rose; you're here for Carissa."

I shake my head. "First of all, Carissa and I are not back together. We just broke up again."

Holly's eyes widen. "She broke up with you *again*?!"

"No, I broke up with her this time. If we were even back together at all." I'm flustered, like the brainwaves are jumbled between my thoughts and mouth. "The only reason I came to this stupid dance with Carissa is because Rose wanted me to."

Holly laughs like I've said the most ridiculous thing in the world. "Rose would never want that."

"Yes, she would. She did. She told Carissa, and Carissa told me." I think about the way Rose whirled away, the hurt in her eyes, the way she said, *I should go find my boyfriend* as if *boyfriend* was the complete opposite of me. I sigh. "She probably wanted to rub it in my face that she has a boyfriend now and I lost my chance."

Holly tilts her head slightly to the side. She looks at me as if she's never seen me before.

"What?" I finally ask her.

"Did you just say what I think you said?"

I fiddle with an abandoned dessert fork, drawing invisible patterns on the cream-colored tablecloth.

"Because it sounded," Holly continues, "like you want to be with Rose."

I shrug. "It doesn't matter. She has a boyfriend."

Sadness floods back into Holly's face. "I guess now we both know how Rose used to feel, huh?"

"Yeah." I take a long sip of punch.

Then her words sink in. I set my glass back down on the table.

"Wait—what? What do you mean, *how Rose used to feel?*"

Holly rolls her eyes again. "C'mon, Brad," she says. "Use your brain. You know exactly what I mean."

And suddenly, it's like my life is a giant puzzle and the last two pieces snap into place. Those conversations I had with Rose in the kitchen as I waited for Carissa to come downstairs. The night I drove Rose home from the radio station, when I felt that charge between us and could have sworn she felt it, too. The tears welling up in her eyes when she said, *You never gave me one thought before all this happened.*

Holly looks at me like I'm an idiot, but there's a hint of a smile in her eyes.

"Are you saying...*me?*" I ask her. "Rose felt that way about me?"

Holly leans in closer. "You're the reason Rose needed me to come to this stupid dance. It was too hard for her, seeing you and Carissa back together. She needed me here as moral support."

I think of my dad in that hospital room with the chemo treatments dripping into his veins. I think of my mom, covering him with a blanket when he falls asleep in his recliner—the most comfortable spot in the house, he says—and how sometimes my mom will sit there in a chair beside him, holding his hand as he sleeps. *No regrets, son. All you get to take with you at the end are the memories you made with the people you care about.*

I stand up from the table. "I've got to find her."

Holly points to the door. "I think she went outside. With Daniel."

I glance over. "Isn't that him coming in now?"

Holly follows my gaze. "Yeah, it is. Huh."

"Rose isn't with him," I say.

"So... I guess now's your chance."

I take a few steps away from the table, but then a thought hits me. I run back. "Hey, Holly?"

She looks up in surprise. "Yeah?"

"You're a really good friend."

She smiles. "Thanks."

"What did you mean when you said that we *both* know how Rose used to feel? I thought you didn't like Leo that way."

"I don't. It's—" She waves me away. "It doesn't matter. Now, go! Find her!"

I squeeze her hand as a thank you. And then I'm off.

Chapter 46

The truth is, I liked Brad for more than a year before he started dating Carissa. I sat behind him in World History. Whenever he passed back papers, he wouldn't fling his arm backward over his head like most guys do. No, Brad would always turn and flash me a smile as he handed over whatever photocopied worksheets or reading material we were assigned that day. Sometimes he'd ask a question about the homework or make a quip about our teacher, the terrifying Miss Gustaf, who was always snapping her ruler against the side of someone's desk and shouting at us, "Wake up, people!"

I found myself looking forward to fifth-period World History all day, and on Fridays I would feel a twinge of sadness that it would be two full days before I saw him again. Looking back, it was pretty obvious I was smitten.

But I kept my feelings buried. I didn't even admit to myself that I was crushing on Brad until Homecoming, when he came to our house to pick up Carissa. A huge pit opened up in my stomach as I watched him carefully slip the corsage onto her wrist. In that moment, I wanted more than anything to be my sister.

That was when I knew I had a problem. Because I'd sworn to myself that I wouldn't go down that road. Not again. I had spent pretty much all of middle school envying Carissa and wishing I were more like her. That road only led to disappointment.

In sixth grade, Bobby Mayers asked me to the end-of-the-year dance. I was giddy with excitement. I hadn't expected to be asked to the dance, and Bobby Mayers was one of the cute boys on the basketball team. I didn't have a crush on him before he asked me to the dance, but I developed one immediately. During the first slow song, he put his arms on my waist and looked into my eyes. I remember how happy I was in that moment. It was a pure, innocent happiness. And then Bobby shattered it by saying, "So, what's your sister like? Do you think she would go out with me?"

It was like I'd been punched in the stomach. He'd only asked me to the dance because Carissa was already taken. I spent the rest of the dance alone in a bathroom stall, crying and texting Holly.

The rest of middle school was a vicious cycle of hopes and heartbreaks: in my eyes, I never measured up to Carissa, and the more time that passed and the more I kept trying, the worse and worse I felt about myself.

And the worse I felt about myself, the more I turned to food for comfort.

It's hard to pinpoint exactly when or how my weight issues began. As long as I can remember, Carissa and I have been locked into roles. She's the outgoing one, while I'm the shy one. She's always had a wide circle of friends, while I'm more comfortable in small groups of people. I guess at some point, those personality traits turned to physical traits in my mind: Carissa was the pretty, popular twin, while I was...the quiet, overweight twin.

Like many things, my weight gain began slowly—at first, unnoticeably. I'd played soccer and basketball as a kid, but I wasn't good enough to make the middle school teams, so I stopped exercising as much. I got really into baking, and pretty soon I was busting out my mixing bowls and measuring spoons as soon as I got home from school. Baking was something Carissa had no interest in—something I had entirely to myself. And I was good at it! Holly and my parents raved about my homemade icing. I searched for the most outlandish recipes I could find and resolved to try them all. Pretty soon, one small taste of each dish I made as it cooled on the counter had snowballed into snacking on cupcakes before dinner.

At some point, I began eating as a way to try to fill a deeper hunger inside of me. More like an emptiness. And it only got worse when Carissa started dating Brad. It was easier and safer to stay inside the role of "the fat, shy bookworm"—not risking anything. That way, I always had an excuse for why things weren't the way I wanted them to be. It was easier to tell myself the reason I had never been kissed or asked out on a date was because of my weight. Being overweight was the scapegoat for all my problems.

I remember how Doris asked me if I only liked Brad because, deep down, I wanted something that was Carissa's. I was worried she was right. But it's actually the opposite. For so long, I've been trying to push away my feelings for Brad because of Carissa. For so long, I've been trying to build a completely different identity for myself other than Carissa Hayward's sister. I didn't want to be anything like her. I didn't want anything she had. I was tired of being compared to her. Tired of competing with her. Tired of judging my own identity as her twin.

So I kept pushing away my feelings for Brad. I told myself that if he wanted to be with Carissa, then I didn't want to be with him. I tried to pretend that my crush was a silly little fantasy and that I was completely over it. Deep down, I think I wanted Daniel to be my boyfriend as a way to convince myself that I had moved on from Brad. Daniel and I should have only been friends all along.

These past few months I've been imagining that as I lost weight, I would shed my feelings for Brad too. But somehow, my pull toward him has only grown stronger.

Now I don't know what to do. Because Brad's never going to change. He's never going to like me that way. Never.

I sigh, kicking my bare heels against the graveled path. The fountain gurgles behind me. Crickets chirp sadly, as if in commiseration. Maybe I'll hide out here until the dance is over. I can't bear to see Carissa and Brad slow-dancing together.

Chapter 47

I find Rose in the garden, sitting by herself on the ledge of an ornately tiered fountain. My shoes crunch on the gravel. She looks up and meets my eyes.

"Hey," I say. My heart hammers. At the sight of her, happiness wells up in my chest.

"Hi," she says. "Why aren't you inside dancing?" The words *with Carissa* hang silently above her mouth like one of those cartoon speech bubbles.

"I was looking for you," I tell her. "Can I sit down?"

She nods and moves slightly over, even though there is already plenty of room beside her.

I sit down. My legs are shaky.

"Listen, Rose." I take a deep breath. "I want you to know, Carissa and I aren't back together. We never were back together. At least, I don't think we were. Or, if we were, we just broke up." The words aren't coming out right. I stop talking.

Rose doesn't say anything. I wish I could read her thoughts, but I can't.

Around us, the crickets hum and the air smells of the ocean. A breeze stirs the fabric of her dress, which billows up slightly around her waist. I want to pull her close. I want to run my hands through her hair. I want her to say something, anything.

"Carissa broke up with you *again*?" she asks.

I laugh, a nervous laugh. "Why does everyone keep saying that? No, in fact, I broke up with *her* this time."

Rose fiddles with the corsage on her wrist. It's a pale pink rose—pretty, but it doesn't fit her. She doesn't like the color pink. At least, she didn't used to. She picks a petal off the rosebud and drops it on the ground.

"Carissa and I weren't right for each other," I say. "We never were. I don't know what took me so long to realize it. But I did. I do. Now."

Rose picks off another petal. I can tell my words aren't enough. She doesn't believe me. Not that I blame her. For nearly a year she watched me hang all over Carissa. I remember how my attention used to snap over to Carissa as soon as she entered the room. Even if I was in the middle of a conversation with Rose. As if Rose didn't even matter.

What a jerk I was. I swallow, try to plan out what to say next. What can I say to make her understand that I've changed? I open my mouth, but nothing comes out.

Then I think, again, of my dad in that hospital room. And it's him and my mom I'm picturing when I say, "You know what I've realized these past few months? Love—real love—isn't striving. It isn't hard. Real love is feeling comfortable around someone. Like you can be your true self, because that person *gets* you, and underneath everything else they're your best friend."

Rose nods, still not meeting my eyes. Is she angry? Does she want me to go away? Maybe Holly was wrong. Maybe I've never been anything more to Rose than her sister's annoying boyfriend.

But, deep down, I know that's not true. If Rose is upset at me—if she doesn't want to be with me anymore—it's entirely my own fault. Maybe I'm simply too late.

Rose plucks off another dusky pink petal.

"Why are you picking apart your flower?" I ask.

"I don't really like this color," she says.

A spark of hope flares up inside my heart, giving me the courage to do what I do next.

"Rose, I meant what I said before. You're beautiful."

Finally, she stops fiddling with her corsage and looks up at me. Her eyes are red-rimmed and her mascara is a little smeared. She wipes her nose with a crumpled napkin. "You mean because I've lost all this weight?" she says softly.

"No, no," I say, scooting closer. I want so badly to take her hand, to kiss her face. Instead, I hold my own hands in my lap. "You've always been beautiful. But it's like, now you're beautiful *and* happy. You're practically glowing."

She smiles. "Really?"

"Really." I swallow, forcing myself to push forward, to get the words out. "Must be because of Daniel, huh? He seems great."

"He is. He's wonderful." She looks off toward the ballroom, as if hoping he'll appear.

This is agonizing. My hands are shaking. This was obviously a mistake, coming out here to find her. She is happy with Daniel. I had my chance—lots of chances—and I blew them all.

I want to sit with her like this for hours, yet at the same time I can't get away fast enough. I stand up to leave.

She wipes her nose again and looks up at me. "But, I mean, we're only friends. Me and Daniel."

My brain is bubble wrap, thoughts *pop pop popping* everywhere. I sit back down beside her. "But I thought... Carissa said you two were a couple."

"Well..." Rose says slowly. "Carissa doesn't always know what she's talking about, does she?"

I smile at her, remembering when those very same words came out of my mouth. It seems like an eternity ago. So much has changed since that day. Back then, I was a guy who thought he had everything: a seat at the popular lunch table, a voice on the school airwaves, and the perfect girlfriend. I thought love meant working hard to change yourself into who you thought you *should* be, who the person you loved wanted you to be. As if who you already are is never enough. I thought love meant you gave up pieces of yourself in order to win the love of somebody else.

Now I know better. Love means gaining pieces of yourself that you never knew existed. I am the same person I've always been—only now, when I'm with Rose, I feel like *more* of myself than I ever was before. Maybe it's because she could always see this more confident, purposeful, happy version of myself. She saw it before even I could see it.

Deep down, where it matters most, I am still the same Brad I always was. Rose is still the same Rose. Yet how strange it is, to be sitting on this fountain ledge with her in this night-hushed garden at the Winter Formal. Everything seems so different, and yet so comfortingly familiar.

Rose kicks her bare feet against the gravel. Her toenails are painted the same shade of purple as her dress. There is so much I still want to say to her, but I don't know where to begin.

Chapter 48

I'm looking at my feet, studying my pedicure as if the answers to all life's mysteries are hidden in the nail polish, because I'm too nervous to meet Brad's eyes. My secret is out: Daniel and I are not together. I have no one to hide behind; I have nothing left to make him jealous. All I have is myself.

I will never be Carissa. I will always be Carissa's sister.

I will always be Rose.

And, the surprising thing is...I am actually grateful for that. I am proud to be myself. For the first time since I was a little girl, I *know*, deep down, that I am worthy—and not because I've lost all this weight. I am enough simply because I am me. I am beautiful because I am shining my own light. On the outside as well as the inside.

All night, everyone has been saying how great I look now that I can fit into this designer dress. But it hasn't meant anything.

What makes me jittery and exhilarated and terrified is this: when Brad says I'm beautiful I can tell he actually means it. He sees beyond the surface. I think he's always seen who I am—who I really am, at my core. Maybe that's why, in spite of everything, I've never been able to let him go.

Brad says my name, and I look up from my feet. The expression in his eyes is so intense I have to look away, at his nose, his ears, his hair, his chin.

"There's something I need to tell you," he says. I watch his chin move up and down with the words.

He pauses. I force myself to meet his eyes, grayish blue like the ocean on a cloudy day. He clears his throat.

"When I'm with you," he says, "I am my best self. My true self. Nothing other than myself."

Usually when I cry I can sense the tears building up within me—a hot pressure burning behind my eyelids. But this time, the tears come without any warning. I duck my head to hide them.

But Brad sees. His forehead wrinkles.

"Hey. Hey now," he says, and there is a tenderness in his voice, that same tenderness I heard when we sat together in his car that night after the radio show. He reaches out and wipes tears off my cheeks with his thumbs. His hands are warm, cupping my face.

My heart is beating wildly, but I am not afraid or anxious. It feels completely normal to be in this moment. It feels right.

I am not thinking about Daniel. I am not thinking about Carissa. I am not thinking about numbers on a scale or fat content or calories burned or waist measurements or body mass indexes or food eaten or food not eaten.

I am only thinking of Brad. Of Brad and me. His fingers brush my cheeks. His thumbs wipe tears from my face. His voice is a whisper.

"Rose."

"Brad."

"There's something else I need to tell you," he says.

Chapter 49

Rose stares into my eyes, waiting for me to continue. I wish I could hit "freeze-frame" on this moment.

"I think..." I begin.

I swallow. My heart is a frantic hamster racing in its wheel. I take a deep breath.

"Rose, the truth is, I think I'm..."

"Rosie?" a voice calls. "Rosie? Are you out here?"

Stacey hurries down the gravel path. Rose and I look at each other like, *Can we hide? Will she go away?*

"Rosie!" Stacey calls. "It's an emergency! Carissa needs you!"

Rose gives me a look like, *I'm sorry.* Then she pulls away from me, stands up and waves. "Hey—over here!"

Relief washes over Stacey's face. She runs over and grabs Rose's hands, pulling her toward the ballroom. "You need to come with me. Something's wrong with Carissa. She's hysterical—I've never seen her like this."

"Oh no." Rose glances at me, a question in her eyes.

"Is this because of me?" I ask. Guilt knots my stomach.

Stacey waves me away. "I don't think so. She didn't mention you. She was crying and crying. Now she's locked herself in the bathroom and she won't come out. Mr. Marshall is threatening to suspend her. They're convinced she's drunk."

Rose puts a hand to her forehead. "Is she?"

"Drunk? No. I don't know where she would have gotten the alcohol. I think she's having a panic attack or something."

Rose slips on her shoes and follows Stacey down the path toward the ballroom. I tag along.

"I'll try to help, but I don't know what I can do," Rose says. "I mean, you're her best friend—if she won't listen to you, she's definitely not going to listen to me."

"No, you don't understand," Stacey says. There's genuine worry in her eyes, and I realize that underneath the apparent shallowness of Carissa's friends, they actually do care about each other. At least, Stacey cares. Maybe she actually cares about Leo, too.

"What don't I understand?" Rose asks.

"Carissa's asking for you. You're the only one she wants to see."

"Me?" Rose says.

"You."

"Really?"

"Yes. All she keeps saying is, 'I want my sister.'"

Rose breaks into a run. The ballroom door is open and a rectangle of light shines out into the dark garden. We all hurry toward it. The gravel is slippery under my dress shoes. Thumping bass music grows louder and louder.

In the doorway, Rose pauses and turns to me.

"Listen, Brad, I think you'd better stay away, in case Carissa's angry at you. I'm sorry. Can you find Holly and Daniel? Tell them we might have to leave soon?"

"Of course." I reach for her hand and squeeze it.

She squeezes back. "Thanks. I'll talk to you later, okay?" Then she releases my hand and follows Stacey toward the bathroom.

I make my way back to our dinner table in the hope that Holly is still there, maybe Daniel too. But no such luck. Our table is empty except for Leo.

"Did Stace find you?" he asks.

"Yeah, she and Rose are going to talk to Carissa right now. Hey, have you seen Holly? Or Daniel?"

Leo points toward the writhing mass of dancing bodies. As if on cue, the thumping bass of the rap track fades into a slow R&B song. "This one's for all you lovebirds out there," the DJ says.

I thank Leo and plunge into the crowd.

Part of me feels guilty about Carissa. Is this really because of me, because I broke up with her? I hope she's okay. In all the time we dated, I never once saw Carissa cry. Stacey said she was "hysterical"—I can't even imagine that. Carissa Hayward, Queen of the School, always has it together. Always.

The other part of me is suspicious that it's all an act. She's throwing a fit because she's tired of Rose being the center of attention. That part of me is ticked off at Carissa. If she wasn't cooped up in the bathroom, refusing to come out, maybe I would be shuffling around this dance floor with Rose in my arms right now.

Then I see them.

In the far corner of the dance floor.

Holly and Daniel. Slow-dancing together.

Her head rests on his shoulder, her eyes closed. His head leans against hers, his fingers stroking her hair.

Holly's words from earlier flit through my mind: *I guess now we both know how Rose used to feel, huh?*

She wasn't talking about Leo. She was talking about Daniel. She likes him.

And from the looks of things, he likes her, too.

Both of them are smiling so big, it's magnetic. Like they're the only two people in the world.

The way I feel when I'm with Rose.

I back away and slip through the crowd before either of them notices me.

Chapter 50

I am nervous as I open the door to the giant Hotel Del Mar bathroom. It's got a large, fancy "powder room" with a long wall of mirrors, a counter and little stools where a handful of girls in floor-length dresses are talking and touching up their make-up. One of them looks my way and elbows her friend, who also turns to stare. It's like the cameras are still rolling, like I'm perpetually onstage. When will life stop feeling this way? Soon, hopefully. I'm not like Carissa. I don't like being the center of attention.

I hurry into the bathroom area, past the row of porcelain sinks, to the very last stall. Where Stacey said she would be.

"Carissa?" I knock softly on the stall door. "It's me."

Nothing. A few stalls over, a toilet flushes.

I knock again, louder this time. "Carissa? You in there?"

"Rosie?" Her voice shakes. It doesn't even sound like her. Stacey was right—this is serious.

"Yeah, it's me," I say. "Can I come in?"

I hear shuffling, the swish of fabric. The clop of a high heel on the tiled floor. Then the sound of the lock sliding open. The stall door opens inward, and there's my beautiful, flawless, always-together twin sister.

Except...she's a mess.

Her face is red and splotchy from crying. Her eye make-up is smeared. Her mascara has become goopy black smudges on her cheeks. Her hair has partly fallen out of her bun. Straggly pieces stick out from her head, as if she just rolled out of bed. What happens next is pure instinct. I open my arms wide and pull her to me.

Her body seems so small and fragile. She sobs into the front of my dress, and I stroke her tangled hair and make soothing noises, the way our mom used to when we were little and had nightmares. Carissa used to have nightmares a lot. When we were in second grade, a German Shepherd almost bit her at the park, and she was terrified of big dogs after that. She'd dream about dogs chasing her, jowls snapping at her feet. I'd often wake up to her crawling into bed beside me, crying, shivering from fear. I'd wrap my arms around her and smooth her hair away from her tear-stained face. Eventually we'd both drift off to sleep again, huddled together under the covers. Back then, we really did look identical. Carissa and I were two halves of the same whole.

What happened to those two little girls? How did we drift so far away from them?

Behind us, someone turns on the faucet at the sink. Whoever it is, I can picture her curious gaze in the mirror, the way she'll return to her friends bursting with gossip. *Carissa's drunk and crying in the bathroom...*

For the first time in a long time, I am filled with the need to protect my sister. I gently push her back into the stall and follow her in, squeezing the door shut behind both of us. I lock it.

Carissa sits down hard on the toilet seat. She's still crying. I rip off some toilet paper and hand it to her. "It's okay," I murmur. "It's okay. I'm here." Eventually she calms down enough to blow her nose. I hand her more toilet paper and she smiles a little.

I squat down so I'm at her eye level. Five months ago I wouldn't have even been able to bend like this, but now look at me—my legs are *strong*! I'm learning to take pride in all the things my body can do that used to be impossible.

"Caris, what's wrong? What happened?"

She wipes at her eyes. Make-up smears onto her fingers. "Everything," she says. "My life's in shambles, Rose."

She's never called me *Rose* before. Holly and Brad are the only ones who call me that. The name I prefer. Growing up, Carissa was Crissy and I was Rosie, and then in middle school Crissy switched to Carissa. I tried to drop the "i" and become the more grown-up sounding Rose. But it didn't catch on. Even Carissa kept calling me Rosie. Like I was still a little girl in pigtails, innocent and invisible.

"What's in shambles?" I ask. "What do you mean?" I gear myself up for a tirade against Brad. I try to push away the image of his serious blue eyes, looking into mine.

Carissa's lower lip quivers, the way I remember from when we were kids and she'd try to hold back tears. "I didn't get in," she says softly.

"What do you mean? In where?"

"I didn't get into Stanford."

I feel like the first time I tried to bench-press—like there's a giant weight pushing down on my chest. Only this one is an emotional weight. A heavy bulk of awfulness.

"Oh, Carissa," I say. She's always wanted to go to Stanford. *Always*. For as long as I can remember she's had her future all planned out: graduate high school with straight As and a zillion extracurriculars, go to Stanford, become a famous microbiologist or engineer or surgeon or whatever her passion happened to be at the time, live happily ever after. She's been wearing our dad's old Stanford T-shirt around the house for years.

"I didn't tell anyone," she sniffles, "but I applied Early Decision. And I didn't get in. They don't want me. Stanford rejected me, and now everything I've worked for my whole life is a total pointless waste!"

"It's not a waste." I gently rub her arms. "Don't say that."

"It *is*. What am I gonna do now? I'm such a loser."

Carissa and *loser* are two words I never thought I would hear in the same sentence—much less a sentence uttered by my sister herself.

Tears roll down her cheeks. "I tried so hard, Rose, but I'm not good enough."

"Caris, you are amazing. If they don't see that, they're idiots and you don't want to go to their lame school anyway."

"But I *do* want to go there!" she wails. "I don't want to go anywhere else!"

I try a different approach. "Any college would be lucky to have you. You're going to end up at the right school. I know it. Everything is going to work out."

"You really think so?" she sniffles.

"Yes. I really do."

She sighs, flinging a mascara-streaked piece of toilet paper onto the tiled floor. "It feels like my life is *over*. I thought getting back together with Brad would make things better, but that backfired, too. He doesn't feel that way about me anymore. And to be honest, we were never the best fit. Our relationship was always more about surface stuff."

I think about all the conversations I had with Brad at our kitchen table. He'd be all excited, waving his hands around and talking about his YouTube videos and his radio dreams, but when Carissa came into the room he would clam up. One time, I tried asking why he did that, and he shrugged and said, "She's not like you. She gets bored with this stuff." And I remember thinking there must be something wrong with me. That maybe I should pretend not to care, too.

"I'm not like you!" Carissa says. "I'm never going to find someone who loves me."

"For the record," I interject, "Daniel and I broke up. We're better off as friends."

Carissa blinks at me. "I'm not talking about Daniel."

My face grows hot. "What do you mean, then?"

"C'mon, Rose. I've seen the way Brad looks at you."

I stare at the pen-graffitied walls of the bathroom stall. Even in a nice bathroom like this, people still feel the impulse to uncap their pens and mark their territory. *Celine + Bert 4ever. Erica was here!!! I love A.D.M.*

"That's nothing to do with Brad," I tell my sister. "Everyone's staring at me. People are surprised at how different I look now."

Carissa shakes her head. "No, I don't mean since you came back from the show. Brad's always looked at you that way."

I can't believe what I'm hearing. I bite my lip. My heart pounds in my chest like a frantic animal.

"I used to get so jealous of the way you'd laugh together," Carissa continues. "All your inside jokes. Your deep conversations. Brad actually talked to you about things that were important to him. It wasn't like that with us. We were always trying to perform for each other. I told myself it didn't matter, but it did. Deep down, I always knew the two of you had this...special connection."

I'm speechless. *Carissa, jealous? Of me?*

Carissa's brown eyes are flecked with gold, a mirror image of my own. "That's partly why I broke up with him," she says. "I knew I could never compete with you."

I can't help it—I start laughing. This is too ridiculous. I glance around the bathroom for hidden cameras. Is this all an elaborate ruse for the show? The producers trying to stir up more drama?

But Carissa looks hurt. "You don't have to laugh," she says. "I'm trying to be honest with you."

I stand up—my legs are killing me—and lean against the wall of the bathroom stall. "I'm sorry for laughing, but seriously, do you even hear yourself? You, competing with me? You, jealous of me? It's ludicrous! You're smart, gorgeous, funny, popular... I could never measure up to you!"

Carissa holds up her hand. "Stop it right there. You're the one person who always sees through my crap. Don't pretend otherwise now."

"I'm not pretending."

"Please. You've always looked down on me and my friends. You think we're shallow, that we care too much about fashion and celebrities and decorations for stupid dances like this."

"That's not true."

Carissa's voice steamrolls over mine, like these words have been bottled up inside her for a long time and now there's no stopping them: "Well, you know what? I admit it. I care too much about what other people think. I wish I could be more like you. I wish I could be brave and go after what matters to me. I wish I didn't waste so much time worrying and trying to be 'perfect,' whatever that is. You're the one who has her life together, Rose. Not me."

I reach out and touch Carissa's shoulders. "Four months ago, my life was a mess. My relationship with food was super unhealthy and it was making me miserable. I had a hopeless crush on someone who was completely off-limits. My self-esteem was in the dumps. I encouraged other people to go after their dreams, but I didn't have the confidence to go after my own. I couldn't even walk across campus without feeling out of breath. And the more down I got, the more junk I ate. You were the one who broke that cycle for me, Caris. I know at the time I hated you for signing me up for the TV show, but now I am so grateful. You helped me get my life back."

By now I'm crying, and so is Carissa. She puts her arms around me and draws me into a hug. I rest my head on her shoulder like I used to do when we were little, watching a Disney movie together on the couch. She lays her head on top of mine.

"I'm probably getting mascara all over your dress," I tell her.

"It's okay, I don't care."

"I love you, Caris."

"I love you too."

"I'm sorry that I said you ruined my life."

"I'm sorry, too," she says. "For a lot of things."

And we stay like that for a while, hugging in the cramped bathroom stall. It feels like we've been reunited after a very long time apart, and neither of us wants to be the first to let go.

Chapter 51

Everyone gets home safely from the dance. The others take the limo; I order a rideshare for myself.

I want so badly to talk to Rose, but she's with Carissa, convincing Principal Marshall that no one is drunk. So I keep my distance. I don't want to set off another crying jag, if it does turn out I am to blame for Carissa's meltdown. Apparently the rest of the student body thinks as much. Girls I don't even know are giving me the evil eye. When my ride arrives I say goodbye to Leo, hop into the car, and flee.

The next morning, I think about texting Rose. I keep writing out messages and then erasing them. Carissa surely hates my guts. What if Rose does, too?

I spend the whole day practicing guitar. My phone remains maddeningly silent.

At ten-thirty, I grab my guitar case and drive to the radio station. Big Wave Dave's Christmas Tree Lot is open. Main Street is decorated with white icicle lights—pretty much the closest thing we get to snow around here. I can't believe the holiday season is here already. Last Christmas, I spent all my saved birthday money on a Tiffany's heart necklace for Carissa. She got me a button-down shirt. Rose and I got each other the same thing: a DVD of this hilariously awful '80s movie we'd talked about one time. I remember we joked about watching it together, but we never did. Carissa thought it sounded lame.

When I get to the station, the studio is dark and quiet. Rumor is, Meghan's got a new boyfriend; she hasn't been around much lately. I kind of miss seeing her, despite the awkwardness. I wish we could have been friends. I think we would have made pretty good workplace friends.

Maybe in time, we still could be. I mean, look at me and Carissa. A few months ago, I thought she had ruined my life. I loved her, and then I hated her, and then I never wanted to see her again. Now, I feel pretty neutral toward her. Like my emotions have finally stabilized. She has her faults, but doesn't everyone? Despite her occasional snobbery and controlling tendencies, deep down she's a good person.

Who knows? Maybe we'll settle into a friendship of sorts. Unless, of course, she never wants to see me again—a distinct possibility, considering the disaster of Winter Formal.

I sigh, flick on the lights, and set down my guitar case in the corner. I don't even know why I brought it. A weird impulse, like my fingers couldn't bear to be away from the strings. I cue up a long playlist of music to be ready for my airtime in ten minutes. I don't feel like talking tonight. I'm still tired from all the talking I did during the emotional rollercoaster that was yesterday.

Thinking of Rose, I head into the back room to microwave a mug of water for green tea. Only two tea bags left in the box. I take one, wishing Rose was here to take the other.

All day, her smile has been flitting through my thoughts. Her smile, and her bare feet kicking the gravel, and her slow teasing voice saying, "Well, Carissa doesn't always know what she's talking about, does she?" And her surprised eyes, welling with tears when I told her that she makes me feel like my best self. She seemed happy when I said that. I think. Already, my memories are becoming tinged with doubt. I remember the way I squeezed her hand and she squeezed mine back. To me it was a promise. A *"to be continued..."*

But now I'm not so sure.

What if it was a *"goodbye"*? Or an *"I'm sorry"*?

Why haven't I heard from her all day?

The microwave beeps. I carefully slide out my piping hot mug and dunk the tea bag, watching the light green diffuse into the water.

My eyes land upon an envelope, slid mostly under the microwave, just a corner peeking out. It must have gotten pushed under there accidentally, lost in the chaos of fan mail, complaint letters, advertisements, and bills that deluge the studio mailbox daily.

Curious, I wedge the envelope out. As soon as I see the handwriting, my heartbeat quickens. No return address, but I immediately recognize the writing as Rose's. The letter is addressed to me, in care of the radio station. *Why would she send me a letter here? She sent her other letter from camp to my house. Maybe she wanted to surprise me?*

The date stamp is two weeks ago. The envelope weighs next to nothing, much thinner than the comic she sent me before.

I tear open the flap and pull out a single sheet of paper torn from a notebook. Carefully, I unfold it.

Dear Brad,

    Carissa told me she doesn't have real feelings for Ryan. If you ask her to the dance, I bet she'll say yes.

    Sincerely,

    Your Fairy Godmother

I read the letter once, twice, three times. Hoping that one more read-through will somehow change the words on the page. Unveil some new hidden meaning. But, even after a fourth reading, the meaning remains the same. Written out in Rose's hand, in stark black ink, unmistakable.

She wanted me to take Carissa to the dance.

She wanted me and Carissa to get back together.

This whole time, that's been her motivation. Nothing more.

My phone alarm beeps. Five minutes to show-time. But I stand there a little longer, green tea steaming on the counter, Rose's note in my hand. As if the words won't be true until I walk back through the door into the studio.

I am sick to my stomach. Already, the magic of last night has receded. All this time I thought Rose and I had a special connection. But I was wrong.

I think back to that summer day when Carissa broke up with me. This is even worse. Rose and I had all this potential for something amazing, but we didn't even get the chance to begin.

I guess that's only my perspective, though. Even if Holly's right and Rose had feelings for me at one point, she's obviously over it now.

Two minutes till I'm on-air. I leave my tea on the counter and head into the studio. My routine is the same as every week: sit down in front of the soundboard, put on my giant headphones, tilt the microphone toward me. Normally this is the time and place I feel most alive. But in this moment, I am numb. The show's about to start and I don't even want to play any of the music I've cued up.

All I want to do is play my guitar.

So I grab it out of its case, adjust a mic close to the strings, and strum a few notes as a warm-up. Then I lean into my own mic and say, "Welcome to your Countdown to Midnight! This is your host, Brad Hoffman."

I clear my throat. *Am I really going to do this?* I've only been playing guitar for three months, and I've never played in front of anyone else, not even Leo. *What if I'm terrible? What if I mess up and make a fool of myself on air?*

But then I picture Rose's kind eyes watching me, her smile encouraging me. Every time I go on the air, every time I'm nervous or unsure of myself, she's the one I think about. And she always makes me feel better. Despite everything, I know we're friends. True friends. A few scrawled lines on a sheet of flimsy notebook paper doesn't change that.

I strum a little more. "Tonight," I say into the mic, "I've got a little something different prepared. Hopefully it will be a treat. I should warn you, there might be some mess-ups. There definitely will be. But please know that I'm doing my best. In the end that's all any of us can do, isn't it?"

I lean back, close my eyes, and begin to play.

Chapter 52

Rose

By the time I escape upstairs to my room and collapse onto my bed, it's already 11:42. Crap, I've missed most of Brad's show. I turn on my stereo. The dial is already set to his station from when I listened to WAVE 104.3 the last time I was home. I remember singing along to the Top 40 tunes as I got ready, trying to calm my nerves, waiting for Brad to come pick me up. That was the night I went on his show. Strange how long ago it seems.

Tonight, I'm surprised to hear a folksy guitar song. This can't be the right station. I check the dial—yep, it's turned to 104.3. Is Brad off tonight for some reason? The melody sounds vaguely familiar... maybe it's a new recording of an old song?

Then the lyrics come in, a male voice singing gently, almost a whisper. I sit up so fast I feel dizzy.

I know that voice.

It's Brad.

I recognize the song now, too. The lyrics are about love and wanting to do anything you can to show the other person how much you love them, even if it's futile, even if they don't feel the same way. It's a sad song. Some of the lines are hopeful, but there's a rawness in Brad's voice that makes it seem like his hopes have already been crushed.

A couple days ago, I would have assumed Brad was singing about Carissa. But last night, when we talked in the garden, it seemed like he was completely over her. I remember looking into his earnest blue eyes. When he cupped my face in his hands and carefully wiped my tears away with his thumbs, my heart was a fountain overflowing.

What had he been going to say next? What would have happened if Stacey hadn't come up right then and interrupted us?

All day I've been checking my phone, hoping for a text. Why hasn't he contacted me? He disappeared last night while I was in the bathroom with Carissa. I remember the way he squeezed my hand right before we separated. It seemed like a promise, like he was saying, "See you soon." But then why did he leave the dance so suddenly?

The possibility that Brad regrets last night keeps flitting through my mind. I try to push away the doubt, but with every hour that my phone remains silent, the doubting part of my brain grows more insistent. *What if he didn't really mean those things he said? Or what if he did mean them, but he's changed his mind?* It happens. I changed my mind about Daniel. Maybe Brad's feeling awkward about Carissa, or maybe he doesn't want to get into a new relationship. All day, I've been picking up my phone to call or text him, but I always set it down again without doing either. If he wants to contact me, he will.

I really thought he would have by now.

The song winds to a close and Brad says, "That was 'To Make You Feel My Love' by Bob Dylan, a song that was also famously covered by both Adele and Garth Brooks. This is Brad Hoffman with your Countdown to Midnight. We'll be right back." A commercial comes on for a new brand of laundry detergent.

Maybe Brad was busy today. I mean, I was busy. He probably was too, right?

My day was a hectic juggling of people: Daniel, Holly, Carissa, my parents. Holly stayed over last night and before conking out we debriefed the basics: I broke up with Daniel, almost-sort-of confessed my love to Brad, and had my first real conversation with Carissa in years. Holly squealed at all the appropriate moments. Then, once I was finished talking, she brought up Daniel again. Even in the dark, I could see the wrinkle in her forehead, which meant she was worried or unsure. "So...you really don't have feelings for Daniel anymore?" she said.

I knew exactly where she was going. "I think Daniel and I were always meant to be friends," I told her. "Actually, I think subconsciously I brought him to the dance because I wanted him to meet you. He's totally into you, Hol."

A smile spread slowly across her face, as if she was trying to hold it back but couldn't. "Really?" she whispered. "You think so?"

"I know so. It's super obvious."

"And you're really okay with it?"

"One-hundred-and-ten percent." I squeezed her hand, thinking about Brad. About crushes. About what a funny, uncontrollable thing the heart is. How I tried for so long to squash my feelings for Brad, but I never could.

This morning, a bunch of us went to the beach. Leo and Stacey came, but Brad didn't show. I kept pulling out my phone to text him and then putting it away. I wanted to ask about him, but it never seemed like the right moment. Daniel and Holly splashed each other in the waves, a cute couple already. I sat on my beach towel beside Carissa. I even took off my shirt to display my new swimsuit. At first I was self-conscious, but then I closed my eyes and relaxed. The breeze felt nice against my bare skin, and the sun was comforting and warm.

For the first time in forever, I didn't wonder what I looked like. Instead, I was simply *me*. Laying on a beach towel in a two-piece swimsuit, breathing in and out beside my twin sister.

The rest of the day flew by. Taking Daniel to one of the beachside shops to buy souvenirs for his family. Teaching my mom how to make a healthy pasta recipe for dinner with spaghetti squash instead of pasta noodles. Being there for Carissa when our parents wanted to know why Principal Marshall called them in for a conference on Monday.

Now—finally!—my family is in bed. Holly and Daniel are sitting outside on the porch together. This is the first time all day I've had a few moments to myself.

The commercials fade out and Brad comes back on the radio, reading a list of local events that are happening around town this week. The sound of his voice takes me back to last night. I close my eyes and it's like I'm right there, sitting beside him.

I wish I would have kissed him. I think of his hands on my face, our eyes locked, and I want to kick myself. Why didn't I go for it? At least then I would have kissed him. At least then something tangible would have happened between us.

Something *did* happen, but it's in that murky indefinable area. A conversation is not a kiss. A conversation can be forgotten, ignored, pushed away. What if the next time I see Brad, he acts like nothing has changed? I don't know if I'd be able to take it. I can't go back to being just friends now. Can I?

"Well," Brad says. In the background, I hear papers shuffling. His guitar bangs into something. "It's getting to be that time. I have one more song to play for you all tonight. Actually, it's a song I want to play for one person. A very special person to me. I don't know if she's even listening, but in case she is..."

He clears his throat. "Rose, this one's for you."

Immediately, I recognize the song's opening chords. James Taylor's "Something in the Way She Moves."

My thoughts are all smeared together. I feel like my life has slowed down, or maybe sped up. I stand up, then I sit down again. Brad's voice breaks in the middle of the chorus, and it's the most beautiful thing I've ever heard.

I turn off the stereo before the song is finished.

Then I grab the keys for the Green Dragon and run out the door.

Chapter 53

Brad

In the first chorus of the song I'm singing for Rose, my voice breaks. It's utterly humiliating. I sound like a sixth-grader going through puberty. A large part of me wants to stop the song right there and sign off for the night. I'm sure Rose isn't listening. Probably no one is listening. But my fingers have a will of their own: they keep holding down the chords and strumming the strings. So I keep singing.

For some reason, I think about the Self-Improvement Plan I made after Carissa broke up with me. I haven't thought about it in a long time.

Do all my homework. Get a job. Check and check.

Wake up early and go for a run every morning before school. Check.

Learn to play the guitar. Yep, playing it right now.

Read a thick, impressive book. I'm more than halfway through *Infinite Jest.* The Old Brad would have quit after page two.

Or...maybe he wouldn't have. Maybe I don't give The Old Me enough credit.

That's the thing about hanging around with someone who acts like you're not good enough: you start to believe her. You start to think you *are* a loser. The truth is, there is no such thing as "The Old Brad"—I was the same person then that I am now. But I have different priorities now that I believe in myself.

I remember the day I wrote down those goals. Such a daunting list of tasks that seemed incredibly difficult, if not impossible. Winning Carissa back was the only reason I was doing any of it. But somewhere along the way, that changed. I stopped doing things for Carissa, and I started doing them for *me*. These days, I wake up early to go for a run because it makes me energized the rest of the day. I do my homework because I like walking into class knowing that I can answer a question if that dinosaur Ostertank calls on me. I work at the radio station because it's my passion, not because I'm trying to impress Carissa or anyone else.

After I play the final melody of the song, I am exhausted. My heart is broken and my fingers hurt. "That's it for your Countdown to Midnight. Thanks for tuning in. This is Brad Hoffman, signing off. See you next week."

I switch on some auto-tracked Top 40 tunes, turn off the mics, and set my guitar back in its case. My throat is sore from all the singing. I head into the break room, remembering my mug of green tea. I put it in the microwave to warm up for a minute. The logical part of my brain says to throw away Rose's note, but I open up the folded paper and study the words one more time.

Dear Brad,

Carissa told me she doesn't have real feelings for Ryan. If you ask

"You really should lock the front door. Anyone can wander in."

I look up, and there she is.

Rose.

Her cheeks are flushed from the cold, and her eyes shine.

"Hey," I say. My mouth is dry. The microwave beeps, but I ignore it.

"I caught the end of your show," she says, walking toward me. "I mean, I wanted to listen to the whole thing, but today has been really hectic and I didn't get a moment to myself until like twenty minutes ago..." She stops a couple feet away from me and leans against the counter. "Anyway, what I'm trying to say is, it was beautiful. Your song."

"*Your* song," I tell her. "I played it for you."

"I know." She smiles, but then she sees what I'm holding and her smile fades. "Is that the note I wrote you?"

"Yeah, I just found it. The envelope got lost under the microwave, and I didn't see it until tonight."

The microwave beeps again. I open the door to make it stop.

"So this whole time," I say, "you wanted me and Carissa to get back together?"

"No!" Rose takes a step closer. "That's the opposite of what I wanted."

"Then why did you write this note telling me to ask her to the dance?"

"Because I thought that's what *you* wanted! I was trying to be a good friend to you. Because I knew that's all we would ever be."

I feel stung. "Just friends?"

"It seemed obvious you were in love with Carissa, and I needed to stop living in a fantasy world." She studies her shoes for a moment, then looks up and meets my eyes. "I had a hopeless crush on you for *years*, Brad. Years."

Adrenaline surges through me. Time has slowed down. I can't believe I'm standing here with Rose, hearing these words from her lips.

I touch her arm gently. "I had no idea."

She nods, wiping at her eyes. "Yeah, well…secret's out, I guess."

"I'm sorry I was such an idiot."

"Don't say that. You're not an idiot."

"I am, though. I'm a little slow on the uptake. Because the truth is, I've been falling in love with you for a long time."

She looks down, and my heart sinks. That's when I realize this whole thing between us really is over. Rose heard the song I played for her on the radio, and she came here to tell me she doesn't feel that way about me anymore. Right now, she's trying to figure out the nicest words to let me down easy.

Then she looks up, and she's smiling this amazing smile that lights up her whole face—a genuine, full, beautiful Rose smile. She reaches over, takes the note from me, and tosses it on the floor.

"Brad." Her voice is nearly a whisper.

I look at her. Wait for her to say whatever it is she came here to tell me.

But she doesn't say anything else. She steps forward and presses her lips against mine. Just like that.

Chapter 54

"I've been falling in love with you for a long time," Brad says.

I've never seen him look so serious. This isn't a joke. This isn't pretend. This is real. There are no cameras or microphones capturing this moment. There's only us.

I reach over and tug the note from Brad's fingers. Then I crumple it up in my fist and let it drop to the floor. He smiles at me. I smile back.

I have too many words filling me up, too many words to squeeze a single one out. I have loved Brad Hoffman from the moment I met him in World History, when he turned around in his seat and asked if he could borrow a pencil. I loved him when he came to our house to pick up Carissa for the Homecoming dance and told me a joke about parakeets as we waited for her to make her grand entrance, and we laughed together like we were already friends. I loved him in our kitchen and at the gym and in his car and at the airport and when I was thousands of miles away on a secluded ranch in Texas. I loved him when both of us were dating other people. I loved him at the Winter Formal, when his tie was crooked and the back of his hair stuck up adorably. A secret part of me has loved him all this time, even though I thought it was fruitless, even though I thought he would never love me back.

And now here he is, saying he loves me, too. Looking into his kind eyes that I know so well, I can see it. He truly does love me exactly as I am. Carissa was right—he always has. I was never an ugly duckling to him.

"Brad," I say.

But no more words will come.

So I just do it. What I've been dreaming about doing for the past two years. What I was dying to do at the Winter Formal and in his car parked in front of my house and a hundred other days and nights before.

I step forward and press my lips against his.

Immediately, Brad wraps his arms around me and pulls me closer. His lips are soft and warm. Lightning flashes through my insides. I feel like this moment has been here all along, just waiting for us to arrive.

Discussion Guide

1. In the first chapter, Brad vows to win Carissa back. What did you think of this plan? Have you ever tried to win someone back? Has someone ever tried to win you back? What was that experience like?

2. Carissa asks Rose if she is perfectly happy with her life the way it is now, and Rose answers, "Well, no—but can anyone honestly say that? I'm happy enough." How would you respond if someone asked you this question right now? Do you agree with Rose, that no one is perfectly happy with their life as it is?

3. Why do you think Carissa nominates Rose to be a contestant on the TV show?

4. When the novel begins, both Brad and Rose feel like their lives have shifted off course, no longer going according to plan. Have you ever felt this way in your life? What happened, and what did you do as a result?

5. In order to win Carissa back, Brad makes a "Self-Improvement Plan." Did you think he would accomplish everything on his list? What would you have added to—or removed from—his list?

6. Brad and Rose both have a secret dream of going into radio. Do you have a secret dream? Have you shared it with anyone?

7. Rose develops a crush on Daniel, even though she still has feelings for Brad. What did you think of Rose and Daniel's relationship? Have you ever tried to push away

feelings for someone by diving into a relationship with someone else?

8. Brad reads a book out loud during his dad's chemo appointments. What books have been a comfort to you during tough seasons of life?

9. Why do you think Carissa wanted to get back together with Brad? Were you surprised? Why do you think Brad decided to go to the Winter Formal with her?

10. At the final weigh-in, Rose realizes: "Instead of being filled with disappointment or shame, like I always expected to feel if I gained weight here at camp, I feel... *free.*" Why do you think she feels free? What transformations did you notice in Rose during her time on the TV show?

11. At the Winter Formal, Brad realizes: "That summer day, when it felt like she ruined my life, maybe Carissa was simply trying to do the right thing even when it was hard." Share about a time in your life when you did the right thing, even though it was hard.

12. What do you imagine would have happened between Brad and Rose in the garden at Winter Formal, if Stacey had not interrupted their conversation?

13. Rose and Carissa have a heart-to-heart in the bathroom at the Winter Formal. How do you think their relationship will be different moving forward? How do you think it will stay the same?

14. At the end of the book, reflecting on his "Self-Improvement Plan," Brad realizes: "Somewhere along the way, I stopped doing things for Carissa, and I started doing them for *me.*" What do you think was Brad's biggest transformation over the course of the book?

15. Reflect on a time when you felt like your life was ruined, but things ended up working out for the best. What

lessons did you learn from that experience? How did it shape you?

16. What do you think happens next in Rose and Brad's story?

Acknowledgments

Thank you to the entire Immortal Works team for your unending belief and support in this book. Special thanks to Beth Buck for plucking my manuscript from the slush pile, Holli Anderson for your extremely insightful edits, and Ruth Mitchell for all the publicity help.

So much gratitude to art director Ashley Literski and cover designer Rebecca Barney for creating the cover of my dreams that perfectly captures the essence of my book.

Thank you to Jeffrey Dransfeldt for taking such lovely author headshots for me.

A big hug to Holly Mueller, my wise friend and first reader, for all of the exclamation-point-filled emails cheering me on as first I drafted this book more than a decade ago. Thank you for falling in love with Rose and Brad's story and for encouraging me not to give up during all the years of rejection along the way.

Writing and revising this novel many times over many years played a huge part in my evolution to rewrite my own story with food, body image, and self-love. I am beyond grateful to Courtney Wyckoff, Susan Hyatt, Corrine Dobbas, Robyn Nohling, Brianna Wilkerson, and Amy Day for their wisdom, teachings and resources that have helped me learn to wholly love my body, fuel it happily and intuitively, and appreciate the miracle it is.

Thank you to all of my teachers, classmates and friends from elementary school onward who have encouraged my writing over the years. Too many to name, but you know who you are!

Thank you to my students and clients, who continually remind me of the joy and magic that comes from unleashing words onto the blank page.

Thank you to my family, and to friends who have become family, for your loving support: Jess Ahoni, Allyn McAuley, Laurel Shearer, Colin McAuley, Frank Paschal, Mary Blasquez, Ann Silvestri, Arianna Silvestri, Amanda Rackley, Julie Hein, Melissa Kaganovsky, Erica Roundy, Dana Boardman, Lauren Baran, Carand Burnet, Chidelia Edochie, Michael Swaidan, Ben Raynor, Connie Halpern, Susan Goodkin, Kay Giles, Wayne and Kathy Bryan, Tavis Smiley, Barry Kibrick, Julie Merrick, Rima Muna, Patti Post, Lenore Pearson, Shana Lynn Schmidt, Justin and Rose Nishioka, Alicia Stratton, Tania Sussman, Henry Fung, Joan Redding, Anna Frandsen, and all of my aunts, uncles, and cousins.

Thank you to my dear friend Céline Lucie Aziz and my grandma Auden, for teaching me that love knows no tense.

Special thanks to my aunt Kym Woodburn King for your constant love and enthusiasm.

Thanks to Grandma and Grandpap, Mary Lou and Gene Paschal, for always making me feel like a best-selling author.

Thank you to Gramps, Dr. James Dallas Woodburn II, for all the phone calls and stories.

Forever gratitude to my generous mother-in-law, Barbara McAuley, for your fierce belief in me and my writing—and the countless hours of babysitting Maya to give me time to write!

A big hug to my sister-in-law and favorite librarian, Allyson McAuley, who gives the best book recommendations! I treasure our conversations, and your faith in my writing means the world to me.

To my brother Greg: thank you for believing in me and building me up when I felt discouraged through the decade-long journey to this book's publication. I am eternally grateful for your wisdom, humor, and unconditional support. Your handwritten cards always come at just the right time when I need your words most!

Thank you to my mom, Lisa, for being my role model and teaching me to treat my body with love, gentleness and gratitude.

Thank you for all the runs, walks and hikes together as we talk about anything and everything. You are the best listener. Thank you for always making me feel understood and loved.

Thank you to my dad, Woody—my favorite author. Thank you for being my cheerleader and supporter for as long as I can remember, and for taking my writing dreams seriously even when I was just a kindergartener. You are my #1 editor, first reader, go-to brainstormer, and superfan.

To my husband, Allyn: thank you for being the real-life inspiration for all of my fictional love stories. From our very first date, you made me feel completely seen and loved for who I am inside. Thank you for being my true partner, my forever love, and my very best friend.

To my daughter, Maya: thank you for the joy of being your mother. Your boundless curiosity and care for the world inspires me as a writer, and as a human being. I hope you always know how worthy and special you are. I love you infinity.

✧ About the Author

Dallas Woodburn's debut novel *The Best Week That Never Happened* was the Grand Prize Winner of the Dante Rossetti Book Award for Young Adult Fiction. She is also the author of the short story collections *Woman, Running Late, in a Dress* and *How to Make Paper When the World is Ending*. A former John Steinbeck Fellow in Creative Writing, her writing has been honored with the Cypress & Pine Short Fiction Award, the international Glass Woman Prize, and four Pushcart Prize nominations. When she's not writing, Dallas hosts the podcast Overflowing Bookshelves, teaches writing classes for teens and adults, and unapologetically bakes pumpkin-spice everything all year round. She lives in the San Francisco Bay Area with her husband and daughter.

This has been an
Immortal Production